RICK PARTLOW
TERMINUS
CUT

AETHON
BOOKS

TERMINUS CUT

©2019 RICK PARTLOW

PROLOGUE

J aimie Brannigan walked alone.

It was the lot of the Guardian of Sparta, the fate he accepted when he shouldered the burden. He'd thought, for a while, he might avoid both the burden and the fate, despite the circumstances of his birth. His father had been a hale man, sure to live another century and perhaps have more sons and daughters who would take up the mantle while he, even as the eldest, might remain a simple soldier with a wife, a home, and a family.

The Lamberts had changed all that, taken it away from him, he thought in the darkest hours of the night. Others assured him the coup attempt by his cousins was a blessing, an opportunity to use the gifts Mithra had given him. The portrait of his wife hanging on the wall just outside the chapel reminded him those opportunities came at a steep price.

His breath still caught at the sight, at the memory. She had been so strong, so beautiful, and remained so to this day in his heart. What would she think of him now? What would she think of the course he had set for their sons?

He entered the chapel unaccompanied, no guards or caretakers this deep inside the palace so early in the morning. It was just after sunrise, and the first golden glow reached the confines of the private temple through the skylight, diluted by stray wisps of smoke from the sacred fire. He took strips of sandalwood from a bowl beside the door and presented them to the priest, his face covered by a mask to prevent his breath from corrupting the ceremony. The old man had served his father here since before Jaimie was born, the lines and creases of a hundred and fifty years in service to God etched around those perceptive green eyes.

The wood burned well in the sacred fire and Jaimie knelt to receive the ash, to have those strong, old fingers smear it across his cheeks as the priest uttered the ancient ritual. Had this been a public ceremony, he would have been expected to be dressed in the traditional robes, to bathe beforehand right here in the temple instead of back in his quarters, and to tie and untie the sacred knots, but allowances were made for his position and schedule.

Great Mithra, Lord of Light, he prayed, feeling the rough warmth of the ash on his face like the presence of God, *take care of my boys. Forgive me for the danger I have placed them in and I beg of you, please don't punish an old man for the foolishness of his youth.*

"You ever study up on how Zoroastrianism came to be the state religion of the Empire of Hellas?"

Jaimie tried not to indulge in the anger swelling in his chest. It wouldn't be appropriate here, which was probably why Constantine had chosen this place to corner him. Jaimie Brannigan rose from his knees, pulling out a cloth to wipe the ashes from his face and murmuring an apology to the priest before he turned toward the unwelcome voice.

General Nicolai Constantine was a weapon waiting to be used, a dagger held low and ready for a disemboweling strike. Even stretched out in an almost disrespectful sprawl across the worship bench, he had the look of a coiled spring or, perhaps more aptly, a snake ready to strike.

"What do you want, Nicolai?" he demanded.

"It's incredibly interesting, if you ever bother to look into it," the man insisted, ignoring Jaimie's question. "My grandparents were followers of the Old Way, you know? What used to be called 'Christianity' before the Empire banned it."

"I would say you should know better than to speak of the Old Way in a place of worship," Jaimie said, a slight tremble to his voice at the barely-contained rage, "but obviously there are many things you should know better about, but have proceeded to do anyway."

"Christianity, Buddhism and an old religion called Islam basically split the world between them once. Whole societies were built on the foundation of these religions, systems of law and government based on their tenets. And Zoroastrianism, well...it barely survived, a curiosity with a handful of followers. And it wasn't like this," he pointed out, waving a finger at their surroundings.

Jaimie checked behind them surreptitiously, making sure the priest had left. The old man knew conversations such as these weren't his place to hear.

"Mithra wasn't even the chief god of Zoroastrianism back then; he was an angel, one of the *Spenta Mainyu*. When Emperor Ericka took power, she wanted to combine Zoroastrianism with the worship of Mithras, to turn it into a soldier's religion. That's why the Old Way was banned, because too many of its followers are pacifists and even those who weren't didn't take kindly to the idea of a religion not merely sponsored by the state but nearly created from whole cloth simply to ensure loyalty to the Empire." The General smoothed down the front of his uniform jacket, regarding the Spartan seal on his right breast carefully.

"I sometimes think," he said, the casual arrogance of his dark-browed face sinking into something brooding, "in our efforts to recapture the glory of the Empire, we forget the cost."

"Nicolai, you have been a friend and supporter for longer than I care to remember. So, I won't give in to my baser instincts and have you taken out to the lake and weighed down with stones, despite the fact you knew Terrin was leaving to stow away on the cargo ship supplying Logan's mission and did nothing to stop it." Despite his resolve not to give sway to his rage, Jaimie's voice rose until he was almost shouting the last few words and his hands had clenched into fists.

"By the time I learned of his plan, that ship had sailed." Constantine snorted, though there seemed little humor in it to Jaimie. "And I didn't tell *you* about it until after it was a *fait accompli* because you would have thought with your heart rather than your head and cancelled the mission to get him back."

"Be that as it may," Jaimie ground out, the growl rumbling from somewhere deep in his massive chest, "I don't think either of us wants to go over that same ground again, and I doubt you came here to give a lecture on comparative religions. So, what do you want, Nicolai?"

"We've had our first report back from Wholesale Slaughter."

There it was, the other shoe. Jaimie Brannigan shook his head, falling into the seat next to Constantine's.

"I still can't believe I let him get away with naming it that."

"Oh, it's colorful, certainly," the Intelligence chief admitted, "but it's exactly the sort of thing a mercenary company commander would do, particularly a young one. It attracts attention; it's free advertising. Though nothing advertises a mercenary company as well as success." He grinned close-mouthed, the last thing an elk saw before the wolf pounced. "They've had their first job. They were hired by an independent colony out beyond Spartan space in one of the nooks and crannies between us and Clan Modi. A place called Arachne."

Constantine barked a laugh, scornful and dismissive. "They were being extorted by some two-bit, wannabe warlord who

4

called himself 'Captain Magnus.' He'd pulled together a cluster of outlaws and rejects and convinced them they were a pirate band he'd named the 'Red Brotherhood.' What a moron. They took him down with minimal casualties, from the reports I've heard."

"That's good news, at least," Jaimie allowed, hissing out the breath he hadn't realized he'd been holding. "Have you heard anything else?"

"Their success hasn't gone unnoticed. They're already on their way to their next employer in the Dagda system, right at the edge of Starkad space." Constantine steepled his hands, tapping the fingers together. "Unfortunately, I don't think this job is going to be quite so simple."

1

"Three habitables in one system is pretty rare," the man who called himself Jonathan Slaughter mused. "Especially out here in the Periphery."

He had to tear his eyes away from the viewscreen, away from the deep blues and welcoming greens of Rhiannon, passing by slowly as the station rotated for the faux gravity of centripetal force. Dagda gleamed in the ever-night, its ferocity muted by the filters of the cameras, a G-class star. He blinked automatically despite the barrier of the video wall, and looked back to the oval table at the center of the—*what had Vasari called it?*—oh, yeah, the "situation room." It seemed pretentious to him.

Jabbar Vasari had also labelled himself a "designated negotiator," which also seemed pretentious and Jonathan wondered if it was something about the culture out here. He was a spare, slender man, not young but not yet at middle age, either, his dark and intense face unlined and unweathered. It was the face of a man who didn't spend much time outdoors. His features could have been painted on for all the emotion he'd shown since they'd arrived on the orbital station. He wasn't exactly cold or unpleasant, simply reserved and calculating.

Desirable qualities in a "designated negotiator," I suppose.

"Honestly, I'm surprised you can stay independent this close to the Supremacy," Jonathan added, wondering if he could provoke a reaction from the man.

He couldn't. Vasari's answer was as calm and unemotional as everything else he'd said.

"Lugh and Fiachna are just terraformed moons around the gas giant Fand," he said. "They don't offer much besides a habitable place for the men and women who maintain the gas mines to raise their children." He shrugged, the movement stiff and almost robotic. "The mines themselves are what keep our economy going, but the Dagda system is at the dead end of a jump-point node. We're not on the way to anywhere else and shipment costs would be too high to justify the expense of annexing us...for the Starkad Supremacy."

Finally, he allowed a frown to mar his sculpted features, eyes losing focus as they stared through the table in front of him.

"Unfortunately, it also means we aren't worth defending."

"Well, that's why we're here, isn't it?" Jonathan smiled, mostly to hide the tension. He was alone with the man, and he wasn't certain he was ready for it. Lyta had insisted, though. Maybe she was trying to make up for usurping his authority with Magnus, though the details of what had happened remained their secret.

"You're in charge," she'd told him in the docking bay, and yet somehow it had still seemed like an order.

"I wouldn't expect the Jeuta to be active this close to the Supremacy border either," Jonathan ventured, stepping back over to the table, leaning on it with the heels of his hands but not sitting down. It was a trick he'd learned from his father; it put people off-balance. "They're risking retaliation, aren't they?"

"According to what they've told their interpreters, they're independent from the Jeuta Confederation, a splinter group looking to set up shop for themselves somewhere further away from the central government. And we're their means to that end."

"What do they want?"

"Fuel, ore and ships." His carefully held face twisted sourly. "More than we can continue to give up and still turn a profit. We considered simply hiring escorts for our barges, but they've threatened to go after our production facilities if we resist. A consensus has been reached." Jonathan stifled a laugh at the intricately-crafted passive voice of the sentence; Vasari was going out of his way to avoid saying *who* had made the decision. "We believe their ultimate aim is to simply take over our production machinery and, eventually, our worlds."

He smiled, as thin and insincere as the expression could possibly be.

"And that's why you're here, isn't it?"

Kamehameha-Nui Johannsen whistled softly at the images playing out across the readout screen. Osceola understood why. The ship was old, centuries old perhaps, but she wasn't a converted commercial craft with strapped-on weapons; she was military, born and bred.

"That's a Reconstruction War era destroyer," Osceola confirmed with a nod toward the surveillance image of the angular, wedge-shaped starship. "Maybe Mbeki, maybe Shang construction. Can't say she has her original load-out, but just the hull is a weapon itself, thick as it is." He shot Lyta a rueful grin. "No wonder these damned plutocrats don't want to mix it up with the Jeuta their own selves."

Lyta Randell looked as if she wanted to pace, but it wasn't practical in microgravity, even with the magnetic boots the four of them were wearing. Kammy always seemed ridiculous in them, wobbling this way and that against the magnetic anchors like some sort of parade float. The kid, Slaughter—*Good God, what a dumb-ass name*—stood stock-still, hands clasped behind his back, frowning in concentration.

"This is going to be a damned sight harder than those half-assed bandits," Osceola added for the kid's benefit. "Jeuta don't fuck around, Wihtgar can tell you that. And they ain't got no inflated ego like that dumb-shit Magnus."

"He's right about that," Lyta admitted, eyeing Jonathan Slaughter sidelong. "Plus, the Dagda Commercial Investment Council doesn't have any idea where the Jeuta are operating out of. They know it's not anything one jump out, and that's about it." She shrugged, an awkward, full-body thing in free-fall. "Maybe we should pass this one up."

Osceola knew that wasn't happening even before the kid shook his head. He might have been a wet-behind-the-ears company commander, but he had focus.

"We need this job."

Jonathan glanced around the bridge carefully before he went on, as if to assure himself the four of them were the only ones there. Osceola had dismissed the duty shift for the meeting since the *Shakak* didn't have anything that could rightly be called a conference room or an operations center.

"This gives us a legitimate reason for heading through Starkad space. If we turn it down, we'll have to bum around waiting for another job to pop up, and then we'll *have* to take the next one, no matter where it is, or risk looking suspicious."

It was a legitimate point, Osceola had to admit.

"Granting that," he interjected, "we still got the problem of how the hell do we find them? 'Cause I'm telling you right now, we ain't gonna be taking *that*..." He motioned at the destroyer. "...on head to head in open space with this ship if we wait for them to come to us. If we ain't surprising them, we ain't winning this fight."

"I got an idea," Kammy said, surprising even his Captain and longtime friend. The big man was wagging a finger at the image of the destroyer, bobbing in the air with each motion. "There's one ship we know they'd take back to their base."

Lyta was way ahead of him, grinning broadly at the First Officer.

"The one Dagda is giving them!"

"We gotta put a tracker on it," Kammy agreed, nodding. "But it can't activate until it gets to the system they're heading to." He nodded toward Jonathan. "Maybe your..." He frowned. "Brother? Cousin? Whatever, maybe Terry can help come up with something. It's gotta' launch on compressed gas, maybe have some kind of radar-absorbent shield it can slough off once the enemy is out of range, then start broadcasting a unidirectional beacon back at the jump point."

"God damn," Osceola murmured, scratching behind his right ear absently. "The only way we could find it is to head down every jump track one after another until we hear the signal. It could take days...even weeks."

"Unless we come up with something better, it's what we're going to have to go with," Jonathan declared. The kid was very decisive, which Osceola found damned annoying. He motioned back toward the main view screens at the commercial space station turning slowly against the blue arc of Rhiannon in the background. "I told them we'd have a tentative plan for them in six hours and that was four hours ago."

Osceola blinked at him, mouth falling open.

"Well, why the hell did you tell them that?" he demanded. "What if we hadn't been able to figure out a plan?" He waved a hand at the image of the destroyer. "Besides, even if we do track down the system they're using for a base, what the hell are we gonna do about it? Build another damned nuke?"

"That won't work on the Jeuta," Lyta said grimly, shaking her head. "They don't get mad, they get even. And they don't have a human's ingrained fear of radiation. They're more resistant to it than we are. Dagda has too much to lose to risk the Jeuta coming here for payback and you said yourself, we can't beat that destroyer if it comes to us."

"Then what?" he asked helplessly. "What are we gonna do?"

Jonathan smiled with an infuriating confidence that made Osceola want to punch him in his too-handsome face.

"We'll figure something out," the kid said. "The way I see it, we have days...maybe even weeks."

"Yeah, and I suppose you're going to let *us*," Osceola motioned back and forth between Kammy and himself, "do all the work hunting down the signal while you do what? Sit here on your ass and think?"

"Hardly. We're going to have to find a training area where we can offload the mechs and the ground troops and run through some training scenarios. But before we do all that..." His eyes went back to Rhiannon and his smile grew wider. "That's a really pretty place. And I'd hate to come all this way without getting a look at it."

"You're nuts, you know that?" Katy shouted in his ear, her voice barely audible over the rush of the wind.

He laughed. He was sure she couldn't hear it, though maybe she could feel it in his shoulders. Her arms were wrapped around his waist, her body pressed against his back and it took a concerted effort to concentrate more on the handling and feel of the motorcycle between his legs, rather than the woman clinging to him. The mountain road twisted under the wheels, the switch-back curves hanging out over a thousand meters of wispy clouds, blue sky, and nothing but bare rock almost vertical beneath them.

Mount Doral stretched high into the morning sky, a grey monolith hiding the city of Westport in its shadow, sheltering her from the storms rising up on the east side of the range. Jonathan had seen her for the first time flying in to Westport to negotiate for a training and staging area for his company, and she'd seemed to be challenging him, inviting him. The first question he'd asked the rep for the Dagda government when she'd picked them up at the shuttle port was, "Is there a road up the mountain?"

He'd waited till later to ask about renting a motorcycle. Didn't want to seem unprofessional.

"You're a pilot!" he yelled back to Katy, feeling the wind trying to worm its way beneath his driving goggles. "I thought you'd like this shit!"

"I *do* like it!" She laughed wildly and kissed the side of his neck. "That doesn't mean you're not crazy!"

As much as he loved the ride and the view, and the company, Jonathan had to admit it was getting damned cold the higher they went, and even his insulated flight jacket wasn't doing enough to shut out the chill wind. He felt a sense of relief when they reached the summit overlook and he slowed the bike to a stop, shutting down the motor and kickstanding it.

"The road just ends here," Katy said, swinging a leg off the bike behind him. She took a few, tentative steps off the paved parking area, to the carefully-arranged boulders lining the over-look. "Do you think they built it just so you could drive up and see the view?"

"I've heard worse reasons to build a road," he said, coming up beside her, slipping an arm around her shoulders as he took in the incredible vista below.

From up here, he saw all of the sprawling city of Westport

from the foothills right down to the ocean. There was little in the way of a metroplex here; it wasn't needed. Most of their business was done off-planet and it made sense to have the centers of business and administration closer to the production. He'd seen images of the colony on Lugh, one of the habitables orbiting the gas giant Danu, and it fit much closer to what he would expect from the capital of something called the "Dagda Commercial Investment Council." The cities there were enclosed and inclusive, domed and shielded against the climate extremes and the background radiation, more useful and practical than orbital facilities simply for the convenience of gravity, a breathable atmosphere and liquid water.

Rhiannon, by contrast, was an outdoor place, a planet of warm oceans, rugged mountains, and rolling planes. Executives who worked on Lugh vacationed and retired on Rhiannon, and the super-rich built their mansions here and forced the nose-to-the-grindstone types to come here to do business with them. He saw the mansions dotting the hillsides near the beach and wondered how much each of them cost in relation to, say, a mech like his Vindicator.

"Things are different here than on Sparta," he said, knowing it was inane but not afraid to sound that way with Katy. With her, he still felt more like Logan Conner, what he hoped was the *real* Logan Conner, and not the made-up, cocky mercenary captain Jonathan Slaughter. "The money's more concentrated, but the population's smaller on the actual planet. You almost can't see the machinery running, the gears being greased."

"Sparta has a government founded on providing military stability after the Fall and the Reconstruction Wars," Katy replied, staring down at Westport with an expression he thought might have been wistful, as if she hated the thought of leaving even though they'd just arrived. "This place, and others like it, are built on business, on making a living, because they were too far away from the wars for security to be a factor...until now."

He laughed, miming applause.

"Wow, aren't you the government and history expert? And here I thought all pilots were math nerds."

"I *am* a math nerd." She punched him lightly in the arm. "My parents are the social sciences experts." She sniffed. "They think so, anyway. I've never thought there was much science involved, just a lot of guesswork and opinions passed off as fact."

"You sound like my mom." He wanted to chuckle at the thought, but he couldn't, not even after all this time. "She always said science was something you could falsify, something you could reproduce, but the human experience was always different, never really something you could replicate."

"I think I would have liked your mom."

Katy's fingers traced a line down his jaw, touching his lips, followed the touch with her lips. Jonathan pulled her close, relishing in her warmth against the chill bite of the wind, feeling wild strands of hair teasing his face.

"I wish this could last," she breathed into his ear, her cheek pressed against his. "Being here, away from everything else."

"This mission won't be forever," he assured her, not wanting to let go of her. "We'll be able to go somewhere for a while if you like, when it's done, maybe a couple weeks..."

She snorted, skepticism in her eyes when she pulled away to regard him. "And then what, Lord Guardian? Are you going to keep me around as your personal pilot on every assignment?" She poked a finger into his ribs. "I have a career too, you know?"

Jonathan felt a very Logan-like roiling in his stomach at the thought of the two of them apart, and a million possibilities began bouncing off each other in his head, none of them very satisfying. He wanted to say something logical, make a plan, present her with a reasoned and well-thought-out argument, but he couldn't seem to wrap his mind around one.

"I don't know," he admitted. "I just know I don't want to give up."

"You're a soldier. Even if you weren't...." She bit down on something sour, and he knew she was trying not to break operational security. "Even if you weren't the *other* things you are, you'd still be a soldier, and soldiers go where they're told. Pilots, too."

He tried to form an objection, but she put a finger over his lips.

"Let's not worry about the future. That's just a good way to ruin the present."

"Did your parents teach you that?" he wondered, trying to sound light and bantering even though the roiling in his stomach just wouldn't go away.

"No." She buried her face in his shoulder and her grip on him tightened. "I learned it on Ramman."

2

"I swear to the Spenta Mainyu, if we have to spend another week crawling between jump-points in this crate, I am going to fucking shoot myself."

Terry didn't even look up from his meal. He'd heard the complaints every tedious, endless day of the search and, while he sympathized, at least the crew had something to do. The complainer this time was one of the Spartan Navy personnel, though at this point the only discernable difference between the two groups was their accents. They'd fallen into their new duties and shifts on the *Shakak* and there hadn't even been any fights since the battle at Arachne.

If you could call it a battle. He'd been on board the ship and it had seemed more like an execution. The bandit ship was poorly armored and while it had been rigged up with a heavy mining laser and a crude mass driver, its targeting systems were laughable compared to the *Shakak's*. In moments, there'd been nothing left of the bandit ship but an expanding cloud of plasma. He wished he could say he'd found it disturbing, but it had been far too antiseptic for that, like watching a history documentary.

He wasn't sure why he'd volunteered for the point-to-point search for the tracer signal instead of staying back with the ground force. Jonathan had negotiated them an island on the moon Fiachna to train for the battle. He could have been bored and restless somewhere with a breathable atmosphere, a consistent gravity and a little bit of privacy, but he'd fancied once they found the system, he might be useful... somehow.

So far, all he'd managed to accomplish was reconfiguring the ship's long-range surveillance gear to optimize for planetary analysis, and developing a curious taste for the imitation chicken pad thai the ship's auto-kitchen could concoct from soy paste and spirulina powder. The stuff was addictive. It had taken him a while to go from grabbing it and eating it in his assigned cabin to actually hanging out in the mess, and he still hadn't talked to anyone but the technicians he was helping with the surveillance package. He just kept his head down, ate his food, and listened.

Which was why he noticed the sudden end to the bitching by the spacers at the table behind him. He glanced up and saw the reason squeezing through the hatchway into the mess, massive and seal-grey and inhuman. Wihtgar ignored the stares from the table full of Spartan Navy spacers and went to the auto-kitchen, punching in a program code and grabbing a plate from the dispenser. Terry found the Jeuta fascinating. He'd never seen one in real life before, but everyone knew their story, how the Empire had created them as a slave race, designed to be resistant to cold, heat, radiation, and even vacuum for a short time, to replace humans in dangerous jobs.

It had been tried before with sentient AI, and had led to a war devastating enough to end the old Consensus government and along with it, any hopes of controllable artificial intelligences. This time though, the Empire's biological researchers had been sure they could engineer something strong and capable enough to handle brute force tasks but not smart enough to revolt.

It hadn't turned out quite the way the Imperials had hoped.

"I can't believe Captain Osceola lets this freakshow eat with real people," one of the Spartan sailors said, loud enough to make sure Wihtgar would hear it.

Terry winced. The Jeuta was big and powerful, but there were six of the Spartans, five men and a woman, and he wasn't sure if Wihtgar could take them all if it came to a physical fight. The one who'd spoken was a junior enlisted, a tall, broad-chested man maybe a year younger than Terry. The name "Nellis" was printed on his duty fatigue blouse and Terry had seen him before, had *heard* him before, which wasn't hard given how loud he was. He didn't complain as much as explain to anyone who listened how things *should* be run, how he would run them if he were in charge.

Nellis was half out of his seat, fists balled up, staring at Wihtgar with hate in his eyes.

"You heard me, Freakshow!" he yelled at the Jeuta, pounding his hand against the table. "I don't feel like eating with one of you around!"

"You should take your food to your quarters then," Wihtgar suggested, the tone of his voice as calm and even as any of the few times Terry had heard him speak.

If the Jeuta had been looking to defuse the situation, he'd swung and missed. Nellis was out of his seat, with his friends rising behind him, a couple of them looking uncertainly at the size of the non-human, but still backing him up. The mess wasn't crowded and there didn't seem to be any other of Osceola's crew in the compartment.

Terry stood before he realized he was doing it, stepped in front of the enlisted man, hands at his side.

"What do you think's going to happen here, Nellis?" Terry asked him. His voice was surprisingly calm, especially given his stomach was tied into a veritable Gordian knot.

"Get out of my way, egghead," Nellis snapped, looking as if he wanted to push Terry out of the way but hesitating.

He probably knows "Jonathan" and I are related.

"You think you're going to beat a Jeuta in a fight, Nellis?" Terry asked him, wracking his brain for something to get through to the man. "Even with your friends backing you up? A *Jeuta?* And what if they don't? What if it's just you?"

"His kind killed my grandfather," one of the other Navy spacers interjected. It was the woman, Ortiz, and she wasn't much smaller than Nellis, nor a bit less intimidating. "My father told me stories about what they did to him. I don't like being on the same ship as one of the damned things."

Terry had been acting without thinking too much to this point, but the intensity in the woman's face scared him. Nellis was just a blowhard, but Ortiz might not care if he was related to the boss. He should just get out of the way and go call Osceola.

But what if someone gets seriously hurt? What if it causes a real problem and we have to cancel the whole operation? What if I have to go home and face Dad without having actually accomplished anything?

That prospect was even scarier than facing down angry spacers. Terry raised his hands to chest-level, palms out and sent a pleading look over his shoulder at the Jeuta. He had no idea what the expression on the thing's face meant. Wihtgar could have been angry, sympathetic or constipated.

"Even if you don't get your asses kicked," Terry said to the spacers, hoping his pleading look would work better on them, "you know how pissed Major Randell is going to be. What do you think *she'll* do to whoever starts this fight?"

That seemed to get through to them. They might not be afraid of Jonathan Slaughter, even if they knew who he really was, but everyone was afraid of Lyta. Nellis' jaw worked and his fingers clenched and unclenched before he swept his tray off the table, sending it crashing to the floor.

"Fuck this," he mumbled, turning. "I'll eat in my fucking cabin from now on."

With the slightest hesitation, Ortiz followed him through the hatch into the passageway and the other four spacers at the table filed out behind them, shooting dirty looks at Terry and Wihtgar. Terry watched the last of them vanish around the corner before he let out the breath he'd been holding. His strength seemed to abandon him along with it and he had to support himself against the table, careful not to step in the spilled food. An aged and battered clean-up robot had already detached itself from a nook in the bulkhead down by the deck and was slowly and reluctantly rolling across the deckplates to vacuum up the mess.

"You did not have to do that," Wihtgar said. Terry nearly jumped at the words, having almost forgotten the Jeuta was there.

"I know," he acknowledged. "But there wasn't anyone else, so I had to…"

"I apologize," the Jeuta interrupted. "I speak your language well, but I sometimes confuse your idiom. I meant to say, there was no reason for you to do that. I am ship's security for a reason. I am here to handle situations such as this."

Anger flared in Terry's chest, working its way to his mouth. He had to head it off before it exploded outward because telling a Jeuta to go mate with its mother was unlikely to be received well, and he had grown fond of the current arrangement of his face.

"Maybe you didn't need any help," Terry said when he could trust himself to say something halfway civil, "but *they* did." He jerked a thumb at the hatchway where the spacers had gone. "And we need them doing their jobs."

That sounded very dutiful and dedicated to the mission, like something his "cousin" would say…not Lyta though. She would have thrown in a lot more cursing.

"Anyway," he went on, "them blaming you for everything any other Jeuta does is stupid. It would be like you blaming me for the Imperials who enslaved your ancestors."

"It would," Wihtgar agreed.

He bent down and retrieved the tray Nellis had knocked down. The food was gone, scrubbed up by the robot before the machine had squeaked and groaned back to its hidey-hole, but it had left the plate and tray for someone taller and with more dexterity. Wihtgar tossed it in the recycler from a meter away, not flinching at the loud clatter of the plastic and metal.

Do Jeuta flinch? he mused. *Maybe I'll find out soon.*

"I believe my food is ready," Wihtgar said, then made an obvious imitation of a human nod, a difficult motion for something with very little in the way of a neck. "Have a pleasant evening, Mr. Conner."

Terry stood beside his table, feeling a bit nonplussed, watching the broad, muscular back walking away from him.

"I think," he muttered to himself, "I'm going back to eating in my cabin."

"You think this'll be the one, boss?" Kammy asked.

Donner Osceola didn't snap at the inane question, even though it was the same one his First Mate had asked at every single one of the six jump-points they'd passed through over the last two and a half weeks, because Kammy was quite obviously *trying* to get him angry. It was what passed for sport when you were bored out of your mind with no end in sight.

"Just jump the damned boat, you overgrown infant."

"Aye-aye, Captain." Kammy grinned and hit the control to feed a capacitor burst to the Kadish-Dean drive.

Reality warped itself around them and sucked Donner Osceola through another universe with it. No one knew exactly how long it took to pass through a Kadish singularity. Attempts had been made to measure it, of course, but the results had been so widely disparate, the research had been abandoned long before the Empire fell. Osceola had made more jumps than he could count in a life lived aboard ship, bouncing from one star to another, yet every single one felt different. It was one of the reasons he loved his job.

His mind took a moment to clear after the passage, and he thought at first the ringing was in his ears until he realized it was coming from the Communications console.

"Captain," Nance, the Spartan Navy Commo Technician exclaimed, twisting against her seat restraints to look back at him. "I've got the signal. This is it."

"Thank Mithra," he murmured. It was a turn of phrase. He hadn't been a believer in quite some time. "Helm," he commanded sharply to Tara, "take us to minimum power, shut down the main reactor and reduce thermal output to station-keeping." The rough-hewn woman worked quickly and professionally, despite looking like a drunk on a three-day bender in the worst bar on Gateway. He touched a control on the arm of his command chair and leaned over the audio pickup. "Dr. Conner, get your ass to the bridge ASAP and make that big brain of yours useful."

He wanted to lean back and bask in the glory of not having to go through the mindless tedium anymore, but it wasn't practical in free-fall so he examined the tactical display instead. The system was about as close to worthless as it could get and still have planets in the habitable zone. The star was a red giant and its expansion had gobbled up anything in the original Goldilocks area, leaving what might have once been an Earthlike world burned to a crisp barely a million kilometers out, and a gas giant so close a flow of ions poured off it like a wind, heading for the star. Farther out lay an ice giant with its own selection of frozen moons and if there'd ever been a useful asteroid belt, it had been burned away along with everything else.

"We getting anything but the drone signal?" he asked Tara, trying to decode the streams of data represented on the screens.

"Not seeing anything, boss." She shook her head. "Not that it means much...coulda been a week or even two since the tribute ship passed through."

"You don't think they just passed through here on the way to another jump-point, do you?" Kammy asked him, face screwed up with sudden worry. Osceola knew the feeling; he did *not* want to be out here any longer if he could help it.

"I don't think so." Terry Conner—if that was even his real name—pushed out onto the bridge, not bothering with magnetic boots, probably because they would have been slower.

The egghead squinted at the screen as if that would let him see further, his brows creased under his unruly hair.

"You see the moon there, the big one around the gas giant?"

"Of course I see it," Osceola snapped. "It's as big as a planet, how could I fuckin' miss it?" The moon was in a strangely close orbit to the planet and Osceola wondered if the nova that had birthed the red giant had somehow altered its path. "But good Lord, kid, the radiation there that close to the gas giant would be something fierce."

"For a human," Terry admitted. "Though from what I can see, it's got a damned thick atmosphere and a powerful magnetosphere too, which would alleviate the radiation a little. Enough for Jeuta to live there. For a while, not forever."

"So, they're desperate then," Osceola said. "Probably means they don't have any intention of keeping the deal they made even if the Dagda Whatever-you-call-it gives them everything they asked for."

"What does that mean for us?" Terry asked, big-eyed like the kid he was.

Osceola shot him an annoyed glare.

"It means we get the hell out of here and go tell our fearless leader Captain Slaughter he was right." He snorted a laugh. "We got an invasion to plan."

3

Jonathan Slaughter regarded the construction project with a narrow, skeptical set to his eyes, watching the separate sections of the modular tank being fitted together by construction mecha and welded into place. The foot-pads of the skeletal, unarmored machines kicked up a thin spray of red dust and he coughed sympathetically. The stuff got into everything here on Fiachna, squirming its erosive, gritty way into every joint of every mech, into the actions of every weapon, inside your damn clothes. It turned the sunsets a really pretty color, though.

"Do you really think we can pull this off?" he asked.

"It's what we've been training for these last three weeks," Lyta Randell reminded him, arms crossed, face impassive. "The outer shell should hold a thick enough layer of metallic hydrogen to shield the soldiers and mechs inside from enemy scans. They'll take the fuel down to the planet; they're going to need it for their fusion reactors. Once they're on the ground, well...." She shrugged. "We only need a distraction for long enough to get our drop-ships through their defenses."

"Seems awful small to hold a platoon of mecha and another platoon of your Rangers," he worried. "And environment suits with enough oxygen to keep them alive till they get to the surface."

"Stop giving me that bullshit," Lyta admonished him. "What's bugging you isn't how dangerous it is, it's that you can't be in it."

"I should be," he insisted mulishly, turning away from the assembly crew and stalking back into the makeshift field head-quarters they'd fashioned out of some deserted concrete bunkers left over from before the Reconstruction Wars.

He knew she was following him, but he ignored her, brushing past technicians running spare parts in and out of the clean-room repair shacks where they were constantly trying to remove the grit.

There was a planning center at the rear of the building, hung with old-tech flat-screen monitors, the best they could do out here. Star maps and long-distance shots of the moon where they *thought* the Jeuta base was located were displayed on the screens, red and green lines drawn across them by light pens in late-night planning sessions. They detailed plans based on incomplete intelligence and outright guesswork and the very sight of them ignited a furious frustration inside him.

The grandly-titled "ops center" was deserted, and he heard the door swing shut behind them. He turned to face Lyta, still feeling argumentative.

"If I'm going to order someone else into a death trap like that," he said, pointing in the general direction of the fake storage tank under assembly, "then I should damn well be in it with them."

"Leaving aside the fact you are *not* expendable," Lyta told him, her voice echoing like the snap of a bullwhip in the small room, "you are the commander. Not *just* a company commander. An Armor Corps company commander might be able to get away with leading from the front, but you're the overall commander of this mission, which means you have to stay alive as long as there's a chance of accomplishing it, and you need to lead from a position where you can change the plan if things go to shit."

She mimicked his enraged jab at the construction project outside the walls.

"And you aren't going to be able to command anything or change anything inside that damn Trojan Horse, whether it works or not."

"My brain knows you're right, Lyta," he admitted, hissing out a breath, leaning back against the edge of the table at the center of the room. "But my gut doesn't feel right about this."

"You're in command," she asserted. "I said it and I meant it. If you decide the plan is too risky and call it off, I'll back you. If you decide this whole job is a bad idea and cancel the contract, I'll back you." She took a step closer, almost nose to nose with him. "But you are not going to be inside the container, and I'm not either; I'm leaving it to Lt. Crowe because leading a platoon is his job. So, who are *you* going to assign to the mission, Captain?"

"We can't crawfish on this job," he said with dolorous acceptance.

Who, then? Paskowski had seniority, but the strike mecha were way too big to fit in the Trojan Horse, not to mention lacking in the mobility and versatility of the assault mecha. There was only one choice, if it was going to be someone he trusted to be there when he couldn't.

He hit a control at the center of the table and one of the screens on the wall switched its display to the feed from the drones flying a slow rotation of the training grounds.

Marc Langella's platoon was running full-speed tactical drills against Kurtz and Hernandez out on what they called the South Range, a thousand square kilometers of rolling hills and scrubland, the green of the brush coated with a thin film of frost on this early spring morning. It was basically a game of "capture the flag" played with thirty-to-fifty-ton mecha, their weapons powered down and replaced with laser designators and computer-simulated damage, but it was a good way to hone target-acquisition on the run as well as split-second decision making.

Langella's Golem was pounding through the saddle between two hills, the other three mecha raising a cloud of rust-colored particulates behind them, fifty meters separation between each in their ranger-file formation. Kurtz had noticed the dust rising and settled his platoon into an inverted wedge around the other side of the hill, weapons trained on where he believed Langella's mecha would emerge.

But Marc Langella wasn't stupid; he'd noticed the dust as well, and knew exactly how visible it made him. He and Jonathan had been trained by the same taskmasters, and for all his "dude-bro" exterior, Langella had been paying attention. Jump-jets ignited on the back of the Golems and as one, they soared over the hilltop, barely clearing it before the danger of overheating forced them down on the opposite slope...with a perfect field of fire overlooking Kurtz and his platoon.

There were no explosions, no rending metal, no ionizing gasses, just invisible laser beams lashing out in the infrared spectrum and striking detectors on the vital areas of the opposing force. Damage display screens aligned with the names of each of the pilots began flashing red and actuators began locking up as the combat assessment routine decided the hits from the simulated ETC cannons and missile launchers had been critical in nature.

He hadn't turned up the sound from the platoon commo nets, but he knew Kurtz would be muttering some backwater colony world epithet no one else had ever heard before, something like, "if that don't burn a raccoon's ass." And Marc Langella would be laughing, barely loud enough to hear, a broad smile splitting his face for a moment before he gave the next order to keep his people moving.

30

"There's no real choice, then," he told Lyta. "It has to be Marc."

"Do you think it's been long enough?" Jonathan asked, and it took Terry a beat to realize who he was asking.

His stomach went suddenly queasy, as if he were back in free-fall even though the *Shakak* had been decelerating at one gravity for hours.

"Umm, according to the flight data recorder from the drone we hid on the last shipment," Terry said, trying to sound confident, "the Jeuta took the tribute barge straight back to the gas giant's moon, accelerating and decelerating at over four gravities, and started transferring the cargo modules to the surface. They were back in orbit around the moon within a standard day after passing through the jump-point."

Which wasn't *exactly* answering the question, but it was close enough. They'd spent nearly two standard days hidden in the shadow of Danu, waiting for the Jeuta destroyer to come through the jump-point closest to the gas giant and lock onto the cargo barge. Then another twelve hours poised at the jump-point themselves, just to give the raiders enough time to get lost in their own drive exhaust so they'd miss the *Shakak* coming into the system.

Through the whole business, Jonathan had been antsy and keyed up, not that Terry could blame him. He didn't even want to be responsible for proclaiming the wait long enough and Jonathan was taking the whole weight of a very complicated and contingency-filled military intelligence operation on his shoulders.

Jonathan wouldn't even strap into an acceleration couch on the ship's bridge, moving from one spot to another, hanging onto the back of the seats of each duty station until the crewmember in question finally gave him the stink-eye until he moved on. Terry had only come up to the bridge at Captain Osceola's insistence, and the fact the man *had* insisted came as something of a shock. He'd found a spare fold-down acceleration seat at the far bulkhead, out of the way, and tried to stay quiet until Jonathan's wandering, restless attention had finally fallen on him.

"You sure you don't want to strap in, Captain Slaughter?" Osceola asked, trying unsuccessfully to hide his exasperation behind badly-faked respect. "Be a shame if we had to pull a sudden high-g maneuver while you were pacing around like a Goddamned expectant father."

Jonathan shot him a glare, but fell into the unoccupied seat behind the command station, strapping himself into the gel-padded acceleration couch.

"I hope they don't see our drive flare," Terry said and immediately regretted it when Jonathan's eyes went wide. "I mean, this is the time they'd see it, when we're decelerating..."

"If they're looking," Lyta Randell declared from her place at the Commo board, "they're going to see us."

She'd supplanted the usual technician and switched the board over to an operations control switchboard to coordinate the disparate elements of their attack. Terry knew there was the platoon of mechs and another of Rangers concealed in the cargo container, the two drop-ships full of pre-loaded mecha just waiting for their pilots, the two assault shuttles and the *Shakak* herself, but he wasn't sure if he'd forgotten anything.

"We just have to hope," Lyta added, "that the distraction worked and the Jeuta are too worried about other things right now."

Jonathan had bridled at her certainty they'd been spotted, but her reassurances seemed to calm him down and he settled back into the acceleration couch, eyes darting from one display to another. He was nervous, uncertain, and Terry wasn't used to seeing him this way. Logan—*yeah, I know, it's Jonathan now, but still*—had always been so sure of himself, so confident in his own abilities. It was somehow unsettling seeing him out of his element.

It's his first time. Everything he's doing on this mission, it's his first time doing it. He sniffed a nearly-silent laugh. *Mine, too.*

"We've burned off enough momentum," Osceola decided. "Kammy, cut deceleration thrust and flip us around."

He was glad he'd taken the motion sickness meds when the drive cut off abruptly, shunting them all back into micro-gravity, followed by the loud, persistent banging of the maneuvering thrusters firing for long seconds, spinning the ship end for end to present the swiftly-approaching moon with her armored nose.

"Hey boss," Tara said slowly, hesitantly, almost thoughtfully. Which was, Terry had come to find out in the last few weeks, very unlike her. "I'm picking up something coming around the orbit of the gas giant."

The world didn't have a name; even the system's red giant primary only had a half-forgotten number in some old, Imperial catalog someone had scrounged from a corrupted data disc. The giant planet sulked in dull orange at the disrespect, nearly filling the view in the forward screen, the target moon a small, shadowed disc against the arc of her mother.

"What?" Osceola asked, frowning as he peered at the readouts.

"It's coming across the terminator..." The woman's eyes went wide, her face slack for just a moment. "It's the destroyer!"

Terry felt a surge of panic, immediately at war with a host of ready rationalizations. *Maybe they won't see us, maybe they were just in orbit around the gas giant the whole time, maybe they're moving in because the force in the Trojan Horse is attacking the base down on the moon and the Jeuta called for help...*

"Sound general quarters!" Osceola snapped. "Arm weapons

and get the deflector screens active! Kammy, take us to a quarter-g acceleration!"

"We have an incoming message," Lyta Randell announced, her voice even and calm, but a sense of fatalistic acceptance in her expression Terry didn't remember ever seeing before. "Coming from the surface of the moon."

"Is it Marc?" Jonathan asked, leaning forward in his seat.

"No." Lyta's eyes closed for the briefest of seconds, just slightly longer than a blink, the only hint of what might be going on behind the mask of her face. "It's the Jeuta."

She traced a control line across the touch screen and the image of the gas giant was supplanted by the flattened features and doll-black eyes of one of the creatures. He'd read articles on the ways you could differentiate the males from the females, but he wasn't a biologist and he couldn't have figured it out even if one of them had stripped naked in front of him. All he could tell about this one was it was big and mean-looking and baring its sharpened teeth at them in a feral grin. And unlike most Jeuta he'd run across, it wore jewelry: a golden nose ring piercing through the thing's flattened nostril.

And it spoke.

"I am Hardrada," it—*he?*—declared, his voice raspy, unsuited to the language. "Here, my word is law, and my will is as the will of the gods. Lest you think otherwise…"

The view from the camera panned out to what had to be the surface of the moon, bathed in a crimson twilight with the arc of the gas giant visible in the sky. A corner of a what seemed to be a cross between a tent and a Quonset hut peeked out on one side of the image, but most of the camera view was taken up by what was unmistakably the Trojan Horse cargo module they'd built back on Fiachna. It rested in a cargo cradle brought down by a heavy-lift freight shuttle, and it yawned open, not separated along the explosive bolts they'd built into it but blown apart at a seam by what looked to have been high explosives. Inside, the shadowy, hulking forms of four mecha stood forlorn and unpowered. Outside, nearly three dozen men and women were lined up in rows, on their knees with their hands clasped behind their heads.

Nearly three dozen. Another four were sprawled on their backs, displayed like hunting trophies with no effort made to cover their corpses. Two had obviously been caught in the blast when the Jeuta had blown their way into the module; their Ranger body armor was burned and shredded and covered in blood. Their helmet faceplates had shattered, their arms and legs twisted and shattered. The other two had been shot. Maybe before he'd seen the carnage on Arachne, Terry might not have been able to tell the difference, but he recognized the signs now.

His gut twisted in ways the space-sickness drugs couldn't help and he clutched at the armrests of his acceleration couch, fighting to keep his stomach contents private. The bridge was as quiet as a grave, not a word spoken, hardly a breath taken.

Behind and beside the Rangers and mech pilots arrayed neatly in three lines were Jeuta warriors, their armor segmented and primitive-looking for all it was likely made from modern materials, their oversized hands filled with fat, heavy rifles trained on the humans. He was no better at reading Jeuta expressions now than when he'd boarded the *Shakak*, and Wihtgar hadn't volunteered to tutor him, but he felt sure the Jeuta guards *wanted* the prisoners to resist so they could kill them.

Terry recognized every single one of the prisoners. He wasn't great with names, but he'd seen their faces nearly every day of the last several weeks. He could name some of them. The female ranger with the shaved head was…Russo. She was a sergeant, he thought. He'd always thought he could see himself reflected off her head, it was so closely shaved, like polished mahogany.

Another of the rangers was a short, unlikely-looking man with hound-dog eyes and a jowly face. His name was Mahmoud, and

Terry had wondered how someone who looked as if he could barely lift himself out of bed had become a ranger under an officer as demanding as Lyta, but she insisted he was tough as a piece of old, chewed leather. At that moment, he looked scared shitless.

He knew Marc Langella, of course. He *hadn't*, not before he'd arrived on the *Shakak*, but you couldn't be on the same ship as someone as colorful as Langella and not know him. His humor and overall good mood were infectious and he always seemed to be smiling and joking. Not now. The whole left side of his face was a bruise, his left eye swollen shut, blood dripping from a cut on his cheek, and his jaw was clenched, maybe against the pain or maybe in frustration.

"You and the soft, decadent, spineless filth of the Dagda system sought to deceive us," Hardrada went on, the camera panning back to him in a jerky, hand-held motion. "You sought to kill us by stealth." An expression that might have been a snarl or the approximation of a grin. "I can appreciate that. The scheme was bold and crafty, worthy of the Jeuta. In a gesture of this appreciation, I will give you a choice." He raised a hand, thick-fingered with nails curled into claws, and held it palm down. "You may leave, your tails tucked between your legs in admission of our natural superiority, and we will dispose of these who have failed, who you have abandoned. Or," he turned the hand over and clenched the fingers into a fist, "you will come to us and we will give you the fight you want. Ship to ship, mech to mech, hand to hand."

Terry glanced away from the screen to Jonathan and Lyta. Lyta's face was still carefully crafted, inexpressive, though he knew her well enough to see the pain in the lines beside her eyes. Jonathan wasn't yet as accomplished an actor as the woman they'd once thought of as an aunt. His lips were peeled back, teeth bared, shoulders tensed against his restraints.

"Maybe you think I am soft for making this offer," Hardrada mused, head tilting. "I would not mislead you so."

The camera swung around again, the shaking and wobbling of the view threatening to bring back Terry's insipient nausea. Two of the Jeuta hauled one of the rangers before Hardrada, pushing him to his knees. Terry recognized the man—he was tall and broad-shouldered with a distinctive, sculpted face and close-cropped black hair. Lt. Crowe was his name, one of Lyta's three platoon leaders, the one she'd sent to lead the ranger contingent on the Trojan Horse.

His hands were tied behind his back, and a cut over his left eyebrow dripped blood down his aquiline nose, but his piercing grey eyes remained defiant. He struggled against his captors, but their grip on his shoulders was intractable and all he gained from fighting was a fist clubbing against the back of his neck. He lolled, stunned, remaining upright only because of the powerful hands gripping him.

Hardrada pulled a handgun from a holster strapped around his chest. The weapon was massive, a fat magazine curving down in front of its grip, the muzzle gaping incredibly wide. Terry didn't know much about guns, but he knew physics; Newton's first law told him launching a bullet as big as that muzzle at any sort of velocity would cause a shitload of recoil. Apparently, recoil didn't bother Jeuta.

Hardrada leveled the gun at Lt. Crowe.

Terry wanted to yell at the screen, wanted to yell at the others for *not* yelling at the screen, for not telling the Jeuta to stop. He didn't. It wasn't a two-way transmission; it was probably a recording, unless Hardrada had been standing out there with the prisoners for hours, waiting for them to come into range. And if screaming would have done any good, Lyta and Jonathan would have been doing it.

The shot should have been louder. It was muted by the automatic dampeners on the audio pickup of the camera, but the flash was huge, a ball of fire a meter across. Crowe's head splashed backwards onto the volcanic soil, leaving nothing left above his jawline, and then Terry *did* puke.

It was a damn good thing Osceola had ordered the ship to a quarter-gravity acceleration, because otherwise the stream of vomitus would have floated through the bridge as tumbling globules, drifting with the air currents until they splattered against something. Instead, the mess simply dripped through the gridwork deck plates as if they'd been built for the purpose. And maybe they had. He knew less about starship construction than he did about guns.

When he was able to raise his head again, coughing and gagging still, he saw the Jeuta guards had let Crowe's body topple to the ground. The guards' black and grey armor was splattered with red and pink, but it didn't seem to bother them. Had he been more confident of his interpretation of their expressions, he might have said they were reveling in it, breathing the officer's spilled life like a fine wine.

Hardrada slipped the gun back into place, then absently wiped a drop of stray blood-splatter from his bicep, rubbing the liquid between his thumb and forefinger.

"I await news of your decision."

The screen went black for the space of a second before returning to a view of the moon, even closer now, and the Jeuta destroyer bearing down on them.

Terry wiped at his chin and waited for someone to say something.

"We have to abort," Lyta said definitively. There was a devastation behind her eyes, underlying the professional tone of her voice. "There's no other choice."

"That destroyer'll kick our ass," Osceola declared, and Kammy and Tara nodded in agreement.

It might have been Jonathan Slaughter who'd sat down in the acceleration couch, but the man who rose from it and glared down at the others couldn't have been anyone but his brother, Logan Conner.

"We're going in."

There was no doubt in those steel-blue eyes, none in the square of his shoulders. They challenged anyone to disagree with him.

"You're fucking nuts!" Osceola exclaimed, unstrapping and jumping up to meet him in the center of the bridge. "You're going to get us all killed!"

"Log...," Lyta stuttered, caught herself before she blurted out his real name. "Jonathan," she corrected herself, "I know you want to help them, that you want to save Marc, but we can't throw more lives away, can't throw this *mission* away just to..."

"What *is* our mission, Major?" Jonathan interrupted her, looking past the irate Captain of the *Shakak* as if he wasn't even there. "You know where we have to go, how we have to get there. How do you expect us to get work if we run away from this fight and leave two platoons of our people to get slaughtered? You think anyone's going to hire a mercenary unit run by a coward?"

She hesitated, and Terry wondered how much what she'd seen on the screen was really affecting her.

"You said I was in command," he reminded her, "that you'd back my decisions. This is my decision."

"The *hell* it is!" Osceola blurted, jabbing at Jonathan's chest with a finger. "This is *my* fucking ship, and *my* people on it, and I'm not going to lead them on a suicide run because you feel guilty!"

Jonathan stared at him, silent for so long Terry wondered if he was going to hit the older man. Instead, he nodded sharply.

"Fine. Give us time to get our people and mecha loaded onto

the drop-ships and launch for the moon, then you can take off and make a run for the jump-point."

Osceola stared at him google-eyed, as if Jonathan had grown a second head.

"Boy, that destroyer will blow you out of space long before you hit atmosphere!"

"Probably, with no cover from you," Jonathan agreed.

Terry could see what Jonathan was trying to do. Hell, a blind man could see what Jonathan was trying to do. Osceola certainly did, because his lined and weathered face began to screw up with anger, but Jonathan already had an end-run around that.

"Are you coming, Lyta?"

She met his eyes and Terry thought something shifted in her expression, an adjustment of where the two of them stood with each other.

"Yes, *sir*," she said, standing. She touched a control on her 'link and spoke into its pickup. "Drop-ships and assault shuttles, prepare for immediate launch."

"Lyta, don't *do* this!" Osceola begged her, shaking his head, hands help up imploringly. "Use your Goddamned head!"

"Oh, Don," she said, her voice uncharacteristically gentle, the fingers of her right hand trailing across the stubble on his chin. "Where's the fun in that?"

Jonathan looked over to Terry, nodded in what might have been a goodbye, then headed for the hatchway. Lyta Randell had turned to follow when Donner Osceola cursed long and loud enough for her to glance back.

"Fine! The hell with both of you! If you think I'm going to..."

He trailed off with a snarl of utter frustration, then slammed a fist into the armrest of his command chair before falling back into it and strapping down.

"Kammy," he snapped, sullen and resentful. "Increase thrust to one gravity and bring us as close to that fucking moon as we can get before the shuttles launch." He glared at Terry. "And *you*, bright boy! Start digging into whatever files we have on that class of destroyer! I need a plan of attack in ten minutes!"

In the hatchway, Lyta Randell was smiling.

"I'll see you on the other side, Don," she said.

"Yeah," Osceola murmured, watching her go. "I love you, too."

4

B oost jammed Kathren Margolis back into her seat with thousands of tons of thrust as her assault shuttle screamed away from the *Shakak* and into what seemed like certain death. At least Acosta seemed to think so.

"They're waiting for us," he reminded her, obviously thinking the point was important enough to warrant the effort of squeezing it past six gees of acceleration. "Shouldn't we be running?"

"We are Wholesale Slaughter, Francis," she reminded him through a fixed grimace, unable to turn her head enough to shoot him a baleful glare. "We run *towards* the sound of the guns."

"Yeah, but there isn't any sound in space," Acosta reminded her. "Isn't that like, a loophole or something?"

Now she *did* want to look at him, because she was sure he'd just made a joke, and the man hadn't shown a single sign of a sense of humor in the whole time she'd known him.

"Don't worry, Francis, we'll be in the soup soon enough, and you'll hear more than you ever wanted to."

"I'm reading four assault-class shuttles rising from the surface," he reported, as if he'd been waiting for the right moment to insert it into the conversation. "Their trajectory has them heading toward us, but I'd guess their real target is the drop-ships."

"Gosh, y'think?" she murmured, touching the commo controls by feel and memory. "Slaughter One, this is Cover One, we have four bogies heading your way. We will move to intercept. Instruct your pilots to maintain course and increase speed. Good luck. Over."

She didn't wait for a reply, just hit another switch. "Cover Two, this is Cover One. We will designate the bogies as Gomer One through Four, from left to right. I will engage Gomer One and Two, you will take Three and Four, over."

"Wilco, Cover One," Lt. Lee responded. "Splitting off in five. Over."

She throttled back the shuttle's fusion drive, ramping the boost back to a more manageable two gravities, keeping half an eye on the navigation display and figuring out if and when she'd have to run a deceleration burn before atmospheric entry. It as way too easy to get wrapped up in a fight and find yourself taking too steep an angle, and sloppy piloting could get you killed just as dead as the enemy.

Too much to think about, she griped inside her head, where the whining wouldn't bother anyone else. The *Shakak* was boosting past them, heading to engage the Jeuta destroyer, a bigger and more heavily armored ship. If Osceola couldn't figure out a way to take her down, they'd all be stranded on this radioactive hell-hole in the unlikely event if they won the battle. Jonathan and his company were heading down into what was undoubtedly an ambush, if they even made it down to the surface past the Jeuta air defenses.

And he was in love with her and starting to talk about the future. Somehow that scared her more than the enemy but she wasn't sure why. Okay, maybe she was. It had been months since Ramman and she was still having nightmares. The counsellors had told her she couldn't let what had happened there control her, couldn't let it ruin the rest of her life. It would be like letting the bandit scum victimize her all over again.

Why the hell am I thinking about this now?

"Gomers are launching!" Acosta's voice broke just a bit at the end of the warning, but for once, she didn't blame him.

A swarm of tell-tale thermal blooms shot away from the enemy shuttles, flickering fireflies against the angry darkness of the volcanic moon.

"Countermeasures!" she snapped. He was already launching them, but you didn't take anything for granted.

Dull thumps vibrated through the hull at the launch of the ECM chaff and she saw the sparkling halo of electrostatically-charged particulates spreading out from her bird. She checked the targeting computer, saw the range was still too long for the lasers and armed one of the handful of intercept missiles on the shuttle's weapons load-out. It had been a risk going with the radar-guided anti-ship missiles, taking space away from her ground-support arsenal, but she'd seen from the destroyer these Jeuta had military gear, and she'd had to figure that might mean military-grade assault shuttles.

It had been, she decided, the right call.

"Fox one," she announced, touching the trigger on the control stick.

A solid, metallic clunk sounded, louder and more substantial than the countermeasures, as the radar-guided ASP-7 missile slid forward into the launch bay and separated on a puff of inert coldgas before the quick-burnout solid-fuel rocket ignited. The missile leapt away from them as if they were standing still, streaking out at over twenty gravities of thrust.

"Those aren't military grade." Acosta's comment seemed a non sequitur for a second, until she realized he was staring at the threat display, watching the oncoming enemy missiles.

He was right. You could tell by the acceleration. The enemy weapons weren't boosting at anywhere near what their own were, and they were already veering off course, fooled far too easily by the ECM chaff coming from both her own bird and the drop-ships. Missiles were easy to fabricate, fuel easy to brew, guidance systems not so much. And the material engineering and construction techniques to create combustion chambers strong enough to allow twenty gravities of thrust weren't something that could be worked up in some jury-rigged fab shop on a deserted moon.

Hers was manufactured on Sparta, using the most advanced technology available in the wake of the Fall and the Reconstruction Wars, and it *nearly* made it through the ECM and anti-missile defenses of the enemy bird. It wasn't fooled by the chaff, but the last line of defense was a bank of flechette guns recessed into niches in the hull. Katy couldn't see them discharging, but she knew they'd worked when her missile's warhead exploded half a kilometer from its target, ignited by waves of steel ball bearings expelled by either magnetic fields or perhaps something as crude as gunpowder.

The missile might not have impacted the shuttle they'd designated Gomer Four, but it certainly *had* an impact; the warhead was a more sophisticated version of the missile defense systems, a huge, one-shot flechette gun with its muzzle pointed right at the Jeuta bird. Tungsten penetrators flared against reactive armor on the exterior of the shuttle's fuselage and still penetrated, escaping atmosphere igniting in jets of fire. Gomer Four didn't explode and the drive didn't cut off, but there was a qualitative difference in how it flew. She didn't see it on the sensors as much as felt it in her gut.

Her instinct was borne out when she saw the drop-ships changing course, angling in for atmospheric entry and three of the enemy birds maneuvering to follow…but not the one she'd hit. Its engine was still boosting, but it was running without guidance, the crew dead or incapacitated by the warhead. Lee had launched a missile too, but his had been knocked out by the combined defense grids of the two Jeuta aerospacecraft and everyone was closing into laser range now…slugging distance, her tactical instructors had called it.

The Jeuta weren't using lasers, though, and she found out the hard way when something about the size of her arm, with enough metal in it to register on the radar, passed only a few meters from her cockpit, … traveling at somewhere north of three thousand meters per second.

"Shit!" she blurted, rolling her bird away from the line of fire.

"They got a coil-gun on a damned shuttle?" Acosta said, eyes wide in disbelief. "That's fucking insane!"

It *was* risky, and she could see the chief downside of it already: the shuttle that had fired on them was burning maneuvering jets wildly, trying to course-correct after the recoil from the electromagnetic slug-shooter had propelled them onto a new trajectory. The upside, for the other team, was that it only took one hit and you were capital-D Dead. And if they got off one accurate shot at the drop-ships…

"Lee!" she yelled into the pickup, opening the throttle and nudging the control stick over again, aiming her nose at the Jeuta bird. "They have coil-guns! Close with and intercept now, before they can get a shot at the drop-ships!"

Boost pushed against her chest and she fought to settle the targeting reticle over Gomer Three before it could fire again. Keeping her course too stable was dangerous with the muzzle of the coil-gun yawning in wait, but she didn't even consider the risk to herself. Protecting the drop-ships was the mission, and the mission came first.

"He's lined up on us," Acosta warned her, but she saw the reticle light up green and her teeth showed in a predatory smile.

"No," she corrected him, "we're lined up on him."

She touched the firing control and as far as her senses were concerned, nothing happened. The targeting computer knew better, though, and simulated the burst of laser pulses for her, connecting her shuttle with the Gomer Three for nearly a full second. The Jeuta shuttle was heavily armored and she didn't expect to pierce all the way through to the cockpit or the drives, so she hadn't tried to. Instead, she'd fired at the muzzle of the coil-gun and was rewarded with a rainbow flare of energy as the laser blew apart the electromagnetic coils and took a good portion of the shuttle's belly armor with it.

Gomer Three banked away with a flare of thrusters, turning its suddenly-vulnerable underside away from their guns. Katy ignored Three, confident it was out of the fight. It still had missiles, but they wouldn't be effective against the drop-ships' defenses, and, most importantly, it wasn't going to be able to enter the atmosphere with its belly armor ruptured. She hoped Lee was holding his own with the other two enemy craft because she had enough problems of her own.

She was low, too low, about to hit atmosphere, and way off her safe entry trajectory. This wasn't going to be pleasant.

"Hold on," she advised Acosta, more a verbal tic than useful advice.

She cut forward thrust long enough to yank the stick around, her world tilting on its side to the staccato beat of the maneuvering jets until the moon was behind them and the expanse of open space ahead. Nine gravities of deceleration *hurt*, even just for a minute's duration. She'd been trying to keep an eye on the tactical display, to get a sense of how Lee was doing with the other two Jeuta shuttles, but tunnel vision and a very urgent need to pass out interfered.

All she could concentrate on was tightening her stomach and legs, trying to force blood back to her brain. The only extraneous thought worming its way through was a sense of gratitude her flight suit could absorb pee.

In the end, she cut the braking maneuver a few seconds short, willing to trade coming in just a little hot for a clear view of the enemy. The planet's gravitational pull was stronger and more evident by now, fighting against her skew-flip maneuver as she turned the assault shuttle back into their direction of travel. Acosta was wheezing beside her, but she was too distracted to even make fun of him.

The drop-ships were far ahead of her, already through the upper layer of the moon's atmosphere and into the dark, roiling storm clouds lurking below as if in ambush. Lee was on the tail of one of the enemy shuttles, slicing into its portside wing with a laser-burst even as she watched; but the last, the one they'd designated Gomer Two, was burning hard after the drop-ships, firing shot after shot from its chin-mounted coil-gun.

"Goddamn it, Lee," she murmured, opening the throttle once more, the bird running superheated air through the reactor instead of metallic hydrogen for reaction mass.

The man was a good pilot, but he was too *slow*, too careful, and sometimes you just needed to go balls-out—*metaphorically* —and rush after the bad guys with your ass on fire and murder in your eyes. If they'd had anyone else to pull from, she would have had him replaced, but beggars couldn't be choosers, so she'd just have to take up the slack. *Again.*

She didn't have a target lock, but they were close enough— she fired the lasers and lightning flashed, the thickening air ionizing to plasma as the laser pulses superheated it, forks branching off the glowing trunk. She grinned, feeling like Zeus hurling thunderbolts from Mount Olympus. Zeus, of course, would have hit the enemy on the first try, while her shot missed narrowly. The turbulence from the heat of the ionized air passing only a few dozen meters away shook the enemy bird, though, sending it banking off to the left before the pilot could correct.

She had to give the Jeuta pilot credit: he didn't break off to fight her. He kept with his primary targets and stuck hard on the drop-ships, but just because she gave him credit didn't mean she wouldn't kill him. She'd had no problems killing human bandits since Ramman, and Jeuta were even easier.

She frowned. The thought *had* started to bother her, and she wondered if it had something to do with Logan's talk about the future. *Jonathan,* she chided herself. But then decided, no, the future was Logan, not Jonathan.

The reverie floated over her head like thought-balloons in the manga she'd used to read as a child, disconnected from her actions, the tactical decisions made at an instinctive level. Her hands nudged the stick over, stroked the throttle like a lover, bringing her back onto Gomer Two's tail. He was launching coun-termeasures, radar-spoofing chaff and flares and probably what-ever passed for a toilet seat on a Jeuta shuttle. And it was working. Her radar and lidar were next to useless, thermal was screwed by the flares and even computer optical interpolation wasn't showing much in the flitting, flickering bits of clear sky amid towering castle walls constructed from storm clouds.

She let her finger dance toward the firing stud, but hesitated. The drop-ships were somewhere up there, as well, just as invis-ible due to the ECM machinations of the Jeuta assault shuttle. She couldn't take the risk, but she knew a lack of visibility wouldn't stop the Jeuta pilot from firing blindly. Cursing, she fed power to the jets, the acceleration, pounding her across the ring of the sky was as if she was sparring Lyta back in the gym in Argos.

I could never lay a glove on that woman unless she let me, she admitted. She had better luck sparring with Jonathan in the *Shakak's* gym, though he could have been taking it easy on her.

He insisted he wasn't, and she would have gotten even with him if he'd let on he was. *But you just never know...*

"We're gonna fly right up his fucking tailpipe," Acosta croaked.

"Shut up and watch the sensors," she snapped. It was probably useless, but then so was he. At least it gave him something to do.

She was using what Lyta liked the call her "Mk I Eyeball Sensors," squinting at the darkness and wondering how much was honest cumulonimbus and how much was residue of the volcanos she'd seen on the planetary scans. Volcanic clouds could be dangerous, especially if the ash got into the intake turbines.

It rains on the just and the unjust, she mused. If it was that bad, the Jeuta wouldn't be able to fly in it either.

There. A flash of engine flare, a different visual signature than a drop-ship, something she knew on a gut level. She couldn't use a missile, not in this murky, sensor-fritzing rap. She fired a three-second burst with the lasers, using Kentucky Windage as one of her weapons instructors had called it—the other had been less charitable, referring to it as "shooting by Braille."

The laser pulses set the clouds on fire, lighting up the Jeuta shuttle with their actinic glow, just kissing the underside of the aerospacecraft. Armor sublimated in a halo of burning gas and Gomer Two pulled up with a jerky, desperate haste, not banking away but jinking and deking wildly. She felt a warmth settling over her, the realization that she had him, that he was one trigger-pull away from nonexistence.

"Katy!" Acosta yelled practically in her ear, a grating desperation in his voice. "On our six!"

She knew. She could see it in the rear camera display, Gomer One. They'd gotten past Lee, maybe taken him down or maybe just shaken the damned dithering bastard. They were right there, on her ass and ready to fire. She could break off, pull straight up, maybe split-S and try to get a shot at Gomer One...but then she'd lose Gomer Two, and he had a clear shot at the drop-ships. At Jonathan... Logan.

"Sorry, Francis," she whispered, pulling the trigger.

She never saw the shot hit home.

"Holy hell!"

Jonathan Slaughter didn't know who had cursed over the open company net, and couldn't focus his vision well enough to read the name on his Vindicator's HUD, but he agreed with the sentiment. The mecha were fastened into their cradles by magnetic grapples, which kept them nice and secure, but unfortunately also made them slaves to the maneuvers of the drop-ship, and the drop-ship was thrashing like a bass on the line.

As commander, he had access to the shuttle's sensors readouts, external camera feeds and pilot communications but following all that wasn't as easy as it had sounded. It was like watching someone else play a video game in a virtual-reality neural halo while all you had was a two-dimensional flat-screen and you didn't even know the rules. And two of your best friends shook you violently every three seconds, yelled in your ear, and occasionally kicked you in the nuts.

"Can't shake him," Jonathan made out through the pilot's abbreviated idiom.

He knew the "him" the pilot was speaking of—he'd been able to make out that much in the rear camera feed. It was one of the Jeuta assault shuttles, as angular and ugly as a combat knife. They were firing coil-guns, he'd gathered, and understood why it upset the pilots so much. It didn't make him feel warm and fuzzy, either. He'd seen what a tungsten slug could do to a mech or a shuttle. Sometimes he wished the researchers could figure out a way to make a coil-gun small enough to fit on a mech and still pack enough of a punch to make it worth channeling so much of the reactor's power into one weapon.

And then there's the recoil...

He shook off the debate he'd heard in mech-jock bars since he was in the Academy, not because he had anything better to do but mostly because he was certain they were all about to die. He didn't want his last thoughts to be about something pointless. Instead, he thought about Katy.

"We got a Cover bird behind us!"

The copilot, her name was Jansen he thought. There was hope in her voice, infectious. Was it Katy? Or maybe the other guy, Lee?

Come on, take that Jeuta fucker down, he urged.

"Jamming's bad," the pilot, Lt. Vazquez said. Jonathan couldn't see his face, but his voice sounded like he was chewing on a mouthful of lemons. "Can't even read the damn IFF."

"Hell, I can't even get a read on Drop-Ship Two."

"Shit!"

The exclamation was synchronous with a spastic, jerking bank to the starboard and Jonathan's restraints bit into his shoulders again, leaving him chafed and sore before he'd even had a chance to leave the damned drop-ship.

"Fucking coil-gun!" the pilot grunted. "He's gonna put a round right up our ass in a second! I'm taking us down hard! Warn 'em back there, Chief!"

"All personnel, secure for violent maneuvers and rapid descent." Chief Nakamura delivered the warning deadpan, as if he were letting them know there was a thirty percent chance of rain and they might want to take a jacket along if they went outside.

"Prepare for violent maneuvers?" Lt. Kurtz said. "What th'hell have they *been* doing?"

"Let's keep the chatter to a minimum," Jonathan snapped. "Platoon leaders, prepare for deployment the second we reach survivable altitude. Ski," he said to Lt. Paskowski, "your heavies are going to need a lower altitude with those strap-on jets. I need to stay with the forward platoons. I want you to link up with Ford and her Arabalests at Objective Alpha, cover her mecha while she lays down covering fire from the table rock we saw on the orbital scans."

"Roger that, sir," Paskowski clipped off.

"Got it, sir," Ford acknowledged. Jonathan wondered if she resented being stuck in the rear with fire support. It was the life of an Arbalest jock but it would have driven him nuts.

"Kurtz, you lead off when we hit the ground. I'll be in-between you and Hernandez's machines. Move fast but stay low unless I order. It's hot as shit down there, so their sensors won't be able to see a damn thing, but neither will ours. Let's not give them a target they don't need sensors to see."

"Gotcha, Cap."

Suddenly, talking was no longer an option. The drop-ship was huge, massive, ungainly, something that shouldn't rightly have been able to stay in the air if it weren't for the ability to pack two fusion reactors into the big lifting body. Raw power kept it airborne, but nothing in the universe could keep it stable in this caustic, roiling, volcanic hellscape of an atmosphere. He was pitching downward, rolling and yawing and even though he'd never had motion sickness a day in his life, he had to clench his teeth to keep his stomach contents inside. He couldn't see anything, couldn't bring himself to even open his eyes to look at the view from the cockpit screens for fear he'd lose his last meal. *Was it breakfast? Lunch?*

He didn't need to see to know they were low, dangerously low, recklessly low, and he wasn't sure they'd be able to pull up. Clipped-off and abbreviated bits of back-and-forth between the pilot and copilot ran past his ears, not catching a firm purchase, until one sentence rang clear and hollow inside his head, the pronouncement of a judge, the slamming of a gavel.

"The Cover bird is down..."

Jonathan felt his blood curdling inside his veins and he fumbled for the commo controls to demand to know *which* bird was down and where, but *something* slammed into the drop-ship, sending it rolling back and forth, and very nearly tumbling forward in a death spiral before the pilots brought it back under control. A transmission from the crew chief blared in his ear, demanding attention, several degrees more urgent than anything he'd heard Nakamura say for the whole length of their voyage.

"Attention all mech elements! Light and heavy, drop now! Emergency drop! Drop! Drop! Drop!"

Oh, sweet Asha preserve us...

They'd been hit and were jumping high and early and he was about to get them all killed.

"All platoons, drop!" he echoed, finding the control for the magnetic locks and slapping it with the heel of his right hand.

The world dropped out from beneath his feet and the wind immediately tried to take him, tried to send the Vindicator tumbling out of control. Jonathan slammed his heels into the jump-jet control pedals as if he were digging them into the fabric of spacetime. Fusion-fired jets roared in defiance of gravity and his stomach recoiled along with a sense of hard-won stability. The map in his HUD had him nearly three hundred meters up, still moving forward at nearly ten meters per second but slowing, coming down over what looked to be an old lava bed, rolling plains, way too open for his comfort.

Between the background radiation, the flare of the storms, and the heat washing up from thermal features all around them, his sensors weren't worth shit. He couldn't even read the IFF signals from his own mecha, could barely *see* them even on infrared.

They were coming down scattered across the lava beds, spread out like the pattern from an ancient bird-hunting shotgun; and from what he remembered, they were at least fifteen kilometers from the objective. Well, *some* of them were, and the rest wouldn't be getting lost easily, not with the big damned volcano sticking two kilometers up over the landscape as an unmissable landmark.

Navigation wasn't going to be the problem. At two hundred meters up, the overheat warnings began flashing and his jump-jets shut down automatically.

"Shit, shit, shit," he murmured to himself, knowing no one else could have heard even if he'd broadcast it on broadband.

It was the background music for a desperate race against automated safety systems, a race he'd never had time to run in combat. Jumps in combat lasted a few seconds, maximum, and if overheating shut down your jets, they were down and so were you. A hundred and fifty meters up and several seconds of free-fall to spare were a luxury he'd never hoped to have, but here it was and happy Yalda to everyone, hope you enjoy the gift...

Thanks be to Mithra he'd been trained by men and women who thought a mech jock should know everything about their machine, not just how to pilot it. The jump-jets were always the first system to overheat and getting them back up and running when you really needed them was one of the first officially-against-the-regs things instructors taught students who they thought could handle the knowledge without blowing themselves up. He'd felt pride at the time, pride in their trust, their faith he wouldn't run his mouth to his father or Colonel Anders and get them written up. Later, he'd realized his father and Donnell Anders had probably been taught the same tricks, but there were certain official fictions that had to be maintained.

All bureaucratic pretense aside, bypassing the heat safeties on the jump-jets could kill you; and the only time you cut that particular corner was when the risk of death by overheating or cockpit fire was secondary to death by crashing into, say, a bed of meta-morphic rock. Like now, for instance.

Red indicators flashed yellow, the best he was going to get for three seconds' work, and he tried again, pressing tentatively at first and nearly shouting exultation when the jets reignited. The yellow indicator bars were still pushing towards red, and this time if they struck the crimson deadline there would be no going back, not in the time he had left. The ground was still approaching too fast, the upcoming impact too hard and he couldn't afford to be crippled after he landed, not if he wanted to get to the objective quickly enough to rescue those hostages alive.

Muttering a prayer to a God he didn't think should be both-ered with trivialities, he shoved the control pedals to their stops. Turbines screamed, tortured beyond endurance, wailing their death cries and then coming apart, their blades heated past the breaking point, blowing out the back of their housings like shaped charges, the front protected by the reactor shielding, as was the cockpit. The thrust disappeared, and the Vindicator's footpads slammed into the ground less than a second later.

The mech sank into a crouch, the last bit of momentum driving its knees nearly into its chest, its articulated left-hand smacking into the jagged, razor-edged lava rock. And Jonathan Slaughter was down.

He let the mech rest in place for a long moment, assessing his own damage before he examined the harm he'd caused to the machine. Blood ran down his chin, the taste of copper in his mouth, and he ran his tongue over his teeth carefully, not finding anything missing but feeling a cut in the side of his mouth. That was going to hurt like a son of a bitch when he had time to think about it. His back was sore, and that would hurt later, too. No broken bones, no torn muscles or ligaments as far as he could tell.

The damage to the machine was easier to read, the injuries highlighted in red and flashing yellow. The jump-jets were a total loss and there was a problematic yellow flash from his missile launch pod. He didn't have an external camera monitor back there anymore, but he'd have been willing to bet the same shrapnel which had taken out the viewer had damaged the launcher.

The Vindicator's hip, knee and ankle actuators were all flashing yellow, but he was confident they'd hold. It wasn't as if he'd be putting them through another jump...

The rest seemed good to go, and he pushed the machine to its feet, feeling the slight sluggishness of the hip motivators but compensating for it automatically. If this had been a planet with standard gravity, he'd have been dead and the mech would have been so much shattered junk, but it was a moon—a damned big moon, but still a moon, and had less than half standard pull.

He looked around, first inside his cockpit and then at the exterior camera views. There was no guidance by satellite, none by signals from orbital ships, or from other mecha. His commo board showed nothing but static and his IFF display was a blank stretch of blue. He had the dead-reckoning map and nothing else.

Outside was nearly total darkness but for the far-away glow, dull red and foreboding, of the active volcano. Infrared showed nothing but barren wasteland for kilometers around him, devoid of life...except for the flares of jump-jets and strap-on landing rigs, flickering fitfully in the night, a swarm of hesitant fireflies in the low-slung clouds.

He pointed himself at the nearest one and started running.

5

"You realize this is probably the stupidest thing you've ever done, right?" Kammy asked, eyes frozen on the screen and the incoming flight of anti-ship missiles.

"Not even in the top five," Donner Osceola assured him, leaning forward in his seat.

That was the great thing about ship-to-ship combat: it was carried out under boost the whole time, not dicking around in free-fall. He was a spacer—he didn't mind microgravity, but it was easier to *think* when your head wasn't stuffed up and you could swallow your own spit without straining and... *Damn, I sound like a groundpounder.*

"Countermeasures launching," Tara reported, not even bothering to tell him what a bad idea she thought this was. She'd gotten it out of her system while the Spartan troops were still launching their shuttles. Kammy, on the other hand, wouldn't shut up.

We might as well be married.

"I'm not worried 'bout the missiles," he mused, more to himself than the bridge crew.

"You're *not*?" Nance asked, looking back from a Commo station that was next to useless at the moment, eyes going wide.

"These things ain't gonna be Dominion tech," he explained, trying not to get impatient with the Spartan. "Not even your ordinary Jeuta military tech. It'll just be whatever they could whip up from black-market parts and the *Shakak* could have taken those down even before you Spartan boys and girls gave us some extra goodies."

As if to prove out his words, one of the Jeuta missiles detonated in a flash of fusing hydrogen, a globe of thermonuclear fire expanding rapidly and fading just as quickly. Another followed, and a third, others simply drifting off into space, their guidance or propulsion systems damaged by the barrage of simple steel ball bearings expelled by chemical propellants from the warheads of the *Shakak's* missile defense arsenal. The anti-missile defense rockets were cheap and easy to make, and a ship this size could carry hundreds of them. Any real military anti-ship missile worth its salt would have an on-board reactor with its own electromagnetic deflector shield, reactive armor, radar shielding and a dozen other countermeasures to fool the countermeasures, but those were all complicated and expensive and hard to get.

"Then what *are* you worried about?" Nance wondered, staring at him as if he were one of the *Spenta Mainyu*, the beneficent spirits, just for having some concept of the enemy's tactical strengths.

What the hell kind of dumbass commanders does the Spartan Navy put out nowadays?

"Ship as big as theirs," he told her, emphasizing the destroyer with a nod, "has enough space for a dedicated reactor to power her weapons. She puts a laser into our flank, it's gonna burn right through our armor."

"She'd have to be pretty close for that." Terry, the kid. He hadn't said a word in nearly a half an hour, having buried his nose in the small readout screen for the tactical files the Spartans had brought aboard, searching for any intelligence on the enemy ship. "Even with a fusion reactor powering them, their lasers would have a fairly short range."

"And if we were running from her, like nice, sane spacers," Osceola shot back, a bit of anger still in his words even though he'd been the one to make the final decision, "maybe that could save our asses. But in case you hadn't noticed, genius, we're heading *that* way." He jabbed a finger at the image of the destroyer. "So please tell me you've fucking found something!"

"It's Mbeki," Terry confirmed. "Early Reconstruction War era. There are some old records about a Mbeki destroyer called the *Durban* that went missing at a battle with Shang near the Jeuta-held worlds. I think this is the *Durban*."

Osceola tried to find patience, but he hadn't used it in so long, he'd forgotten where he he'd last seen it.

"That's all fucking interesting, kid," he snapped, "but I wasn't asking for a history lesson, I was looking for something I could use to *kill* those assholes!"

The kid dithered for a second, playing for time Osceola thought, using a verbal tic he'd learned in school when a professor asked him a question he wasn't sure about. Shit like that was fine in academia, but he'd have to break the kid of the habit if he was going to be useful out here.

"Listen, genius, when I ask you a question, you either tell me the answer or admit you don't have one so I stop wasting time! You got that?"

He was being hard on the kid, and it felt like hitting a puppy in the nose with a broom, right down to the weepy, brown eyes, but some things had to be done. The kid looked gobsmacked and Osceola had resigned himself to the idea it had been a waste of time when the puppy-dog face finally firmed up.

"There's one thing I saw," Terry said, obviously trying to

sound more confident and decisive. He actually seemed more like a little kid pretending to be a grown-up, but at least it was an improvement. "The destroyer was designed and built during the later parts of the Fall, early in the Reconstruction Wars, and they were trying to duplicate an old Imperial design, the *Konigsberg*."

He was talking faster now, as if he were afraid Osceola was about to cut him off.

Not an unreasonable fear.

"But the *Konigsberg*'s design was predicated on using the old Alanson-McCleary stardrive. We don't have any idea how to manufacture the stardrive anymore, but we have a general idea of the physics of it, and one of the effects of the drive is that it warps spacetime around it and that makes it into a sort of energy shield."

Osceola was perhaps half a second away from tossing the kid off the bridge when the implications of the last sentence finally hit him.

"There's gaps in the armor." It wasn't a question, it was a reasonable assumption.

"A few small ones," Terry agreed, an eager grin splitting his face. "And one *big* one, right where the drive propagation disc was mounted on the original. It's right over the primary power trunk from the reactor to the weapons." The kid's smile faded a bit. "They replaced the disc with one for their electromagnetic deflectors though, so it's not vulnerable to a missile or a railgun shot. You'll have to use a laser."

"Shit," Kammy moaned. "So, all we gotta' do is make them sit still while we circle around them at close range and shoot out their deflector dish. I'm sure they ain't got no lasers of their own over there to defend the thing, and we won't be able to use our own laser defenses or we'll attenuate our own beam."

"You're always such a damned ray of sunshine," Osceola told him. He rubbed his palms together, then cracked his knuckles as if he were about to get started on a big job. "Okay, we need them to have a reason to point their deflector dish straight at us and I can think of a damn good one. Kammy, take us to three gravities and aim straight at her. Tara, arm the main gun and prepare to fire when I give the word."

"I love it when you get all aggressive, boss," Tara croaked a laugh. "Gets me all worked up."

"I hope we don't get killed," Osceola said grimly. "Because that is not the image I want to take with me to the afterlife."

The woman was laughing as acceleration pushed them back into their seats and the *Shakak* leapt into battle.

All we need is a fife and a drum, Jonathan mused, thinking of the reproduction he'd seen in the museum in Argos of a painting from the ancient, pre-Imperial days.

The mecha shuffling slowly and painfully through the lava beds reminded him of those wounded foot-soldiers in the picture, slogging on into battle because there just wasn't any other choice. They were a rag-tag lot: besides his Vindicator, there were three Golems including Lt. Kurtz's, two Arbalests though not Lt. Ford's, and ironically enough, Paskowski's full platoon of strike mechs, all four of them as perfect as if they'd stepped right off the production line.

The damn strap-on jump kits don't overheat as quick as the integral kind, he thought with a rueful sigh. Of course, they were only good for one aerial insertion and then they were junk to be recycled, which made them too expensive to use on every mission.

"Sir," Kurtz said over their private channel, "do you think Hernandez and the others will be okay back there?"

Jonathan winced at the question, mostly because he'd been asking himself the same thing for nearly twenty minutes. He'd made the call to leave the mecha too badly damaged to walk or fight with their pilots under the command of Lt. Aliyah Hernandez, whose Spartacus had suffered a catastrophic left knee joint failure. There were four of them, half her platoon and half Kurtz's, plus an Arbalest pilot who'd wandered in, her mech too far away and too badly damaged to reach the others. Lt. Ford was still missing.

"I think they'll be fine," he told Kurtz, trying to sound more confident than he felt. "As long as we win this thing," he amended.

And as long as the drop-ships make it down safely, and as long as Osceola somehow beats that destroyer and is still around to pick us up if we do win down here, he added to himself but not to Kurtz.

He shoved those worries aside and concentrated on the things he could actually control. He didn't like their formation—it was too bunched up, less than fifty meters between mecha. It was a necessary evil, at least in his opinion, because of the terrain. The lava beds had curled into a canyon, carved back at a time when there'd been a river running through there, before the volcanic uplift had changed its course. The walls were less than a hundred meters apart at their widest, the footing rocky and uneven and the visibility beyond those walls almost nil. If they'd had functioning jump-jets, he would have bypassed the whole mess, but doing it all on foot with gimpy mecha along would have added hours to the route. He didn't think they had that kind of time. At least they were close enough they could all communicate with laser-line-of-sight relay, which was reliable even with the background radiation and jamming, and secure as well.

Kurtz was in the lead with the combined platoon from his and Hernandez's mecha while the strike platoon brought up the rear and he stayed in the center with the two Arbalests. He knew it was the right thing to do, but he chafed at the confinement, at the lack of maneuverability. Without the jump-jets, the rocks seemed to drag at the mech's footpads with more gravitational pull than the moon actually possessed and the walls felt as if they were closing in.

"It's widening out up here," Kurtz reported from around two hundred meters ahead and Jonathan fought an instinct to rush up to see with his own eyes.

Instead, he tied into Kurtz's camera feed and saw what the platoon leader was seeing: the end of the canyon and the end of the lava beds. Ahead, the ground was softer, older and much more alive. A polychromatic moss seemed to grow on every rock, every bare stretch of soil, what was probably a mutation of the original terraforming algae the Empire had dropped on the moon a thousand years or more ago, designed to bond with anything and produce arable soil.

It had done its job, even on this volcanic, radioactive hellhole. Short, twisted trees with scaly bark clumped together in thickets, the branches of each so intricately woven with those of the others it was impossible to tell where one left off and the other began. Broad-leaf grasses and thorn bushes filled in the gaps and it seemed as if wherever something could grow, something did.

There had to be insects, animals, and maybe birds out there, somewhere in the rolling hills stretching out towards the mountains, and the glow of the volcano, though they were probably genetically altered to survive the conditions. They wouldn't be showing their faces on a night like this, not with the scream of turbojets and the thunder of mech footpads and the smell of blood and death in the air. Animals had more sense than that.

He recognized the terrain from the mission brief and his mapping software matched it even closer. The Jeuta outpost was on the other side of the hills, three kilometers farther, in a river valley with actual flowing water, something rare and valuable in a place like this. The Jeuta under Hardrada had a fusion reactor and a cleared-out landing zone and at least one prefab, quick-setup warehouse/workshop/fabrication center big enough to reflect a lidar from orbit, and that was the sum total of their pre-launch intelligence.

Things were going to go wrong. He knew it, he had faith in it, he wasn't a bit surprised.

When the ambush came, the only thing that saved them was the bad hip actuator in the point-man's Golem. Warrant Officer Joy Patel was her name, right there on Jonathan's IFF display but he knew her already, knew them all. Her Golem's left leg dragged, slowing her turn into the curve of the path as it turned around the first hill, and the cannon round passed less than a meter ahead of her chest plastron, a streak of light in the pitch-black erupting into a starburst explosion against a stand of trees and setting them afire.

Jonathan knew what it was immediately, knew it from thousands of simulations, a dozen a day sometimes against men and women from all over Sparta, the best the military had to offer. It was someone young, someone eager, someone who just couldn't wait to pull the trigger. A training NCO would have ripped the kid a new asshole, but he had the feeling Hardrada wouldn't be so merciful. He'd put a bullet through the pilot's head, if he had the chance. He wouldn't have the chance.

Valentine Kurtz was a hunter, a good ol' boy and one hell of a snap shot. He fired the ETC like a gunfighter from the old stories, from the hip, and put a hypersonic round into the center of the Jeuta mech's chest. The design was old, as old as the destroyer the Jeuta had sailed in on, early Reconstruction War but obviously made from what materials they could scrounge on fabricators in their local shop. The ETC round cored through the cockpit and on into the fusion reactor, blowing a spray of star-hot plasma out the back as the magnetic containment failed and the reactor flushed.

The rising sun of the core flush lit up the sheltered glade to the west of the trail, spread out over the slow rise heading up the next hill to their right, burnt bare at some point in the recent past. The artificial sun glinted off the grey armor of half a dozen other mecha, crouched down as low as their joints could handle, arrayed in an inverted V formation.

It was an ambush, and there was only two ways to handle an ambush: fire and break contact, or assault through. Jonathan Slaughter made the same decision Logan Conner would have, except maybe a microsecond faster.

"Assault through!" he yelled into his audio pickup, spurring his machine into a bone-jarring run. "Lay down suppressive fire! Arbalests, get to the high ground!"

The Golems charged ahead of him, a line of blockers clearing the way for the quarterback, and absorbing some of the hits in the process. Explosive cannon rounds chewed up the soil, ripped into clusters of the short, scaly trees and paused mecha in their stride, scraping off tons of armor in a single hit. None went down; they seemed to push through on sheer will and momentum, crashing through the lines of the ambush.

Time seemed to slip into slow motion, as if his sprint around the curve of the hill took minutes instead of seconds, as if the incoming streaks of fire wormed forward a centimeter at a time, passing so close he could see the waves of heat distorting the air around them. The enemy positions were obvious, searchlights on thermal since they'd opened fire; he could even count them. Seven mecha in the ambush, all of them assault class, all of them fabricated from designs centuries old and fitted mostly with what looked to be 50mm auto-cannons and 25mm chain guns. If they had missiles, they hadn't launched any, probably because they were too close and couldn't count on the warheads arming in time.

He had no such compunctions and would have happily disabled the minimum arming distance for his own missile, but he didn't trust them, not with the damage to the launch pod. He triggered a burst from the 30mm on his right shoulder and was gratified when it worked; the tungsten slugs chewed into the right knee joint of one of the Jeuta mecha, catching it in mid-step and throwing it off-balance. The enemy pilot wasn't bad. He managed to turn a forward sprawl into a lunge, his left footpad scraping a meter-deep gouge into the soil, but the cannon mounted on his mech's right arm skewed out of line, thrown to the side along with the arm to try to balance the lurching machine.

Jonathan's fired his plasma gun with savage joy, reveling in the chance to just act, to fight instead of sitting back and coordinating others. The blast struck the off-balance Jeuta mech in its right shoulder from less than fifty meters away and the arm spun away in a halo of cascading sparks and sublimating metal. The sudden loss of tons of mass sent the machine tumbling helplessly to its left. Before Jonathan could fire a follow-up shot, Kurtz kicked the thing in the chest, crushing the cockpit and then moving on as if it had been incidental.

Jonathan fought an urge to stand his ground and try to survey the situation, knowing time was a luxury and motion a necessity. His eyes brushed across the IFF display on the way across from rear camera view to front camera view, peripherally aware all of the assault mecha were either inside or through the ambush site, with Joy Patel in the lead, sticking to the weaving trail.

"Val!" he snapped to Kurtz. "Off the trail! Send Patel up the hill to the southeast!"

Kurtz was relaying the order, but Jonathan didn't wait to see if it was followed. Something visceral and instinctive was screaming in his ear, telling him this ambush was too half-assed to be the main effort. Light flared behind him, the residue of high-explosive shells detonating and fusion reactors failing catastrophically, but he pushed upward. Overworked actuators wailed and moaned, protesting the strain, but he ignored those as well, leaning into the climb and using his mech's left hand to pull the massive machine up the slope with an overwhelming conviction that time was running out.

The Vindicator crested the hill and Jonathan paused to let the cameras mounted on the mech's upper body spy into the saddle below. And there they were, lining both sides of the path between the hills, alternating and spaced out fifty meters apart. It was hard to see them with the optical view, even using infrared and computer interpolation; the Jeuta knew this place, knew how to camouflage themselves when they didn't want to be found. But he could see the thermal signatures, and he could read the stories those signatures told.

These weren't cheap copies of Reconstruction War-era mecha crewed by the enemy's most expendable pilots. They were strike mecha, a reinforced platoon of them, five in all, and they were top of the line. Two Sentinels, a Scorpion and two Nomads. He didn't know how well they were armed, but Nomads could carry nearly the missile load of an Arbalest.

They were waiting there, expecting the survivors of the *Shakak's* drop-ships to have to come this way to get to the Jeuta base, expecting them to charge through a half-assed ambush and keep running, cocky and blinded with overconfidence.

And I nearly did, he thought with a shudder.

Kurtz's Golems were coming up the hill behind him, strung out thanks to the mechanical problems some of the mecha had due to the rough landing, and he didn't have much time. When his machines didn't come running down the path as expected, the Jeuta were going to know something was up. He wanted to wait for the strike mecha and Arbalests to arrive, but he knew the sound and heat and motion would be too much.

Only one thing to do. He shared the targeting data from his thermal sensors through Kurtz and down to the others via a laser relay.

"All Slaughter mecha," he commanded, "slave your missile targeting to my mech and launch as you bear!"

Jonathan pulled his Vindicator over the crest of the hill, feeling more than seeing the missiles launching behind him, their fiery trails arcing over the rise, each a glowing green delta in his Heads-Up Display, each slaved to his laser designator. He began a quick trot down the other side of the hill, faster, a gallop, trying to keep the laser aimed at the enemy mecha. They noticed him, swiveling to meet the new threat.

His mech was going too fast to stop, too fast to slow down, to do anything but run right into the teeth of them.

"Over the top, Wholesale Slaughter!" he bellowed, heading straight for the strike mecha, two dozen missiles coming behind him. "Follow me!"

6

Terry nearly jumped out of his skin when the main railgun fired.

"What the hell was that?" he blurted. The whole ship rang like a gong from the vibration, and she jerked backwards, even accelerating at one gravity.

The answer was on the tactical display, simulated by the computer by a streak of yellow.... *No, wait a damned minute... not simulated! That's real!*

"We're in a vacuum," he said, feeling a twinge of embarrassment for stating the obvious. "How can I see a vapor trail in a vacuum?"

The numbers beneath the image on the display were just as unbelievable, half again what he'd seen from the reports on the most powerful rail guns Sparta could field on their biggest cruisers. When the slug impacted the Jeuta destroyer a few seconds later, the flare of liberated energy from vaporized armor was as visible as the flash from the discharge, even from hundreds of kilometers away, though he didn't think the round had penetrated through the thick nose armor.

"That'll get their attention," Tara said, cackling.

"Load up another one," Osceola told her, grinning himself. He eyed Terry sidelong, the grin turning to a smirk. "It's something I picked up from a black-market arms dealer out in Shang, something a corporate research team had dreamed up, but the military didn't want to pay for. The trail you saw is from ionized gas we inject into the emitter and then zap with a high-power laser pulse just before the railgun fires."

"Shit," Terry breathed. "The laser charges up the plasma and it turns into an extension of the rails! That's why the projectile is moving so fast!" He shook his head, speechless for a moment. "That's a brilliant idea!"

"It had better be," Kammy groused, "seeing how much you paid for it."

"They're gonna see how much it got past their deflectors where they're thin up front," Tara expanded, eyes not leaving her control board as she ran the sequence to load another ground-car-sized slug and recharge what had to be some massive capacitors. "Then they're gonna turn side-on to us to get the deflector dish pointed directly this way, to let them get close enough to use their lasers on us."

"Might take another shot," Osceola estimated, rubbing at the stubble on his chin. "We up yet?"

"Still charging the capacitor," she said, then shot a look at Terry. "That's the downside to this gadget, it takes forever to charge and we can't use the main lasers while it's juicing up."

"And they ain't waiting for us," Tara warned just before the alarm sounded and the computer displayed a broad red line connecting the Jeuta destroyer to their bow. "That's their main laser battery."

"Still a bit far for lasers," Osceola assessed, sniffing like a food critic who'd bitten into a poorly-cooked steak. "They can't burn through our armor from there."

"They can make a damn good try of it," Kammy piped up. "Are the capacitors charged yet?"

"Oh, what the living fuck?" Tara exclaimed.

Osceola was out of his restraints and looking over her shoulder before she could say another word, and his expression had turned abruptly from confident to profoundly disturbed.

"We have a power failure down in engineering," he said. "The feed from the reactor to the weapons' capacitor banks has been cut." He shouldered Nance aside at the Commo console and hit a control. "Chief!" he barked into the pickup. "What the hell's going on down there?"

There was no reply and Terry frowned. Chief Engineer Duncan was a reliable, competent man who wouldn't be away from his post in a combat situation. Terry would have been down there himself if Osceola hadn't told him to stay on the bridge.

"Leslie!" Osceola said, trying again. "Come on, you old coot, stop fucking around and answer!" Another pause and he switched to another intercom control. "Wihtgar, are you down there? If you can hear this, I need you to get to Engineering!"

Another long pause with no answer. Terry threw off his restraints and stood, a little hesitantly.

"I'll go check on the Chief," he volunteered.

"Don't just stand there then, kid!" Osceola snapped. "Get down there and find out what the hell is going on!"

Terry was already moving. It was easier under one-gravity boost, and much less crowded when everyone was either at battle stations or off the ship. The passageways were deserted, and the sound of his own footsteps on the deckplates were hollow and haunting. He didn't take the elevators because you didn't, not in combat. The rule had been drilled into him over and over by Jonathan, Osceola, even Duncan. You took the hub, which was a stairwell when you were under boost or a tunnel when you were in free-fall, and you'd better hope to Mithra you didn't have to use it when you were accelerating at high gees or running combat evasive maneuvers. The hatchway was open, though it would slam shut automatically if the ship lost pressure on one of the lower decks, and a fold-up ramp led from the hatch to the landing of the spiral staircase running the length of the ship.

Steel grating banged under his ship boots, echoing off the curving bulkheads of the hub, barely two meters across. When the ship was in free-fall, the steps retracted into the segmented cylinder running down the center of the hub, clearing space for the crew to use the tunnel while floating in microgravity, which meant the steps always seemed flimsy to Terry under boost no matter how much his brain told him they were plenty stable enough. The lack of a safety railing bothered him and his hands kept searching for something to grab and catching only air.

The engineering level was the last one that could be reached through the hub, the last crewed level before the ship's massive radiation shielding, her metallic-hydrogen fuel stores, the main fusion reactor and the drives. It was also the only place you could physically access the primary power trunk from the reactor to the weapons control systems without a vacuum suit, and it was the origin of the fault Tara had detected back on the bridge, and there just weren't those kinds of coincidences.

The hatch to the engineering level was shut, which wasn't a surprise. It was also security locked, which was. Terry frowned, cursing under his breath and fishing his 'link out of his jacket pocket. He'd been issued a security code to get him into Engineering back at the beginning of the cruise, but he'd never had to use it. It took a bit of scrolling through menus to get to it, but when he held the 'link against the security scanner, the hatch cracked open with a pneumatic hiss and he echoed the sound with his sigh of relief. His first thought had been a radiation leak, but the door lock wouldn't have released if the automated safety systems had detected a dangerous level of radiation.

Chiding himself for his hesitance, he pushed the heavy, shielded hatch inward, having to put all his weight into it. Reluctant hinges creaked their muted protest, but he was able to slip through into the short passageway leading from the hub and the lift banks to the engine room. It was a narrow cylinder flattened by deck-plates at the bottom and light panels at the top and it existed mostly as a functional airlock in case of an atmosphere or radiation leak. The light panels were switched off, and through the passage, darkness loomed in the engine room as well, ominous shadows lit only by the readouts from control boards.

Power surge? he wondered. He winced at the thought of what that much electricity could have done to the Chief and the other engineering crew on duty.

A shadow flitted across the floor, deeper and darker than the others, something in motion against the display lights.

"Chief?" he said, his words as tentative as his steps.

He didn't notice the bodies until he reached the end of the passage. They were tossed into a corner, one piled on top of the other, a blob of broken humanity. It took him a long second to recognize them as Chief Duncan and the other two Engineering crew from this shift, Cheryl Mendelson and Kenyatta. His mouth was drawing open to scream or shout a warning over his 'link back to Osceola or Mithra knew what, but he never had the chance.

A wide, meaty hand wrapped around his throat and lifted him off the deck. Denial came first, the refusal to believe what was happening to him. He'd never been in any sort of fight and only had vague memories of far-off violence from the coup attempt that had claimed his mother. When the pain in his throat and the fire burning in his chest penetrated the fog of disbelief, he reacted without thought or plan. Terry tried to yell but he had no breath, tried to hit the arm choking him but it felt as solid as iron. His vision was beginning to blur, but he still saw the face behind the arm, dark, flat, and nearly featureless.

"You should not have come down here," Wihtgar said, voice flat and emotionless, as dead as the darkness behind his eyes. "You meant well, as you humans like to say, and I did not wish it to come to this. Though perhaps it is irrelevant."

The hand squeezed tighter and Terry began to lose consciousness, fire erupting inside his brain.

"You will just die a bit sooner than everyone else."

For all the fearsome reputation of the Rangers in general and herself in particular, Lyta Randell had never enjoyed jumping out of aircraft. She found she particularly didn't care for it when said aircraft was on fire and she was only a thousand meters up over a landscape of razor-sharp lava rock which was also, incidentally, radioactive. She risked a look back over her shoulder into the trackless depths of the volcanic clouds and hoped against hope the drop-ship was still up there, somewhere. It had still been airborne when they'd bailed out, though the urgency in the crew chief's voice hadn't been encouraging.

"You doing all right, Grigori?" she asked, trying not to stare at the man.

Master Sergeant Grigori Denisenko had been limping since they'd left the drop zone nearly an hour ago, and it had only gotten worse since. She didn't *think* his left ankle was broken, but it was surely a bad sprain and they'd probably wind up having to cut his boot off when all this was over.

"Right as rain, ma'am," he assured her. She couldn't see his face through his helmet's visor, but he couldn't hide the strain in his voice.

She resisted the urge to argue. She couldn't leave him behind, not here, and so far, he hadn't slowed them down as much as the terrain had. Maybe mecha didn't have any problem walking over the lava beds, but a foot soldier sure did, especially if they were trying to maintain a minimum interval and not just walk down the middle of the damned path like a bunch of tourists.

The platoon was spread out over a hundred meters across and deep, and she and Master Sergeant Denisenko were near the center, where the ranking NCO and officer belonged, even though it rankled her.

"Major," she heard Sparano's voice, recognized it before the IFF display in her helmet identified it as the platoon leader. "We got movement up here. Don't have a visual, just a thermal signal, but it's definitely biological."

"Everyone hit the prone," she ordered over the general net. She heard a groan and made a point not to notice who it was. She empathized. The rocks were sharp and uncomfortable even through their body armor. "Sgt. Denisenko stay here, I'm going up with the platoon leader."

She knew he was hurting when he didn't protest he should go instead, just barked orders over their laser line-of-sight communications to the squad leaders. She didn't high-crawl over the sharp rock—her boots were already sliced through in two places and there was such as thing as being *too* damned tactical—but she stayed low and moved fast. She had infrared and thermal to guide her, but even those seemed inadequate when every damn piece of this ground looked pretty much like every other piece. Thankfully, Sparano wasn't that far, and she was able to keep track of him with the laser designator in his helmet's comm set.

The platoon leader was up near the front of the formation, huddled up with the Ranger they'd had walking point, crouched behind a meter-high square of grey basalt. Their rifles were aimed around the edges of the rock, at a point about twenty meters away, where the lava beds dropped off into an old creek bed. She couldn't tell how deep it was from this distance, but it was the perfect place for the enemy to try to set up an ambush.

"Haven't seen anything the last few minutes," Sparano reported to her, rifle and eyes still aimed outward, "but there was something in there. Cobb saw it, too."

Private Cobb had been walking point and she jabbed a finger of her support hand to the north, alongside the barrel of her rifle.

"They're coming right up the dry creek bed, ma'am," she confirmed. "They're either gonna pass us by or they're setting up a trap for us further down."

"Cobb," Lyta ordered, "get up there and get me eyes on. If we're walking into an ambush, I want to know."

The woman grunted acknowledgement and began high-crawling forward, her rifle cradled in the crooks of her arms as she moved along on elbow and knee pads, where her armor was at its thickest.

Damn, Lyta thought in mild annoyance. They weren't that far from the enemy base, or at least where the mapping program in her helmet *thought* the enemy base was, but if they were hung up here, the battle might be over before they arrived. And if any of her people died because she hadn't arrived in time...

"Ma'am," Cobb called, startlingly loud in her helmet earphones. Lyta realized with a start she'd been woolgathering for a minute like some damned greenhorn.

She found Cobb immediately, not least because the woman was standing up, her rifle held casually at her side, staring down into the creek bed. Her lips were forming a sharp rebuke when she realized what the private's stance might signify and her heart beat quicker.

"You need to come up here, ma'am," Cobb told her.

She pushed herself off the ground with the butt of her rifle and jogged up to the edge of the creek bed...and stopped short, eyes wide.

Francis Acosta looked as if he'd been dragged behind an all-terrain vehicle for a kilometer and hit every rock along the way. His flight suit was torn in a dozen places, caked with ash and dust and dirt and blood, and more of it matted the hair on the right side of his head, and he still looked better than Kathren Margolis. She was draped over his right shoulder, a deep cut over her right eye, her eyelids fluttering in a semi-conscious stupor, blackened scorch-marks on the legs of her flight suit.

Acosta slowly shook his head, his face sunken into utter exhaustion.

"I am never," he declared, "going to fly again."

7

He knew he was going to die and wondered if it mattered if he died calling himself Terry Conner or Terrin Brannigan. Mom had always assured him Mithra knew what was in his heart no matter what he pretended on the outside, but he hadn't believed in any of that for years. How could he believe in a beneficent deity when life had taken his mother from him?

It would have shocked Dad if he'd known, though Logan probably suspected. He couldn't concentrate enough to remember to call his brother "Jonathan," even if he'd thought it mattered. He couldn't feel the pain in his throat anymore, couldn't feel anything. His vision had narrowed to a dark tunnel directly ahead of him, just wide enough to ensure the very last thing he saw was Wihtgar's shark-black eyes.

There was the sound of an impact, flesh on flesh, coming from far away, and yet somehow, he knew it had actually been close, that it was his fading consciousness making it sound distant. The pressure on his neck ceased and he was falling. He thought for just the briefest fraction of a second that the gravity was gone, that he was back in free-fall, until he realized he was only half-right. He was falling, but there was nothing free about it. The deck smacked him between the shoulder blades and all the pain he hadn't been feeling from his throat returned in a rush of red-hot daggers driven into his windpipe.

Stars filled his vision, but he shook them away, desperation battling fear and pain for control of his mind and body. He had to get up, had to see what was happening…

And abruptly, he could.

It was as if two titans of legend battled for possession of his soul, dim shadows bathing them in mystery, cloaking their motions in an illusion of inhuman speed that was more a function of his oxygen-starved thoughts than reality. Terry would have thought no human could take on a Jeuta hand-to-hand, that no human could match their size and strength and speed and ferocity. He'd never seen Kamehameha-Nui Johannsen fight.

The man was huge, a giant who he'd initially thought of as pudgy, maybe even fat. He'd been wrong. The bulk was muscle, at least 130 kilograms of it, and Kammy knew how to use it. What came naturally to Wihtgar, scriven in his genes by Imperial scientists centuries ago, was the product of a lifetime of practice and work for the *Shakak's* First Mate. Swipes from clawed Jeuta fingers that would have disemboweled had they struck home found only air, missing by millimeters as Kammy swayed like the most agile ballet dancer, turning the close confines of the engine room into his private studio. Fists the size of a cured ham pounded into the gap between the Jeuta's ribs, seeking out weaknesses and punishing them with merciless precision.

Sweat flickered away from Kammy's brow, propelled by the hypnotic, metronome-swing of his dreadlocks, swaying with the movement of his massive shoulders, part of the dance. Wihtgar didn't perspire, not like a human, but his mouth was hanging open, the only outward sign he was growing tired. Blood dripped fitfully from the claws at the tips of his fingers and Terry saw the matching tears on the sleeves of Kammy's ship fatigues. The scratches were ugly and ragged, but only superficial.

"Give it up," Kammy said to Wihtgar. "You're not getting off this ship."

"None of us are," the Jeuta proclaimed, lunging for the big man.

It was clumsy, even Terry could see that just from the little he'd learned in the gym sparring with Lyta these last few weeks. It was the move of someone with little training, someone who relied on their superior strength too much. Kammy seemed to glide out of the way of the attack, his plant leg hopping just a step, his front leg sliding smoothly in an organic, natural motion. Massive hands moved impossibly fast, catching the Jeuta behind the neck, pushing him forward along the direction of his motion and slamming him face-first into the bulkhead.

Wihtgar wasn't out, but he was stunned—too stunned to put up an effective defense when Kammy sank the rear naked choke into his throat. The Jeuta were hardier, stronger than humans, but there were things you just couldn't change and remain a biped with stereoscopic hearing and vision: your brain had to be above your heart on a movable neck, and the blood had to get to the brain with the veins and arteries close enough to the surface to avoid overheating.

If you were humanoid, you could be choked unconscious.

Wihtgar thrashed impotently, tried to claw at Kammy's arm but lacked the strength to do more than leave a few surface cuts. The Jeuta went slack, hands falling away from the big man's arm, but Kammy kept the choke in for another ten or twenty seconds. In a normal human, it was probably long enough to do some permanent damage, but Terry had no idea what the effect would be on a Jeuta.

Finally, Kammy let Wihtgar roll off him and scrambled to his feet.

"Is he…?" Terry tried to say it out loud but his voice didn't seem to want to work and the words came out in a whisper.

"Can you fix what he did?" Kammy asked, his usual good humor lost in strained impatience. "Can you get the weapons back up?"

Terry nodded, pushing away from the deck and stumbling over to the main control board. He tried not to look at the bodies in the corner. He wondered if the Jeuta had killed them with his bare hands or used a gun…

"Terry!" Kammy's sharp remonstration snapped him out of the fugue he'd been sinking into.

He traced the fault on the power distribution display just the way Chief Duncan had shown him, finding it almost immediately. Wihtgar hadn't tried anything fancy, probably because he was more of a strong back than a technician; he'd simply thrown the breakers for the power conduit from the reactor to the weapons systems. Kammy was watching him with one eye while he devoted most of his attention to securing Wihtgar's hands behind him with a pair of heavy metal cuffs.

"You just happened to be carrying those?" Terry asked, moving past him to a closed cabinet, using the code programmed into his 'link to unlock it.

"Naw," Kammy admitted, keeping his full weight pressed against the Jeuta. "I had an itch between my shoulder blades when I heard about the power failure. And honestly, bro…" He shrugged. "I never completely trusted our buddy here."

Terry didn't speak, concentrating on the job at hand. He pulled the breaker board open, counting down and across row upon row of physical fail-safe switches to the designator he'd seen on the display, H236. There it was, manually tripped. There was, he noticed with a twist of his guts, blood spattered on the flat grey surface of it. He gritted his teeth and closed the circuit. Red indicators flashed green and he nodded to Kammy.

"Bridge," the big man spoke into the pickup of his personal 'link, holding the device between thumb and forefinger as if it were a toothpick in his meaty hand, the other pinning Wihtgar's shoulders to the deck, "we're up! You're good to go!"

"Roger that," Osceola answered, his voice sounding tiny through the 'link's external speaker. "Good job."

"And get me a security detail and a medical team down here, boss," Kammy added. "We got casualties."

"If you thought it was him," Terry finally asked, gesturing toward the Jeuta, "then why didn't you bring a gun?"

"I don't like shooting guns in the engine room." Kammy grinned broadly, his reply as flippant and easy as if there weren't three dead bodies lying in the corner.

A rush of loathing filled Terry, an earnest wish he'd never met any of these people, never decided to come along. He pushed it down with effort, telling himself firmly it wasn't that Kammy or any of the others were bad people, they were just in a life that hardened their souls.

"Besides…" Kammy shrugged, seemingly unaware of the play of emotions behind Terry's purposefully bland expression. "I knew I could take him."

Terry felt the deck shift beneath him as maneuvering thrusters fired and he knew Osceola was lining up the rail gun for another shot.

"Go check on the Engineering crew."

He glanced up at Kammy, certain he'd misheard him.

"They might not all be dead," the big man insisted. "I can't let this asshole go until the security team gets here and Mithra knows how long till we get the medics in here."

Terry nodded, acknowledging the reasoning and ethics of the situation if not the conclusion that he needed to be the one to check on the bodies. He cleared his throat, rubbing at the raw spots on his neck where Wihtgar's fingers had abraded the flesh, receiving a very clear flash of how easily he could be just another one of the bodies dead on the floor. They were sprawled one atop the other, as if the Jeuta had discarded them casually, tossing them aside to make room for the work he had to do.

He knew them. He worked with them every day for years.

The body at the top of the heap was Duncan, pudgy, grey-haired, and unabashedly old. He'd told Terry he'd been a junior machinist's mate for the Spartan Navy in the last of the Reconstruction Wars, which would have made him nearly two hundred. Terry wasn't sure he'd believed the man, but it made a great story. Duncan's neck was broken, his head lolling at an impossible angle, his eyes horribly open, staring in white accusation.

Terry clenched his teeth and grabbed the old man's arm, pulling him off the others. The arm was floppy, unnaturally loose as if he were a stuffed doll; Terry jerked away and wiped his hand on his leg instinctively. He cursed at his own stupidity and stepped forward again, checking the next victim.

Cheryl Mendelson was her name. He almost couldn't remember the last name because everyone called her Cheryl and the *Shakak's* crew was fairly casual about rank. She had red hair and a pleasant, open face painted with freckles and barely came up to his shoulder. She'd reminded him of one of the nannies his father had employed after his mother's death, but Cheryl had loved the *Shakak* like it was her own child. Her enthusiasm for the task of keeping a starship up and running had been as infectious as her schoolgirl giggle.

Her throat had been crushed. The flesh there was purple, red welts marking where the Jeuta's fingers had dug into it, and above them her face was blue, the veins in her eyes red and broken. His sight blurred and when he wiped the back of his hand across his eyes, he was surprised when it came away wet. He was crying. He hadn't cried since Mom had died.

"Fuck you, Kammy," he said aloud, yanking on Cheryl's

sleeve, turning her over, turning her face away from him as he pulled her off the last of them.

"I'm sorry, man," Kammy said softly. It sounded as if he meant it. "I'd do it if I could."

The last body was Mwai Kenyatta. Terry had said two words to the man the whole time he'd been on the ship, didn't know him beyond his name and the fact he liked to wear T-shirts with animated images of cats on them. His face was badly bruised, blood streaming from his nose and mouth...and he was breathing.

"Kenyatta is alive," he reported, the words flat and neutral.

He had no idea what to do with the man, no sort of first aid training whatsoever, but he cleared the others off the engineering technician's body and straightened him out.

"He tried to fight me," Wihtgar said, and Terry jumped at the words.

Kammy leaned into the Jeuta as if he expected him to make a move, but Wihtgar stayed motionless, almost impassive, as if resigned to his fate.

"I didn't have the need to kill him after I had rendered him helpless," he elaborated, almost as if he considered it a justification.

"Why?" Terry wanted to know. He turned his eyes back toward Kenyatta, making sure the man's airway was clear, making sure he had no broken bones but unsure of what else to do. "These people gave you a chance, took you in when no one else would have. Why would you do this to them?"

"You are not Jeuta," Wihtgar said, "or you would not ask that question."

Terry waited for him to expound, but the Jeuta said no more. Then security and medical stormed into the room and patient and prisoner were both quickly swept away, leaving him alone with Kammy and the two corpses. He stood there for what seemed like minutes, before Kammy put a hand on his arm and turned him around.

"We should get back to the bridge," the big man said, his rounded face unusually firm. "The fight's not over."

Terry nodded, remembering what Wihtgar had said.

"Yeah. I guess it's not."

The world was exploding around him. The ground shifted beneath the foot-pads of the Vindicator, each impact of the missiles arcing over his head another earthquake, yet he kept it upright, kept her moving forward. Smoke and fire and debris blinded his optical and infrared cameras making thermal useless, but still he kept his laser designator pointed straight ahead, knowing the enemy strike mecha hadn't had time to move.

They were still there; he knew it because they were shooting at him. Not hitting, mostly, because they probably couldn't see him any better than he could see them, but he caught the flare of a laser through the particulate cloud of darkness, saw a streaking cannon round pass by. It was all he could do to keep the Vindicator on its feet and keep the laser designator aligned and he made no attempt to fire back.

He was only fifty meters away when the last missile hit, close enough for the heat to wash through his cockpit, squeezing the air from his lungs with a sudden, searing pain. Something struck the Vindicator's chest plastron with enough force to throw the mech off its stride and he was barely able to maintain balance at the loss of hundreds of kilograms of armor on his right side.

Someone yelled over the headphones in his helmet but the words couldn't penetrate the roaring in his ears. Was it the concussion of the blast, he wondered, or the incipient heat exhaustion? He hadn't decided between the two when he crashed the right shoulder of the Vindicator into the chest of one of the strike mecha at over thirty kilometers an hour.

The straps of his safety harness bit into his chest and shoulders and his helmet pounded into the padded rest surrounding it, and he could feel his easy chair jerking against its moorings. Metal shrieked and roared then tore away, but both machines stayed upright. He had to act before the other pilot recovered enough to make use of the superior mass of his strike mech.

The plasma cannon mounted in his mech's right hand was jammed downward, trapped by the impact, but he was close enough to make out the right leg of the Nomad in the camera view on the gun mount, lined up with the targeting reticle. He fired. More heat, conducting through material designed to be insulating, and the soles of his feet blistered right through his boots. He wanted to scream but lacked the breath. Sun-bright light washed out the camera feed and polarized the coating of his canopy. He couldn't see a damned thing, but he felt the mass of the Nomad falling away from the front of the Vindicator, freeing up its right arm.

He stamped downward by instinct, the impulses going through his neural halo and into the motivator circuits of the mech, felt the crunch of metal beneath his right foot-pad. It was just the sort of feeling a mech's cockpit made when it was crushed. The yellow warnings on his damage display began flashing red, but it was something else he couldn't control and he ignored it.

The swirling cloud of smoke and flame billowed angrily through the saddle between the hills, revealing fleeting glimpses of the carnage surrounding Jonathan. Through one of those teasing gaps in the blackness, he saw the charred wreckage of two of the other strike mecha, one of the Nomads and the Scorpion. They were out of commission, out of the fight, their pilots likely mangled corpses inside the twisted metal.

One of the Sentinels was badly damaged but still on its feet, one arm hanging limp and useless. Its ETC cannon had broken off its mount on the right shoulder and hung down its back by a single power cable as if by a sling.

The last Sentinel was running, and he would have bet a year's pay Hardrada was inside it. He raised his plasma gun, trying to line up a shot on the fleeing Jeuta, but the other strike mech stepped into the line of fire and the blast of accelerated ionized gas took it in its functional arm, blowing it off in a shower of sparks and a halo of vaporized metal. The Sentinel staggered out of the way, pulled off to the side by the dead weight of its damaged arm, leaving him with a clear shot to the other mech. But...

"Shit," he rasped, his mouth full of cotton from the heat. He would have taken a sip from the water bladder built into his suit, but he was worried it might be hot enough to burn his tongue.

The capacitor for the plasma gun would take seconds to recharge and the running strike mech would be out of sight by then, around the corner of the hill. He had one weapon that could stop the Jeuta, and he knew what might happen if he used it—the flashing red warning signal at his shoulder kept reminding him.

"Fuck it."

He switched the targeting reticle to the missile pod and fired. Three of the four missiles in the launch pod streaked out, crossing the two hundred meters between the Vindicator and the Sentinel in less than a second and striking just where he'd aimed them, in the massive, plodding machine's right knee. A wave of heat and concussion radiated outward and armor was stripped to the metallic bones, the joint giving way, sending the mech lurching off to the right, its leg ending above the knee in a ragged, molten stump.

Three of the missiles had launched. The other stuck in the pod, and Jonathan knew exactly what the ear-splitting screech of the alarm and the flashing red warning meant. It was about to cook off. He bit down on his mouthpiece and yanked the ejection levers with both hands.

He had only ever ejected once, in training, and only because no one graduated from mech training without a successful ejection. A "successful" ejection could still involve broken bones, a concussion and internal injuries. An *unsuccessful* ejection meant you were dead. His practice run under ideal conditions had been successful, in that he'd survived with cracked ribs and a broken left wrist.

This wasn't practice and the conditions weren't ideal. The canopy tumbled away on explosive bolts and the cockpit pod punched forward with a gentle chuff of compressed gas. The solid-fuel rockets ignited an acceleration somewhere north of ten gravities and when Jonathan passed out, he figured it was probably for the best.

8

"Am I in Hell?"

The dark, faceless figure hovering above Jonathan could easily have passed for a demon, but as his vision swam slowly into focus, he discerned he was actually staring up at a Ranger helmet visor.

"I should take that as an insult," Lyta Randell's voice replied. She'd been down on a knee, hovering over him, but now she stood and offered him a hand. "But considering your condition, I'll let it slide."

His condition was, he quickly discovered, bruised all over. He took Lyta's hand and let her pull him up because he sure as hell wasn't going to be pushing himself up on his own. She must have already unstrapped him from the ejection pod, because he hadn't done it. The edges of the pod were still smoking, the parachute flapping in the breeze, stretched out behind it. He could barely believe he'd reached a high enough altitude for the flimsy-looking synthetic silk to brake his descent.

"How the hell did you get here?" he wondered, a twinge in his back turning the question into a pained groan. He slowly and gingerly pulled off his helmet, the neural halo coming free with

93

the reluctance of medical bandage adhesive. "How long have I been out?"

"Not too long," she informed him, waving around them demonstratively. "We got here just before the missiles started flying."

Mecha loomed over him, their footfalls sending rhythmic vibrations through the ground as they shuffled into a protective perimeter. Flames ate away at the scaly thorn trees, spreading quickly up the hillside across the grass and underbrush, the smoke merging with the low clouds but the fire remained painfully visible in the darkness.

"Are you okay, boss?"

The voice boomed down loud enough to startle him and he spun to see it had come from the external address speakers on Paskowski's Scorpion. The strike mech was incredibly intimidating from down at ground level and enough heat was still radiating off its plasma cannons he could feel it from thirty meters away.

"Yeah," he said, waving in case the mech's audio pickup couldn't make out his voice. "I'll survive."

He remembered something, looked around and found the remains of the Sentinel he'd used his ill-fated missiles to take down. It was lying on its side a hundred meters away, the remains of its right leg still smoking, and its canopy yawning open.

"Where did the pilot go?" he demanded, spinning around to direct the question to Lyta. "From the mech I hit with those damned missiles?"

"He took off before we could get over to you," she confessed. "I tried to have him taken out, but we didn't have a clear shot with…" She gestured. "…all this shit."

His head was clearing and he noticed she had her people deployed in a defensive perimeter out at the edges of the saddle, where she could be sure their own mecha wouldn't accidentally step on them. He also noticed there were only three squads, and light squads at that.

"How many people did you lose?" he asked, dread clenching at his stomach.

"No one," she said, lifting her visor up so she could look him in the eye. "I've got some walking wounded and I left a squad with them and the other casualties we picked up along the way."

He'd sighed in relief at her pronouncement she hadn't lost anyone, but his eyes narrowed at the mention of other casualties.

"Who?"

"Katy and her copilot, Acosta. They crash-landed their assault shuttle out in the badlands and Acosta had to carry Katy out."

The dread hit again, twice as hard, and he was in the middle of an urgent question when she raised a hand to stop him, answering before he could get the words out.

"She's got a concussion, along with a separated shoulder and a badly sprained knee, but I think she's going to be okay if we can get her to the ship's med bay." She cocked an eyebrow. "If there's a med bay and a ship to get back to," she amended. "Otherwise, we're all dead."

He nodded, forcing the fear down, boxing it away for later. The best thing he could do for Katy was to finish this mission. He patted himself down, but whatever had happened to his 'link, it wasn't on his belt anymore. Lyta noticed and handed him a spare from one of her equipment pouches and he nodded gratefully.

"Slaughter Units, this is Slaughter One," he said. "The objective is three kilometers that way." He stabbed a finger in an exaggerated motion in the direction the enemy mech jock had fled. "They know we're coming, so there's no point in trying to sneak up on them. Paskowski, I want your strike mecha up front. Kurtz, you circle around the other side of the perimeter and work your way inward. Kill any of them you see."

"What about the hostages, sir?" Kurtz asked him.

"That's why the Rangers are here, Lieutenant," Lyta informed him. "They know *you're* here, but they won't know about us."

"I'm walking in with you," Jonathan told her. "No argument, Lyta," he cut off the words he knew were trailing her arched eyebrow. "Trying to kick one of the others out of their mech would slow us down way too much. You got a rifle I can carry so I at least *look* dangerous?"

She regarded him with a scowl, hefting her carbine demonstratively.

"Yeah, I'm carrying an extra one around in my pocket, just in case."

"Well, shit," he murmured, pulling his handgun out of its chest holster. "I guess I should practice more with this thing." He touched the control on the 'link to address the entire force. He didn't want to sound cheesy and gung-ho, but he was quickly finding it seemed to come with the job.

"All right, Wholesale Slaughter, let's go get our people back."

Jonathan thought it might be getting near dawn. It was more of a sense of grey behind the darkness than any real hint of sunlight, but might be as much of a dawn as they got around here. Fog and smoke clung to every hollow, floating through the intertwined branches of the thorn trees, and the only hint he had of the Jeuta base was a faint, yellow halo lingering above the pockets of fog in the hollow just ahead.

"How do you stand it?" he asked Lyta, keeping his voice low but not whispering. She'd taught him that; a whisper carried further than a normal tone spoken softly.

She didn't look back at him, her eyes scanning carefully around even though they were in the center of a double-wedge formation and her Rangers in the lead arrowhead would spot danger long before she did.

"Stand what?" she asked, her voice even lower than his, but still clear enough to understand. "Mech jocks who don't know when to shut up?"

"Very funny. No, being this low, not being able to see anything."

"It's a trade-off. We don't see them, they don't see us." She jabbed a finger to their right. "They can see your people well enough, though, and I'd rather be down here."

He didn't have the thermal and infrared filters built into her helmet visor, but he could still just make out the glint of a distant floodlight off the matte grey metal of a mech, just barely hear the impact of footpads on the hard-packed soil. Something shot upward at the mech, a segmented streak of light, tracers from a heavy machine gun or light cannon, a crew-served weapon on a vehicle or in a bunker. Impacts sparked off the chest plastron, lighting up the mech and revealing it as Paskowski's Scorpion in the brief moment before he returned fire with the lasers flanking the mech's pod-shaped torso. Coherent light burned air into a plasma in a shimmering line and something on the ground burst into flames, ammo cooking off with spiteful pops, and the firing stopped. For a moment. It started somewhere else three seconds later, and the mech moved on.

"They must not have any mecha left," he guessed. "If they did, they'd have them in a last defensive position here."

"Maybe not, but that doesn't mean they're helpless." She raised her visor and shot him an annoyed glance. "You're the CO, sir, but my advice to you in this situation would be to shut up and soldier."

Abashed, he did as he was told and stopped talking, following her as she trailed her first squad and the point of their arrowhead formation, Private Cobb. He was used to the long, ground-eating strides of a ten-meter-tall mech and to him, their pace seemed a crawl. Lyta was keeping them moving at what was almost a reckless speed for her. She probably felt the same sense of urgency he did, the intuition their friends being held captive didn't have much longer.

Finally, they cleared the curve of the hill, past the tangled forest of thorn trees and emerged slowly and cautiously into the hollow. The Jeuta base was smaller than it had looked in the orbital images, the buildings squatter than he'd imagined, and much of the storage was out in the open, covered by camouflage tarps rather than enclosed in one of the sheet-metal warehouses they'd thrown together. Empty, barren patches of flat ground, burned clean of all vegetation, marked the landing zones for their assault shuttles, while their cargo bird rested a few hundred meters away, ungainly and unarmed.

Why haven't they just flown out on the heavy lift shuttle? he wondered. He wanted to ask Lyta what she thought, but didn't want to get scolded again. Somehow, it would be even more embarrassing now that he was the commander.

The answer to his question came seconds later in a rolling peal of thunder, the scream of turbojets whining overhead and the glow of an assault shuttle's engines only a few hundred meters up. It had to be Lt. Lee and he felt an irrational fury at the man. He had no idea how Katy had wound up being shot down, but he'd listened to her complain about Lee's tentative flying in combat before and it didn't take too much imagination to figure out what had happened.

Still, he was here now and he was keeping the cargo shuttle grounded and that might be the only thing keeping the hostages alive, so Jonathan was willing to cut him a break and let Katy take care of him personally once it was all over.

Though maybe that's not cutting him a break, after all, he thought with a shudder. Katy was not someone you wanted to have pissed off at you.

The ripping-metal stutter of Vulcans and the snap-crack of lasers echoed off sheet metal walls and rolled over the open plain; he had to scan the length of the installation twice before he spotted the mecha striding purposefully along, moving up in a pincer movement from both sides and pushing the Jeuta ahead of them.

"Where they're falling back to," Lyta told him, pointing with the barrel of her carbine, "that'll be where they have the hostages."

"Let's go!" he urged, almost pushing past her. She stopped him with a hand on his chest, casual yet strong enough that he couldn't have moved it if he'd tried.

"Slow," she said. "We need to let your people do their work, first."

He nodded, but chafed at the pace, imagining Marc Langella and the others waiting for rescue, maybe injured, dying and he was dragging his feet, waiting for the others to kill off more of the enemy. He gripped his pistol so tightly his fingers began to cramp and he was forced to switch it to his left hand and shake out the right, hoping this wasn't going to be the exact second he needed it because he couldn't shoot for shit left-handed.

Of course, Mithra heard him and small arms chattered only fifty meters ahead of him. He dropped to the ground and Lyta crouched beside him, the barrel of her carbine still at low port. He followed her example and kept his handgun pointed down, trying not to sweep friendlies with his muzzle. The gunfire sputtered out and he thought it was over, but another burst erupted to his right and seemed to flip the switch again, lighting up the whole perimeter with muzzle flashes.

He couldn't see a damned thing, much less anything worth

shooting and he had to relax his jaw to stop from grinding his teeth. This was so much worse than being in a mech.

How the hell does Lyta do it?

It took another ten seconds, but the firing died away and Lyta pushed up to her feet, motioning for him to follow. She said nothing and he assumed the squad leaders were communicating with their throat mics, but it made the coordinated movement seem haunting in the dim light, a platoon of spectral soldiers moving across the battlefield in supernatural synchronization.

Except for the one dumbass mech jock tagging along.

He passed by the body of a Jeuta foot-soldier laid out along the route of their advance, his chest ripped apart by what had to be multiple bursts. Blood was splashed down the front of his armor, a testimony to how long it had taken him to die even under the hail of bullets. The Jeuta's weapon rested beside him, already stripped of its magazine by the troops to the front, a simple automatic rifle with a basic optical sight, fabricated right here at their base, most likely. He didn't know how many others were sprawled out across the wedge of the Rangers' formation, giving their blood to the radioactive soil, but he figured there had to be more.

Had they gotten all of them? Were others running back to warn the Jeuta troops guarding the hostages, to tell them to shoot them?

Maybe Lyta was thinking the same thing, because she'd sped up the march and Jonathan had to run to keep up with her steady, surefooted jog. The buildings were closer now, lacking the sort of security fence he'd seen in the encampments of human bandits. He wondered if it was a practical thing, if they'd never considered anyone might threaten them here, or if it was something about the Jeuta psyche, an unwillingness to admit they might need fences to protect them from their enemies.

They'd certainly grown used to being on the offensive during the Fall, and only fighting amongst themselves had kept them from sweeping through human space like a plague. No fences needed, no walls, no defenses but a hellacious offense. They'd learned that lesson well, and it had cost them tonight. The main warehouse was smoking and charred where missile strikes or cannon rounds had taken out crew-served weapons turrets and bodies—and pieces of bodies—littered the ground. He didn't see a single Jeuta alive, nothing moving but for his own company's mecha and the ghostly shadows of the Rangers moving smoothly from cover to cover.

"Captain Slaughter."

Lyta had skidded to a halt barely a meter ahead of him and he had to dig his heels in and slide to avoid running into her. He couldn't see her face, but he knew something wasn't right by the sound of her voice over her helmet's external speakers. And by the fact she was speaking through them at all; they weren't exactly tactical. She paused, reaching up to pull back her visor.

"I just had a transmission from Paskowski. He wants to see you up front." She motioned forward toward a Quonset hut on the other side of the main warehouse, tucked between it and one of the camouflaged outdoor storage pallets.

She didn't offer to go with him, made no move toward the building and a frozen lump of iron weighed down his guts, a chill of revelation. His mouth worked but no sound emerged. He wanted to tell her no, wanted to walk away.

He couldn't. He was the commander.

Someone was trying to call him on his 'link, but he ignored the buzz, simply placing one foot in front of the other, an automaton drawn to a task against his will. Jeuta corpses smoked and bled out on the soft, crunching soil only meters from him, but he didn't look aside to them, made no move to check if they were still alive. His handgun hung forgotten in his hand, carried loosely at his side; only carefully ingrained habit kept him from dropping it.

Paskowski's Scorpion stood outside the open double-doors to the Quonset hut, crouched low as if its head hung, its canopy open. The man who should have been a captain sat forlorn in the open cockpit, one leg dangling, head buried in his hands. Lyta's Rangers were stepping in and out of the building, having cleared it already, checking diligently for booby-traps before Jonathan entered.

Inside, death waited for him.

The hostages were bound hand and foot, gagged and blind-folded, lined up neatly from front to back. The front rank had been shot through the head, all six of them. They had slumped where they knelt, a couple still grotesquely stuck upright by the position of their arms and legs against the restraints. The second rank...he blinked. The first two men in the second rank had been shot as well, but sprawled over the top of the next in line was the body of a Jeuta. Most of the body of a Jeuta. Below the chest, all that was left of him was a charred skeleton, but there was some-thing about the thing's face he recognized...a small, golden ring passing through its nostril.

It was Hardrada. The same obscenely large handgun he'd used to kill the hostage in his message to them was smoking and charred on the ground beside his right hand. Hardrada had been hit with a laser, and the same blast had killed three of the others bound and lined up beside where he'd stood, burned them down to scorched bone...but the rest were alive.

Ranger medics were picking up the worst cases in stretchers as he watched, hauling them out somewhere away from the over-whelming stink of burnt flesh and vaporized blood. Flash burns seared skin and blackened even fireproof clothing and some of them were in bad shape, but he thought they would live if they got treatment quickly enough. Others were walking on their own, a few sobbing as they were led out of the building. Some were stopping to thank him, grabbing at his hand or offering shaky salutes.

He tried to mumble something comforting, but couldn't find the words. He couldn't tear his eyes away from one of the victims of the laser shot, the one directly in front of Hardrada, the one he'd likely been about to kill when Paskowski had made what would likely be the hardest decision of his life and killed a handful of his own people in order to save the others. The man's chest had been obliterated by the burst of coherent light, but part of his face had survived, a stretch of skin the color of hardwood and tightly-curled hair and just the edge of his familiar, snarky grin, probably when he'd seen Paskowski's mech come up at the doorway and realized someone was about to put paid the Jeuta warlord.

He'd met Marc Langella at the Academy and fate, or perhaps the machinations of his father or Colonel Anders, had thrown the two together after they'd graduated from mech training. He'd dated Langella's older sister for about a month until he decided his friend's snarky wit wasn't genetic and the woman just wasn't interesting enough without it.

He crouched beside Marc's body, trying not to breathe, trying not to smell the sickening burnt-meat stench.

"I'm sorry, bud," he whispered. "I should have been able to get you out of this."

He wasn't sure how long he sat there, eyes closed, dimly aware of survivors and victims being carried out of the room by the Rangers. No one disturbed him, even though Lyta's people had lost friends of their own and it wasn't fair for him to be monopolizing the grief. He only glanced up once the room was empty, even Marc's body removed, and everything had gone quiet. Quiet enough for him to hear the sobbing.

At first, he had the wild thought he was the one who was crying, that he'd been bawling the whole time and not realized it, but he quickly realized the sound was coming from behind him. It was Paskowski. He'd climbed down from his mech and was leaning against the doorway, hands balled into fists, hunched over as if he were about to throw up, sobs wracking his body. Jonathan felt uncomfortable around the naked emotion.

"I didn't want to be a company commander," the man said, finally getting control of himself. "I volunteered for this mission," he went on, his voice shuddering and unsteady, "because I wanted a strike platoon, but also because I didn't want to be a company commander."

His eyes met Jonathan's and there was infinite pain inside them, down through to his soul.

"I didn't want to be the one making decisions that could get my own people killed."

"You did the right thing, Gerald," he told the platoon leader. "If you hadn't taken out Hardrada, he would have killed everyone."

"The Rangers..." Paskowski started to protest, but Jonathan cut him off.

"The Rangers were too far away. You did the right thing." Jonathan emphasized every word, trying to hammer the point through the guilt and self-doubt his subordinate was feeling. He stepped closer, putting a hand on Gerald Paskowski's shoulder. It was skinny, boney even. Paskowski was a small man who wanted to drive big mecha. "Now get in your Scorpion and get your platoon back to work."

Paskowski nodded. "I'm sorry," he said, just before he turned back to his mech. "I know he was your friend."

Jonathan didn't know how to reply to that, so he said nothing. He needed to get back to work himself. The mission wasn't over. He looked back to where Marc Langella had died and had to correct himself.

It's over for some of us.

9

S he doesn't look that bad," Terry said softly, eyes glued to the screen.

The Jeuta destroyer was drifting, unpowered, her drive inactive, but her hull was mostly intact, except for the ugly burnthrough where the deflector dish had been.

"She'd be good salvage," Osceola agreed, shaking his head, regret in his voice. "But she's still got a shitload of momentum taking her outsystem and it would burn up a lot of fuel to match her."

The battle had been an anticlimax. Two more shots from the *Shakak's* overpowered railgun had convinced the commander of the destroyer to cut thrust and maneuver his deflector shield into the line of fire. The Jeuta had probably thought he was being clever, but two sustained bursts from the laser batteries had shattered the deflectors and pierced right through them into the reactor. Thermal readings told the story: the plasma had flushed into the ship, burning through the shields and killing everyone on board. They were already decelerating towards the moon now, prepping shuttles with medics and repair crews, but Terry couldn't help watching the destroyer drift away behind them.

"Now we gotta take care of our other problem," Osceola said, yanking the quick-release for his acceleration couch and standing slowly, deliberately...perhaps reluctantly. Kammy nodded and powered his seat back from the console, following his captain.

"You have the conn, Tara," Osceola said to the woman. His eyes settled on Terry. "Come on, kid. You too."

"What?" he asked, blinking incomprehension.

"You were a witness," Kammy explained. "You have to be there." He waved toward the hatch to the hub and the lift banks.

Terry still didn't understand what the hell was going on, but his throat hurt too much to argue, so he followed the Captain and the First Mate off the bridge. He was hoping for the lift bank since they weren't in combat, currently, but groaned softly and followed when Osceola chose the hub instead. The drumbeat of feet on the metal grating of the steps was an ear-splitting racket in the enclosed cylinder of the hub, but at least they didn't go all the way down to Engineering this time. Instead, Osceola led them out of the stairwell at the main cargo deck, circling around the maze of the hold, past five-meter-tall storage bins for raw soy paste and spirulina powder, past barrel after barrel of powdered metal for the fabricators, crate after crate of replacement parts and ammunition for the mecha.

He was still trying to puzzle out where they were heading when he saw the security guards. These weren't the Spartan Naval Security attached to the ship; they were the more rough-and-ready ship's security called together from other departments to handle matters before the Spartan troops had come aboard. Wihtgar's co-workers, four of them. Big, broad-shouldered men and a single woman, and two of them had guts matching their shoulders but Terry still wouldn't have wanted to face any of them, even with a weapon in his hand. Each carried a stun baton and looked eager to use it on the Jeuta traitor, but Wihtgar made no move to fight against his restraints.

It would have been futile anyway: the cuffs around his wrists and the hobbles at his ankles were made from the same metal as a starship hull, and the cable joining them together was a weave of carbon nanotubes. They weren't taking any chances with the Jeuta.

"Why is *he* down here?" Terry wondered. "Are you going to put him a shuttle down to the moon?"

"He might wind up on the moon," Kammy mused, "depending on gravity and trajectories, but he won't be taking no shuttle."

That was when Terry noticed the proximity of the utility airlock. It was used for maintenance and emergency repairs rather than cargo transfers, the hatches only three meters on a side, just large enough for a work party in suits and the equipment they would use. It was only useful when the ship wasn't boosting, as it was now. Anyone or anything that went out the lock while under boost would fall away, still following the same direction of travel but no longer accelerating or decelerating.

"You're going to just kill him?" Terry asked, his voice breaking in the middle, perhaps from the damage to his throat. "Shouldn't Captain Slaughter be the one to…"

"This is an independent shipping vessel outside territorial space," Osceola reminded him, voice as grim as his face. "According to agreements between the Dominions, the captain retains the right and responsibility to convene judicial hearings and dispense appropriate punishments in accordance with maritime law. Appropriate punishments for murder include banishment, imprisonment or execution."

He nodded to the security detail and the woman, who Terry thought worked in the cargo loading area, hit the control to open the inner airlock door. It swung inward toward them with a metallic grinding of old servomotors and, when it was open far enough, two of the others shoved Wihtgar inside with the business end of their batons. One gave him a shock and the Jeuta jerked away, muscles spasming, sharpened teeth visible in a feral snarl. The woman touched the control again and the door motors complained loudly about having to shut the hatch they'd just opened. It slammed with a finality Terry could feel in his chest, the Jeuta only visible through the thick, transparent aluminum porthole in the hatch.

Wihtgar might have been glaring at them or might not. Kammy stepped over to the airlock panel and switched on the intercom speaker between the outer and inner lock.

"The accused," he said, his normally jolly voice suddenly stiff and official, "is Wihtgar, machinist's mate third class."

"What are the charges?" Osceola asked with equal formality.

"Two counts of murder, two counts of assault with intent to commit murder, one count of sabotage with the intent to commit murder, and one count of espionage." Terry's ears pricked up at the last charge and Kammy expounded, breaking from his officious prosecutor mannerisms for a minute. "We found tools and spare parts hidden in his cabin and we're pretty sure he rigged some sort of beacon on the Trojan Horse to let Hardrada know it was a trick." Back into his imitation of a lawyer voice, Kammy quickly and efficiently summarized the events of the day, as if Osceola had no knowledge of them and needed a briefing.

"Are there witnesses?"

"Myself," Kammy informed him, "Mwai Kenyatta and Terry Conner. Kenyatta is still under emergency medical care and won't be able to testify."

"First Mate Johansen, do you confirm the statement of charges as accurate?"

"I do." Kammy didn't seem to take the answer lightly. He inclined his head as if he were at a funeral.

"Machinist mate third class Conner," Osceola continued, eyes settling on Terry, "do *you* confirm the statement of charges as accurate?"

Terry nodded, then realized he had to speak the words for it to be official.

"I do."

Osceola placed a hand on the bulkhead beside the airlock and leaned in toward the intercom speaker.

"Does the accused have anything to say in his own defense?"

Wihtgar stared at him and Terry thought the Jeuta would remain silent as he had since security had hauled him away from the engine room. Instead, he spoke, short and to the point.

"I wish you had left me to die. It would have been more honorable than the lie I have been living among you humans."

Donner Osceola said nothing for a moment, eyes closed almost as if praying. When they opened, he'd made his judgement.

"The accused is found guilty of his crimes. The sentence…"

For the first time since they'd left the bridge, Terry thought the Captain seemed uncertain. Osceola looked between him and Kammy and slowly shook his head.

"I'm too close to this," he admitted. "Bringing him here with us was my mistake. I'm just as to blame for the deaths of Cheryl and the Chief as he is."

"I backed you up back then," Kammy declared stoutly. "And I still think it was the right thing to do. If you can't make the decision then neither can I."

Terry suddenly, *horribly* realized they were both staring at him. The security detail was, too, as if they knew more about the process than he did.

"You witnessed the crimes," Osceola explained. "You were one of the victims. You're part of the crew and with Kenyatta out of commission, you're probably the only engineering tech we have left on duty."

"And you didn't know them all," Kammy interjected. "Not the way we did. You can be more objective."

"I'm so Goddamned angry I want to kill him right now," Osceola explained. "But I can't know if the fact I've known Duncan…" He paused, closing his eyes again before he could go on. "I *knew* Duncan for fifteen years and feeling as if his death is my fault is clouding my judgement."

He flipped up the safety gate for the outer lock control. It was flashing red, a warning to all that pressing it would explosively drain the air from the chamber.

"If you push this button, Wihtgar is dead. He deserves it, there's no question about it. But this is my ship, and I don't like killing people." He shrugged. "I'll do it, when I have to, and I won't lose any sleep over it as long as they were trying to do me in first, but a cold-blooded execution is a bit harder on the conscience. So, I'm leaving it to you. If you think he should die, you push the button. If not, we'll fly him down to the moon and leave him there. I doubt anyone's going to find him there, but your people probably left enough supplies untouched for him to live, at least for a while."

"The only other option," Kammy said, "is to turn him over to the Dagda government, but they'll just tell us to put a bullet in him and add it to our bill."

Sweat trickled down Jonathan's back despite the sterile chill of the cargo deck. He rubbed at the bruises on his neck, still raw and chafed, and tried to search the cold, dead, black eyes on the other side of the airlock porthole for any sign of compassion, empathy, anything he could call human. There was nothing, not even hatred.

Terrin Brannigan would never do this. Terrin Brannigan was a scientist, an advanced graduate student, a teacher. He would never have considered taking the life of anyone, human or Jeuta. Terrin Brannigan had stayed on Sparta.

Terry Conner pushed the button.

Wihtgar was strong, perhaps strong enough to have clung to the handles built into the bulkhead for use in free-fall had he not been bound hand and foot. The atmosphere trapped in the airlock compartment rushed out into space and took the Jeuta with it. Terry turned away from the darkness beyond, barely noticing the keening of the alarm or the flashing of warning lights or Kammy leaning over to close the outer lock.

The big man was saying something, calling after him, but Terry didn't bother to respond.

There was nothing left to say.

"Who's going to notify the families?"

Jonathan didn't look up from his drink. The answers were in there, lost in the opaque amber of the bourbon, he was sure of it. It was disappointing when the amber was gone and only clear glass remained, which was why he'd kept refilling it. Yeah, that was the reason.

"I am," he declared. The bourbon approved. It didn't say anything negative, so he assumed its approval. "It won't mean a damned thing to them; they don't know who the hell Captain Jonathan Slaughter is. But they'll get a nice, fat check from Wholesale Slaughter, LLC and maybe after all this is over, I'll get to visit personally and explain what really happened."

And won't that be a wonderful experience for the Langella family, finding out their only son followed his friend Logan off on some damn-fool secret mission and died on a nameless, unimportant moon hundreds of light-years from home?

"This wake sucks," Donner Osceola said.

Jonathan finally diverted his attention from the hypnotic darkness of the bourbon, squinting at the ship's captain. He was sprawled across the chair, long legs stretched out halfway into the aisle between their table and the next. Jonathan had considered taking a shot every time someone tripped over the man, but he didn't want to get alcohol poisoning.

"Yeah, I've seen better," he admitted. People were huddled together in small groups of two or three, subdued and depressed and drinking heavily. "I remember General Aberdeen's wake."

"Do you?" Lyta wondered, lubricated enough by a third of a bottle of tequila to crack a grin. "I don't."

She chuckled, leaning into Osceola's shoulder. He wished Katy were here, but the medics wanted her to stay in sick bay another day for observation because of her concussion. She wouldn't have let him get away with being this morose.

"I was still in the Academy," he recalled, "and there was wall-to-wall brass in the palace banquet hall. I was scared shitless, sitting at attention and saluting anything that moved. About four glasses of rum later, me and two Colonels and an Admiral were standing on a table singing Reconstruction War-era marching songs"

"Not much table-singing going on tonight," Osceola observed. The man *should* have been drunk as a skunk in a funk, given how much vodka he'd downed in the last two hours, but instead he simply seemed mellow.

"You got two crews mashed together," Lyta said, "neither of which trusts the other completely, a third of our people are still in sickbay, and we can't even tell stories about the ones who died because most of what they did was classified."

"Like I said," Osceola agreed, "this wake sucks."

"Well, at least Mr. Vasari was happy," Lyta said, downing the rest of the tequila in her glass. "He even okayed paying for the repairs to our drop-ships and assault shuttle without blinking an eye."

"And we got to keep the cargo we found at the Jeuta base."

The captain shrugged, laughing softly, "whoever the hell it used to belong to."

"We salvaged quite a bit from the strike mecha the Jeuta had stolen." She was pouring herself another glass, which made five but who was counting? Certainly not Paskowski, who was snoring loudly, cheek resting on the next table.

"The operation was a success," Jonathan quoted the old saying, unable to keep the bitterness out of his voice, "but the patient died."

"The only way we could have avoided casualties on this one," Lyta told him, "was to turn down the job. And if we'd done that, we wouldn't be heading for our *next* job on the far end of Starkad space."

"I'm sure I'll get a fucking medal for initiative," he said, sneering at the thought. "It's too bad I won't be able to put it in Marc's coffin."

"You can't tell us your war stories, kid," Osceola said, out of nowhere, as if he hadn't been listening, "so let me tell you one of mine, instead."

The older man's eyes lost focus, turning inward towards a memory.

"There was this young officer in the Spartan Navy, almost as young as you. He was, at the time, the youngest man to make captain, to get his own ship command." Osceola shrugged, sipping from his drink. "I understand that record's been broken since, but it was impressive enough to get him noticed. He was at the tip of the spear when the real bullets started flying, never afraid of an impossible task. And you know what happens when you pull off an impossible mission, kid?"

"They give you one even more impossible," Lyta supplied.

Osceola touched glasses with her and they both took a drink.

"Exactly. And you can only keep rolling sixes for so long before your luck runs dry. It's the hottest days of the Lambert

Rebellion, what you folk closer to Sparta call 'the coup.' Every ship is tied up fighting off the rebel forces, and Clan Modi decides it's a wonderful time to try seizing one of our border colonies, a little place they called Vadodara. We named it something different, of course: Plataea."

Jonathan's eyes opened wide and his thoughts clarified with an instant sobriety.

"You were at Plataea?"

Osceola laughed without humor, the expression changing easily to a scowl when he saw his empty glass. He set it down with a flat crack.

"Three Modi cruisers were attacking the colony and the only reason it hadn't fallen before we got there was a fairly robust static defense system...and the fact they wanted it intact. They had too many lifeless, radioactive rocks in their 'holdings' already thanks to the Reconstruction Wars, and they weren't of a mind to just crash meteors into it until the local government surrendered."

He didn't say anything for about ten seconds, just staring at the empty glass. Finally, Lyta grabbed it from him, leaned over to Paskowski's table and stole his half-full vodka bottle, pouring Osceola another shot. The captain took it from her, looked as if he were considering downing the whole thing in one gulp, but then just took a single sip.

"We ran them around the system for two solid weeks, trading potshots, waiting for help that never came. When we realized we were on our own, we had the choice of standing and fighting or just un-assing the situation and coming back to re-take the colony after things had shaken out back on Sparta." Another sip, and a shrug. "Of course, by then Modi would have stolen everything worth taking from the planet, maybe including the people. Back then, the Modi government was into the slave trade, unofficially, you understand."

"They still are," Lyta growled, her face hardening.

"Just so. We…" A wince. "*I* decided to fight. Me, boy fucking wonder. I decided we could take them all on with just our one ship, the *Paralus*."

"The *Paralus?*" Jonathan repeated, disbelief creeping into his voice. "*The* fucking *Paralus?*" He smacked the table. "We studied that battle in the Academy…it was required for military history. But I don't remember any Donner Osceola being part of it."

"Well, kid," the captain said, cocking an eyebrow, "I hate to break it to you, but you're not the first person in the galaxy to use a fake name."

"Mithra," Jonathan breathed. "Then you're…"

"You may be in charge of this mission, youngster," Osceola interrupted him, "and you may be paying the bills, but if you say that name in my hearing, your ass will be doing its best to breathe vacuum." He eyed Jonathan with a sidelong glare, a conviction he meant what he was saying. "You get me?"

Jonathan didn't like being threatened, but an instinct from somewhere in his hind-brain forced him to nod assent. Osceola grunted in what might have been acknowledgement, and went on.

"You know the rest. You know what we did. All the stories about how the *Paralus* destroyed three ships, each twice her size. And maybe you've even read about how much it cost, how we wound up with half our superstructure ripped away, with no atmosphere left and all of us who survived having to live in pressure suits until they could get rescue shuttles up to us."

He drummed his fingers on the tabletop rhythmically.

"What they didn't teach you was how you could hear the crew screaming over their suit radios when the acceleration couch they were belted into was knocked off its moorings by railgun rounds and kicked out of the superstructure into space. You couldn't shut your suit radio off because it was the only way any of us could communicate, so you had to sit there and listen to them scream. What they didn't teach you was how we had to gather the dead bodies and rope them together in one of the compartments so they wouldn't float free of the ship, so we could bring them home. Or how the inside of our helmets began to smell like death after two days straight in it, or how we all ran out of the food paste in the reservoirs after three days..."

The man's voice became more strained, more strident with each word until he snapped his mouth shut on the last, as if he were afraid what he would say next, of what the words were making him remember. His fingers ceased drumming, the hand shaking too badly to continue. Lyta covered it with hers and slipped an arm around him, her expression not so much concerned as forbearing.

A shudder ran through Osceola's shoulders and he visibly gathered himself. A few deep breaths later, he was able to look Jonathan in the eye again.

"After they pinned the medal on my chest and had all the commemorative ceremonies and monument dedications and everything began to get back to normal on Sparta," he went on, voice hoarser, rougher than before, "they wanted to reward my performance by putting me in command of the *Salamis*." Which still was, Jonathan knew, the Spartan Navy's flagship, usually reserved for an admiral. "Instead, I resigned my commission, cashed in my retirement and every favor I had, sold the prime land in Argos that had been in my family for ten generations and put myself deep into hock to buy an old, beat-up piece of shit like this."

The grin twisting his face was far from pleasant. "Because now, when I fuck up and get people killed, I can blame myself for it without someone trying to give me a medal."

Jonathan cocked his head to the side, eyes narrowing.

"Captain Osceola," he said slowly, "that may be the worst fucking motivational speech I've ever heard."

The older man's grim expression cracked, shuddered, then

broke completely and he began to snort, then giggle, before erupting into a full, belly laugh. Jonathan was worried for a moment it might turn into a hysterical cackle but he couldn't help joining in, the catharsis of the laughter so much easier than the sobs he wouldn't allow.

Lyta smiled but didn't join in. Instead, she stood and raised her glass high.

"A toast!" Her voice cracked across the room like a bullwhip, and even Paskowski raised up from the table, a damp napkin sticking to his face, eyes blinking incomprehension.

"Here's to us," Lyta said in cheerful defiance of grief, "and those like us!"

Glasses were raised in salute all across the *Shakak's* mess, ship's crew, Spartan Navy, Rangers, and mechjocks all standing as one. Some smiled, others were grim, and Jonathan thought he saw at least a few tears. But the reply was universal, shouted loud, echoing off the bulkheads.

"Damn few!"

He downed what was left of his drink in honor of the dead.

Fewer all the time.

Colonel Aleksandr Kuryakin scrolled through images of the retirement community on Trondheim with a dolorous resignation. Hot springs and glaciers, beaches and mountains, it all looked supremely boring. When the knock came on his door, he didn't even look up from the screen.

"Come."

Clunky, clumsy, loud, rushed. He would have known who it was even if she hadn't been announced by his office clerk twenty minutes ago.

"Sir, Captain Laurent reports…"

"At ease, damn it," he snapped, interrupting her attempted salute. "Just close the door behind you and stop acting as if you're on a parade ground, Ruth."

"Yes, sir," she said, juggling her tablet and her shoulder bag as she reached back to pull the door closed. She was still in her field uniform and from the look of it, had come straight to his office from the spaceport.

"What was so important you couldn't go home first and change into your office uniform?" He leaned back in his chair and stroked his goatee. "Oh, for the love of God, sit down!" While she was fumbling with her shoulder bag, he turned the screen on his desk so she could see it. "Retirement," he explained. "My wife is constantly bugging me to retire and I am not even sixty. What the hell am I going to do in some Goddamned retirement village? Fish? I *hate* fishing. I will put a gun in my mouth if I have to sit around and fish day in and day out..."

"Sir," she interrupted him and he instantly knew it must be something important. Captain Laurent wouldn't have dared try to speak over him otherwise. "There's a new report about Wholesale Slaughter."

"Well, I assumed so," he said, waving a hand at her. "Otherwise you wouldn't be back already. Out with it, Ruth!"

"I was out at the Periphery, sir," she began, "searching for information on..."

"Cut to the chase. I know what you were doing, I assigned you the mission."

Laurent sucked in a breath and appeared to be trying to organize her thoughts.

"Wholesale Slaughter took a job out in the Dagda system. It's an independent colony technically within our claimed borders, but not worth the effort to annex due to the low rate of return in their gas mines." She tapped a sequence into her tablet and a star map slid over onto his desk screen.

He nearly sighed at the uselessness of it; he knew where the damned Periphery was. But he dutifully noted the location of the system and the arrangement of the habitable worlds.

Three, he thought with just a hint of surprise. *Don't usually see three habitables in a Periphery system.*

"A band of Jeuta raiders was trying to shake them down," she explained, and he nearly came out of his chair.

"Jeuta!" he exclaimed. "Within our fucking borders? And this is the first I'm hearing of it?"

"It's not a force from the Regency," she amended hastily, blanching at his outburst. "These are outcasts, raiders, just a single ship and a few mecha. They haven't threatened our shipping, just attacked outlying worlds not under our direct control. I, uh…I don't know why no one has asked for military action against them…"

The why was obvious, he thought with cynicism born of years dealing with politicians. *If we let them harass the non-aligned systems, it gives them more reason to align with us.*

"Go on," he told her, keeping the sentiment to himself. "What happened?"

She summarized the campaign from what sounded like the perspective of the local press in the Dagda system, which was probably her source.

"They took some losses," she summed up, "but not unacceptable ones given the forces they faced and the situation. And they more than made up for them with the salvage."

"A commander who's willing to risk his people but not waste them." Kuryakin nodded approval. Then frowned, disturbed by that very sense of approval. "Very unlike most mercenary units I've seen. Most of them are risk-averse. Understandable given the thin margins they live on, but…"

"We did manage to get some footage of the Wholesale

Slaughter command staff from local news footage," she went on, sliding another image from her work tablet to his station.

Kuryakin's face froze in the middle of a suggestion she should get sources closer to the action. The image on his screen was of a slick-back weasel in a business suit speaking to two military types, a younger man and a middle-aged woman. She was tall and impressive and he had the feeling he'd seen her face somewhere before, though he couldn't place it. The man, though...he *knew* he'd seen that face somewhere. He shushed Laurent when she tried to proceed, wracking his brain for connections.

Someone he'd seen at a conference? A treaty signing? A negotiation? Was it Gensai? Cordhaven? No, no, earlier. Atlomina? But that was ten years ago. This man would have been a teenager and what would a teenager be doing at a peace conference... Aleksandr Kuryakin's blood froze in his veins and he pushed himself out of his chair, stepping away from the screen as if it were poisoned.

"Where are they now?" he demanded, his tone sharp and unyielding.

"They have a new contract with a system in the Shang Directorate," she answered quickly. "They're heading across Starkad space now; I think they'd be at the outer Blarheim jump point by now..."

He stabbed the intercom control, nearly snarling as he waited for his office clerk to reply.

"Yes, sir?" Petty Officer Greuner sounded efficient, professional, serious, everything he demanded of his staff.

"What's the largest Naval combat vessel we have insystem right now?" Kuryakin asked him, knowing he'd have the information at hand, without having to search for it.

"The cruiser *Valkyrian*, Colonel. It's scheduled to head out on a routine patrol in three days." Perfect.

"Send this message, text only, to Captain Kessler of the

Valkyrian: Colonel Kuryakin sends codeword 'lycanthrope.' Be prepared to receive troops, orders to follow in person. End message."

"Yes, sir." Greuner repeated the message back to him for confirmation, then signed off.

"Sir," Captain Laurent asked, staring at him wide-eyed, "where are you going?"

He grinned at her and a savage, joy filled his chest, something he hadn't felt since he'd traded a mech's easy chair for this fucking desk.

"This information stays eyes-only," he told her, tapping the tablet. "*My* eyes only, you got that, Laurent? No one sees this without my okay."

"Understood, sir!" she responded smartly, coming to attention like the by-the-book marionette she was.

"Oh, and don't bother to unpack," he decided. "You're coming along."

"Yes, sir," she said automatically, then frowned. "But *where*, sir?"

He wasn't listening, thinking instead about the hot springs at Trondheim.

"Retirement my ass," he murmured, chuckling. *Logan Conner, by God. The Guardian's son...*

He was done with this job, all right. In a month, Lord Starkad would be appointing him to the fucking Ministry.

10

Y ou're sure you can't fix her?"

Jonathan cursed under his breath, angry at himself for the plaintive tone in his voice. What importance was a machine when he'd lost real *people* in the battle? And yet, seeing what remained of his Vindicator in pieces on the deck of the *Shakak's* cargo bay seemed to bring home all the death and loss of the battle two weeks ago in the way no wake or memorial could.

"'Fraid so, sir." Chief McKee rubbed at his hands with the stained red cloth he usually carried in his back pocket, as if he were wringing them in anguish. He seemed loathe to admit there was anything he couldn't repair, but one look at the shredded remains of the cockpit made it evident. "The reactor flushed and the plasma did too much damage. I was able to salvage some of the weapons, but the rest is a total loss."

"Well, damn," he sighed. He'd been piloting the Vindicator for a long time, and his had been the only one on the mission. "I suppose I can use one of the Golems..."

He trailed off. The Golems Marc Langella had taken with him on the ill-fated Trojan Horse mission had all been recovered intact. The Jeuta would have converted them for their own use eventually, but they hadn't had enough time to begin ripping up their control boards to remove the fail-safes. The thought of piloting Langella's mech, though...it wasn't so much disrespectful as it was *ghoulish*.

"Well, that's why I called you down here, sir," McKee said, a distinct cat-ate-the-canary passing across his doughy, soft-edged face. "Me and the salvage crew, we've been working on something and I wanted to let you have a look at it."

A twinge of suspicion passed across the back of Jonathan's neck, but he followed Chief McKee out of the repair bay, through a maze of equipment and stacks of spare parts, on in to the mecha storage area. The huge machines were restrained by magnetic harnesses, monsters in some mad scientist's lair, hidden away ready to be unleashed on the world. Some of the harnesses were empty, their mecha still being repaired, and some were occupied by mecha he hadn't seen before, which he figured were salvage from their jobs.

The mech the Chief led him to wasn't in a harness. The salvage crew had brought it out especially for his visit, he was sure the second he saw them all gathered at its feet. It was a Sentinel, towering fifteen meters tall, bipedal and upright, an ancient knight in shining armor, except...

"Was this Magnus' mech?" he wondered, running a hand across the cold metal of a tree-trunk leg.

"The chassis," McKee confirmed, nodding with a hint of pride in his eyes. "Though as you can tell, we did give it a paint job."

That they had. Gone was the gaudy, boastful red of the bandit chieftain, replaced by what had become the official company camouflage pattern, grey and black and brown, with a subdued "Wholesale Slaughter" scrawled in cursive across the upper right chest plastron. And the color scheme wasn't the only change.

"What the hell?" Jonathan muttered, stepping around the machine, eyes craned upward toward the strike mech's hands.

Where the normal setup for a Sentinel was an ETC cannon mounted like a pistol, this one carried a plasma gun, which lacked the range of the projectile weapon but wouldn't run out of ammo as long as the fusion reactor was running. The other hand was articulated but also heavily armored, suitable for use as a massive club. The rest of the mech's armament was fairly standard: a missile launch pod on one shoulder, a 30mm Vulcan on the other and twin lasers at the hips.

"I knew you liked the plasma gun better," the Chief said, wringing out the hand cloth again, obviously nervous about presenting the mech to his commanding officer. "And totally honest, we didn't have a spare ETC we could fit to the mount here."

"No, no, the weapons load is fine," Jonathan assured the man, a smile slowly spreading across his face.

It wasn't what he was used to, and it would be hard getting acclimated to the lack of jump-jets, but Sentinels were chosen by unit commanders for a reason: their command and control suite was unparalleled, they had nearly twice the armor of an assault mech like his Vindicator, a reactor with half again the output, and an automated missile defense system.

"It's the mech the commanding officer of Wholesale Slaughter should be piloting."

He spun around, recognizing Valentine Kurtz's voice and was surprised to see his other platoon leaders with the man—Ford, Paskowski, Hernandez and brevet-Lieutenant Summer Prevatt, all one-and-a-half meters of her defiant in her new officer's rank, her spiky red hair stuffed under a mech pilot's black beret. She'd taken the position as First Platoon leader and one of the cross-trained salvage techs had stepped into her spot in the platoon, but replacing someone like Marc Langella wasn't nearly so easy. She'd been spending hour after hour in the simulator since she was given the job, despite the fact she'd only been discharged from the infirmary a week ago.

"What are you guys doing here?" Jonathan asked them, keeping his tone light, trying to keep the melancholy thoughts of his friend off of his face. He glanced from the platoon leaders to McKee and his band of mechanics. "Is this a surprise party or an intervention?"

A smattering of weak laughs told him it was more the latter, and he sighed in resignation.

"Sir," Kurtz said with more hesitance than he'd ever heard from the man, "it's just we kind of been feeling you're blaming yourself for what happened to Marc, and…"

"You shouldn't," Paskowski interrupted, voice stern and definitive. "You were a hundred percent right when you told me I'd done the right thing firing on that Jeuta prick because I had to do it to save more lives. You did the same thing and just because we had a traitor on board doesn't mean you didn't make the right decision."

"I appreciate the work you've done on the new mech," he said to McKee, "and I really appreciate the thought." That to his officers. "But I'm the commander of this unit, which means everything that goes wrong is my responsibility, whether it's an act of treason or an act of God."

"It's your responsibility, sir," Hernandez agreed, "but it's not your fault." It surprised him to hear her chime in; she was usually tight-lipped and taciturn, not showing up for social functions unless required, not sharing anything personal with the other officers. "Soldiers die in combat, even when everything goes right."

"Sir," Prevatt piped up, her voice high-pitched and squeaky in a way that somehow didn't come over on the comms from her mech, "I was in the Trojan Horse. I was in that damned Quonset hut when Hardrada started killing us, one by one. When Lt. Paskowski's Scorpion appeared outside the door, I was hoping he'd squash the damn Jeuta bastard like a bug, even if he took me with him. I was sure I was dead. And after the laser fired, I hurt so bad I almost wished I *was* dead."

Pain tugged at the corner of her mouth and Jonathan flinched, remembering the red, weeping burns on her left leg and side when he'd gone to the casualty collection point to check on the wounded.

"And not once," she went on, her pixie voice gaining steel in the telling, "did I ever regret I'd volunteered for this assignment, or the mission. Not once did I ever blame you, sir. I knew you'd come get us out of there, and you did."

"We've accomplished something out here," Hernandez declared. "Whether we ever find this Terminus Cut or not, we've made two different systems safe for thousands of innocent civilians. It's why we all signed on."

"I signed on for the money," Kurtz admitted in a sardonic drawl. "But the people we've been helping are a lot like my family and friends back home, and I like working to keep them safe a lot more than I like trying to maintain the 'balance of power,' whatever the hell that might be."

"Me and the crew," McKee added, gesturing at the other salvage techs, "feel the same way, sir."

"So do the pilots."

He didn't know where the hell Katy had been hiding, because she appeared behind him as if she'd always been there, a hand touching him on the shoulder. She seemed fully recovered from the crash, not even a limp or a stray headache, but she'd been impossible to live with until the Dagda mechanics had gotten her shuttle repaired.

"Well," she amended with a wry smile, "all the pilots except Acosta. He thinks we're all nuts and keeps saying he wants to go home."

When Lyta approached he wasn't surprised at least; she

walked in from the same hatchway to the lift station where the others had come from. She walked, he noticed not for the first time, like a sauntering lioness, a promise of violent action in every step.

"You should already know this," she told him, giving him a baleful glare, "but the Rangers feel the same way. No one blames you for what happened, including me. You're our commander."

"Except when I try to get myself killed," he reminded her with a rueful grin. "Then you'll protect me in spite of myself, right?

"We're heading into the middle of Starkad space," she said, shaking her head grimly. "I don't think I'm going to be able to keep that promise."

"Oh, I really don't like this," Osceola murmured. Jonathan had to agree there was a lot not to like.

Gefjon wasn't *quite* the center of the Starkad Supremacy, but it was close enough: only three jumps to Baldur and the Supremacy Core on Jormungandr. Close enough for it to be the busiest interstellar hub system in the Five Dominions.

"With all this space," Katy said, standing beside Jonathan on the bridge, looking over Osceola's shoulder at the main view screen, "you wouldn't think it was possible to have a traffic jam."

Yet here they were, decelerating at one gravity with ten other starships within visual scanning range, no more than a hundred kilometers between them, almost danger-close in terms of space travel.

One mistake, one slip-up, Jonathan thought, feeling an itch running down his back, *and we could have an actual collision. It's fucking ridiculous.*

And yet this was a rare jump-point hub, a spatial coordinate where over a dozen of the gravito-inertial lines of force between stars intersected; if you wanted to go anywhere on the other side of Gefjon, you had to travel to one exact location relative to the elliptical plane of the system.

"Literally thousands of ships pass through this system every day," Osceola said, though Jonathan wasn't sure if it was an explanation of the situation Katy had brought up or simply an expansion of what he didn't like about their current circumstances.

"There's an agreement about licensed military contractors, right?" Terry asked.

He didn't sound nervous about it, just curious. Jonathan wondered what he was doing on the bridge instead of back in Engineering, since that department was down to a skeleton crew after what had happened with Wihtgar. He seemed at home in the spare acceleration couch off to the side from Kammy's helm position, and Osceola hadn't said anything about him being there.

"Yeah," he answered his brother's question. "It's been in place for over a century. All our licensing is in order; we should be fine."

Terry shrugged as if it would be the same to him either way and Jonathan frowned.

"What the hell is with him lately?" he whispered to Katy. "Is he still freaked out from Wihtgar trying to kill him?"

"Tell you later," she promised, and he grunted in dissatisfaction.

"How far away are those Starkad patrol ships, Tara?" Osceola asked his tactical officer, fidgeting slightly, as close to nervous as Jonathan had seen the captain on the bridge of his ship.

"Still hanging out around ten thousand kilometers away," the woman reported, scowling at the sight of the two military vessels on the long-range scanners. "Not getting any closer, but they're matching velocities with us and the other ships heading for the jump point."

"We got another hour before main engine shut down," Kammy supplied from the helm station. "That's not counting the time we're going to have to spend waiting around for our turn at the jump point, which might mean another braking burn."

"You're sure that business with the New Sainters isn't going to get your registry flagged with Starkad?" Jonathan asked, for what had to be the fifth time in the last three days. "Or the gunfight at Gateway?"

"The only laws I broke," Osceola ground out, his strained patience coming through every word, "were local to Canaan, and as big and monolithic as Starkad is, I still don't think they're interested in collecting bounties for two-bit independent religious colonies, do you?"

He half expected Lyta to try to smooth things over, but she had decided to spend the transit through the Gefjon system with her Rangers. Jonathan suspected she was staying off the bridge in an effort to emphasize to him her declaration recognizing him as the commander, but her absence bothered him. She was a security blanket, a guardian, and a confidant from his childhood and he'd perhaps come to depend on her too much on this mission.

I need to work on cutting loose, he thought. But he would have been happier working on it once they were out of Starkad space.

"Sir," Nance said, turning back from the communications console with distress written large across her face, "we're getting a transmission from one of the Supremacy cruisers, text only. They..." she tripped over the words as if she hated to admit the reality of their existence, "...they're saying they want to send a customs inspection team over in a shuttle, and we need to give them full access to our cargo, stores, personnel, and ship's logs. Any resistance will be considered a violation of our charter as a licensed military contractor and will result in our arrest and the forfeiture of the ship and everything in it." Her uncertain gaze moved from Jonathan to Osceola. "They said we should maintain current course and deceleration profile and their shuttle will match velocities with us after we reach engine cut-off hold for rendezvous with the jump point." She swallowed hard. "Any deviation from those directions will result in our ship being disabled."

"Fuck me." Osceola spat the words.

Jonathan couldn't even curse. His head was swimming through a sea of possibilities, each worse than the last. This *could* be routine, some stick-up-his-ass functionary in system Customs pulled with every mercenary company coming through just to show them who was boss. Or they could be just fishing, looking for some violation of the Bremerton Accords so they could slap a huge fine on the mercenary trash. Or they could be after Osceola, either because of the various smuggling and black-market weapons dealing he'd done in the last twenty years, or because they knew who he really was.

Or they had spies deep enough into the Spartan government to realize Wholesale Slaughter was a cover for a Spartan military intelligence operation.

Or they knew who he was.

Or, worst of all, they knew who he was *and* why he was there.

Katy nudged his arm and he suddenly realized Osceola was staring at him. No, *everyone* on the bridge was staring at him.

Damn.

"I don't suppose," he asked Osceola, "there's any way this ship could jump before those cruisers could intercept us?"

Kammy snorted, a sound that might have originated in the chest of a Percheron stallion, and Tara brayed a mocking laugh.

"These ain't pirates or bandits, kid," Osceola scoffed. "They got missiles that'll pull thirty, thirty-five gravities for a short range like this, with tungsten penetrators for warheads if they don't want to just nuke you to vapors. And just in case you think the deflectors have a chance against those, they got laser batteries fed by their own dedicated reactor just as big as our main drive reactor and they'll core us like a damned apple."

"I'll take that as a no," Jonathan said, the dry humor more of an attempt to calm himself down than to impress the others. "There's no choice, then." He nodded to the Commo technician. "Send a reply. Tell them we're heaving to and preparing to accept their inspection team."

He felt Katy's hand slip into his and squeezed it gratefully.

"If there's anything we need to hide," Jonathan said, casting a suspicious, sidelong glance at Osceola, "we better get started now."

11

W hat a dump."

Aleksandr Kuryakin snorted a laugh, less at the frank assessment and more at the fact it had come from Captain Laurent. She had, he reflected, loosened up a bit over the two weeks it had taken them to reach Gefjon. Not enough for him to share his secret with her; that sort of trust wouldn't come in weeks, if ever. But at least she wasn't insufferably tentative with every word she spoke, which was a distinct improvement.

She also had a point about the ship. The vessel was functional, but only just. He'd seen it first on the way up from the docking bay, seen the cargo pods carelessly strapped onto pallets half their size, the loose fasteners and restraint cords and food wrappers orbiting in the currents from the air vents.

"Welcome to the *Shakak!*" the big, goofy-looking First Mate had greeted them with cheerfulness he would have thought forced and fake if it weren't for the vacant stupidity evident behind his piggy eyes. He hadn't even looked sideways at the twenty armed and armored Supremacy Marines who'd filed out of the airlock behind Kuryakin and Laurent, smiling at them like the entertainment director on a cruise ship. "I'll show you to the bridge."

133

He'd clanked off in his monstrously oversized magnetic boots, his gait as clumsy and awkward as a toddler just learning to walk, leading them to the hub. His fat, stubby fingers had hovered over the call button for the lift car before he'd finally looked back and seemingly just noticed the Marines, then looked comically at the lift door, realizing they wouldn't all fit inside.

"Call the car for us," Kuryakin had supplied impatiently. "My troops will take the hub tunnel and inspect the ship."

Mithra alone knew what the Marines would find , but what he was seeing on the way to the bridge from the hub only confirmed his initial observations. Maintenance hatches hung loose or were missing altogether, probably stowed away somewhere because the power junctions they'd covered shorted out often enough to make it not worth the effort to conceal them. Bypasses and splices hung out of the open niches, held together with tape and good wishes, and carbon dust hung in the air from jury-rigged repairs. About a quarter of the light panels were dark and inoperative, and if the emergency seals for the bridge had ever worked, they certainly didn't at the moment, not with the guts of the motors hanging out.

He hadn't seen any of the crew along the way to the bridge except for Johansen, the First Mate, but there were eight of them on the bridge. Most were strapped into the acceleration couches at their stations, except for the man he assumed was the captain of the ship from his position beside the empty command station and one other…the one he'd come here to see.

The captain was everything Kuryakin had expected from the master of this junk heap. He was ragged, a piece of leather chewed up and spat out by life, his hair long and stringy and streaked with grey, his flight jacket threadbare and worn at the elbows, as if it weren't important enough for him to have another fabricated. Kuryakin wasn't sure how it was possible to slouch in free-fall, but Osceola was managing it, one elbow hooked around the armrest of the captain's chair, legs crossed. There was apathy in his stance and in his eyes so pure and unadulterated it couldn't have been faked.

"Colonel Kuryakin," Johansen said, mangling his name worse than his instructors in basic training had over forty years ago, "this is Captain Donner Osceola."

The introduction was pointless, a formality they could have skipped to save time, but time spent on this ship wasn't wasted, so Kuryakin nodded curtly to the spindly, leathery captain.

"This is my aid, Captain Laurent," he added politely and just as pointlessly. He knew she would have felt slighted if he hadn't mentioned her, though, and he didn't need her crawling back into her shell. "It is my duty to inspect all licensed private military contractors before allowing them to pass through Supremacy territory." He smiled genially. "We can't take the chance of our enemies using the Bremerton Accords as a cover to smuggle their troops past our borders, can we?"

"Do all Supremacy Customs officers have such active imaginations, Colonel Kuryakin?"

It was *him*. Even seeing the news footage, Kuryakin hadn't been one hundred percent sure, but seeing that taut smile, hearing his voice, it was as if he were seeing Jamie Brannigan's visage laid over that of his late wife. Kuryakin was a man used to reining in his emotions, keeping them far from his face, but it was hard this time. He wanted to yell, he wanted to crow, he wanted to leap upward and bounce off the overhead.

Instead, he forced himself to regard the younger man with the sort of annoyed disinterest and vague distaste a Supremacy military officer might show for typical mercenary scum.

"You must be the leader of this colorfully named mercenary company, then," he said, shaping the words with obvious disdain.

"Captain Jonathan Slaughter, President and CEO of Wholesale Slaughter LLC, at your service, sir."

There was just a hint of a grin beneath his perfectly serious face, as if some inner part of what was still a young man enjoyed the ludicrous, over-the-top nature of his cover.

"And how long have you been in the business, Captain Slaughter?" He knew the answer, of course, both the real one and the one they were using as a cover, but interrogating an enemy operative was similar to cross-examining a witness at a trial. You never asked a question you didn't already know the answer to.

"Just a few months," the man calling himself Jonathan Slaughter told him. "Though I'd been planning and raising funds for the company for months before that, of course."

"Yes, I believe I heard you are especially passionate about the plight of independent colonies suffering the predations of bandits and raiders." He waved a hand, inadvisable as a gesture in free-fall but for his magnetic boots. "An admirable sentiment, I suppose, though one wonders how it became such a passion for a Spartan military officer."

The cool, genial demeanor the younger man had been projecting curled away in a puff of smoke like paper singed on a fire.

"I've lost people I cared about," Slaughter told him, his voice suddenly harsh. "I've had people I love hurt very badly. I have more than enough passion for this subject, Colonel Kuryakin."

"I believe you do, son," Kuryakin acceded, nodding slowly, almost unwillingly. And he did. The hatred in the young man's voice could no more have been faked than the apathy in Osceola's demeanor. "Surely, you could have done more with the resources of the Guardianship military behind you, though?"

"The Five Dominions don't see bandits and raiders as a threat to their national security, Colonel." Bitterness too, astride the anger. "They use them as political tools against each other, and no one is truly interested in hunting them down. Other military contractors even, they're more interested in jacking up their fees and protecting their assets than fighting." Grey eyes flashed in the dim shadows of burned out light panels. "I am in business to kill bandits."

Kuryakin regarded the man he knew to be Logan Conner, uncertain for the first time since he'd left Jormungandr. He'd felt sure this was some sort of intelligence-gathering mission, something desperate for Jaimie Brannigan to risk the life of his oldest son on it, but he had the sense now this was something else, something even bigger. Definitely something more personal to Logan Conner.

He felt the weight of his 'link in his pocket, knew he could order the Marines to arrest the crew and end this now under the watchful eyes of the *Valkyrian*. He left it in his pocket. This required flexibility.

"Well," he said, clapping his hands together with cheerful finality, "I think our work is done here. Everything seems in order." He turned and shot a significant glance at Laurent. "Captain, if you would go see to the bill of lading for their records?"

It was a code phrase, one he'd given her in the briefing, and he hoped like hell she had a good memory. The glint of realization in her eyes told him she did.

"Yes, sir," she said, nodding firmly. She headed back out the bridge hatch, raising her hand to stop the First Mate when he tried to escort her. "I can find my own way, thank you."

Kuryakin gave her a moment to clear the bridge, hoping she'd be smart enough to use a secure text message instead of making a voice call someone might overhear over the ship's intercom pickups.

"I understand your next contract is in the Shang Directorate," he told the man calling himself Jonathan Slaughter.

"That's right," he confirmed, just a hiss of breath escaping his nostrils to indicate the relief he was hiding. "It's actually on Mingtiao, a colony near the border. Nothing profitable or populated enough for Shang or Starkad to care about their ore shipments being raided by bandits."

"These people can't be paying you much, Captain Slaughter." It took every ounce of self-control Kuryakin possessed not to imbue the name with the scorn he felt for it. "How can you afford to pay your pilots, the crew of this ship?"

"I have enough cash reserves to work at a small loss until we build a name for ourselves."

The answer was well-rehearsed but unconvincing.

"You're certainly on your way to that. And what a name it is." The sneer wouldn't be repressed this time. "Wholesale Slaughter indeed."

"It's memorable," the younger man argued. "Potential customers will remember it now…and pirates will know it pretty soon. When we come into a system, they'll leave without a fight."

"A business model I can appreciate." Kuryakin offered a hand, stripping off his black leather glove first. Logan Conner's grip was firm and dry. "Good luck in your endeavors, Captain."

"And you in yours, Colonel."

There was something in Logan Conner's expression…or maybe it was Jonathan Slaughter he was talking to, after all. Something knowing, something challenging. He could read the words as clearly as if the man had spoken them: you don't know why I'm here and you can't stop me.

We'll see about that, boy.

"I will take my leave then." He motioned to the First Mate, Johansen. "Lead on." A baleful glare back at Osceola. "Captain Osceola, your ship is a pig-sty."

"Yeah, nice meetin' you, too, Colonel Crackalackin," the ragged man murmured.

Kuryakin didn't bother answering. He had the answers he'd come for.

"What are you supposed to be? The zero-g ballet?"

Lyta Randell ignored the question, concentrating on her form, bouncing off the gym's padded overhead and twisting her body in mid-air to bring her feet back beneath her before she impacted the deck. She clicked the heels of her magnetic boots together just before she hit and the heels stuck to the deck, leaving her standing, facing the Supremacy Marine standing in the hatchway.

He was wearing standard body armor except for the helmet, which was hinged back off his head, resting negligently against the emergency air supply in his backpack. He carried a Gyroc carbine, meant for use in zero-g, a recoilless weapon that fired spin-stabilized mini-rockets. He had it slung across his chest, one hand resting on the optical sight atop the receiver. She immediately loathed the man—helmets were meant to be worn and weapons to be held at the ready, especially on a ship potentially full of hostiles. She loathed him even more when she saw the captain's bars etched into his chest plate. Captain Jeffries, Pasqual R.

The man's an officer and this is the sort of example he's setting?

"Did you want something?" she asked, retrieving a towel from her belt and wiping away the sweat persistently beading against her skin in the microgravity. "Or have the Supremacy Marines never heard of free-fall combat training?"

Pasqual Jeffries had one of those faces, too handsome for his job and cocky enough to know it. She saw it in the smug tilt of his head, the way his eyebrow twitched up as he looked her over.

"Seems like an odd time to be training," he judged, "right in the middle of a customs inspection."

"Not so odd," she told him, tucking the towel away. "You're a waste of our time, and I don't like to see time go to waste. You never know how much of it you have left."

"Is that a philosophical observation or a threat, Ms...?" That tilted brow again, as if he thought he was being clever, or possibly even charming.

"Major," she corrected him, stepping over to the lockers set in the wall. "Major Randell." She pulled her fatigue blouse on, sealing it down the front. It didn't say "Spartan Rangers" anymore, the sign and the seal replaced by the Wholesale Slaughter crest. *For the time being.*

"Major of what?" Jeffries wondered. "You aren't a mech jock. You can always tell a mech jock by the way they walk, the way they stand. You're a crunchie, like me."

"We're private military contractors," she reminded him, stomping up to the hatchway, magnetic boots clacking loudly on the deck. "Gotta' be versatile. Versatility starts on the ground."

"Ooh," he mimed clutching at a shot through his heart. "I think I'm in love." He laughed at his own joke, another sure sign of a narcissistic asshole. "Any chance you got time for a little unarmed combat with a Marine?"

She was almost nose to nose with the man, only a few centimeters shorter than his meter-eight. She could smell the overly sweet musk of whatever he was using for cologne.

Just douchebag alarms sounding everywhere.

"I already told you, Captain Jeffries, I don't have the time to waste. Now if you wouldn't mind moving out of my way?"

He fixed her with a stare, hard and humorless. She thought perhaps she'd pushed past his limit for rejection and began formulating ways to take the carbine away from him and put a round through that high forehead.

"All right, Major Randell," he said, finally, stepping back a pace to let her through. "But I get this feeling we're going to see each other again."

"I'll be seeing you," she assured him, then cupped her hand like a gun-sight and put it to her eye. "I'm not sure you'll be seeing me."

He was laughing as she stomped away, just a bit too loud to be genuine.

"There they go," Aleksandr Kuryakin said, watching on the main screen of the *Valkyrian's* bridge as the *Shakak* disappeared in the rainbow ring of a jump-point transition.

His voice sounded a bit wistful to his own ears. Had he made the right decision? It would have been so simple to seize the ship, arrest Logan Conner and presented him to Lord Starkad as a gift, the ultimate bargaining tool to force concessions from that loud-mouthed clod Jaimie Brannigan. Aaron Starkad would have owed him, perhaps enough to write his own ticket.

His gut had told him no, and he'd learned over the last thirty years to listen to his gut.

"Are you certain the trackers won't be detected?" he asked Laurent. It was nerves; he knew what she'd say.

"Not unless they make a visual inspection of the hull," she replied, nodding toward the blank spot in space where the tramp ship had been a moment before. "There are enough transponder drones to leave a trail for the next four jump-points." She shrugged diffidently. "Though it may take a while to check every possible jump-line…"

"Time well spent, Ruth," he assured her.

Captain Kessler was trying not to stare, trying not to look resentful and failing miserably at both. The woman didn't care to have her cruiser hijacked by some flakey military intelligence spook and it couldn't have been more obvious had she worn a sign around her neck. She'd like what came next even less.

"Captain," he told her, "have your navigator draw up a grid search up to four jump-points out." He grinned at her discomfort. "I'm afraid we have a long trip ahead of us."

⊕

Donner Osceola didn't spend much time in the ship's gym if he could help it. Lyta kept bugging him to stay in better shape, telling him he spent too much time sitting around and drinking on his off hours, and his reply was always "that's feature, not a bug, darlin'."

But the message on his 'link from the kid, Jonathan, had asked to meet at the gym. Why the hell he wanted to meet *now* was the question. Every hour was a working hour on a starship, but he kept track of the sleep cycles of the crew—it was part of his job—and he knew the kid should have been sleeping by now, snuggled up with that hot pilot girlfriend of his.

Osceola snorted. Least the kid had good taste.

The gym was deserted, the lights turned off and this time not because he'd had his crew rip the circuits out for the benefit of the Starkad inspectors. The glow of chemical strip-lighting was pale and ghostly, throwing shadows across the padded walls and floor, but nothing moved inside.

"Well, fuck," he muttered, checking the time on his 'link. If the kid was messing with him…

Donner Osceola had felt the business end of a gun against his neck before, so he had no trouble figuring out what the cold, metallic pressure just beneath his right ear was. He froze in place, keeping his hands in front of him, fingers spread, careful not even to breath too deeply.

"Hey now," he said slowly and calmly, "let's not do anything we'll regret…"

"Shut up."

He frowned. His first thought had been another traitor or a Starkad plant, his second a disgruntled crewmember and his last a jilted ex-lover. None of those thoughts had involved Jonathan Slaughter putting a gun to his head.

"Kid, what the fuck are you…" He tried to jerk around, but a grip stronger than he thought a mech-jock would have jerked the back of his flight jacket and kept him in place, the barrel of the handgun jabbing painfully into the bone behind his ear.

"I said shut up."

Osceola was many things: a gambler, a drunkard, a womanizer, a liar, a thief, a smuggler…

Hold on. Where the fuck was this going? Oh, right…

…but he wasn't an idiot and he recognized a serious threat when he heard one. He shut up.

"Osceola," the kid went on, his voice low but as hard and unyielding as the muzzle of his large-caliber handgun, "this is your ship. I won't tell you how to run it. If you want to hold your little kangaroo court in the cargo bay and chuck one of your own crew out the airlock, I don't give a shit as long as it doesn't interfere with my mission."

A harsh rasp of breath and the grip on Osceola's collar tightened with a cracking of knuckles.

"But you don't involve my fucking *brother* in your little mind games. Terry might be working in your engine room, but he's part of *my* company, part of *my* mission. Maybe you think you're giving him closure, giving him a chance at revenge for his friends, toughening him up as a man, whatever…I don't give a damn. It's not your place. Maybe you're a famous war hero or maybe you're just a tramp freighter captain and a part-time criminal, but you don't *get* to be his mentor, or his teacher or his father figure."

Jonathan spun him around, slamming him back against the

bulkhead, the very, very large-caliber muzzle shoved directly between his eyes.

"This is the only warning you get. You fuck up my mission, our contract is void, we part ways and you lose all that money and all that salvage. But you fuck with my *family*, I don't care if I have to fight my way through your whole crew afterwards, I will put a bullet right through your forehead. Am I making myself clear?"

He wanted to be angry. He wanted to shout the kid down, gun or no gun, wanted to tell him no one threatened him on *his* ship. He wanted to try to explain he hadn't done it to play any games with Terry, he just...

Shit.

"I'm sorry, Jonathan," he said instead.

The muzzle of the gun lowered a few centimeters, the furl in the kid's brow evidence that whatever he'd expected Osceola to say, an apology hadn't been among the possibilities.

"I mean it," Osceola insisted, chewing on his lip. "I wasn't trying to hurt your brother." *Hadn't he called the boy his cousin? Just another bit of cover story, I guess.* "I trusted Wihtgar, I liked him. I made a mistake and I was afraid I was going to make another if I decided what to do with him." He shrugged, misery dragging down his face. "I let him choose because I thought he'd be more likely to do the right thing than me."

Jonathan Slaughter, or whatever the hell his name really was, lowered the pistol slowly, almost reluctantly, as if he didn't want to give up on being furious. But the anger seemed to slide away from him in a sigh. He shoved the handgun back into its holster.

"I believe you. It doesn't make it right."

"No," Osceola agreed. "I guess...I like the kid. He knows he doesn't belong here, but he came along anyway." He waved a hand helplessly. "I'll let him alone, you have my word." *For what it's worth.*

"No, you don't have to do that." Jonathan had relaxed, but now his expression hardened again. "But I'm in charge of this mission, and of my people. I need you to tell me you understand that."

"I do. You're the boss."

The words were sour, but he had to say them. He had to mean them. Not for Jonathan Slaughter, but for Lyta. He'd screwed up a lot of things in his life, wasted a lot of chances. He wasn't going to waste this one.

12

Y ou know," Donner Osceola said, pausing to spit a stream of brown liquid into a flip-top bottle, "I have been sailing longer than Junior there," he nodded at Jonathan, "has been alive, and I don't think I have ever been anywhere this far from settled space."

Lyta scowled at him, gesturing at the spit bottle in a secured cupholder fitted to the captain's acceleration couch.

"When the hell did you start chewing again?" she demanded.

"When you dragged me through fucking Starkad space on a spy mission," he retorted, giving her the same stink-eye back, "and then out here past the middle of nowhere and right up to the very ragged edge of anywhere." He leaned back in his chair and propped a leg up, draping his elbow across it. "Tends to put a man on edge."

"You bring that shit to bed you can find somewhere else to sleep," she warned him.

Jonathan tried to shut out their banter, staring at the flashing yellow line on the navigation display. It was a searchlight leading them on, through three jump-points and nearly a hundred light years past Starkad space, beyond the Periphery colonies, and well into the Shadow Zone, the inner reaches of the old Empire where kinetic-energy strikes and nuclear weapons had sterilized all living planets in the senseless and spiteful destruction of the Reconstruction Wars.

"How many more systems?" he asked, speaking to a point somewhere between Kammy and Nance. The two were huddled together, trying to mesh the data from the Communications console with the navigation computer. "How many more before we reach the source of the signal?"

You'd think it'd be easy, he grumbled to himself. *We know how old it is, we know it was... traveling at the speed of light...*

But of course, they didn't know *exactly* how old it was because it was an automated replay of a recording. The recording was 423 years, seven months and three days old, but the transmission itself could have been years later. And years at the speed of light meant light-years of distance, which they had all been finding out to their chagrin over the last few weeks.

"I am thinking..." Kammy answered his question with the absent-minded tone of someone concentrating hard on something besides talking, trailing off for a moment before he turned to Jonathan with a huge smile splitting his huge face. "None. This is it."

There was a surge of humanity across the bridge—*Hell, it feels like across the whole damn ship!*—towards the navigation screen, the whole bridge crew and Jonathan and Lyta all staring at the giant yellow arrow pointing through the system to a black and rocky world. Too far from the too-dim orange dwarf star at the center of the system, the world roamed alone, moonless and seemingly dead.

"It's Terminus," Nance breathed the words like a prayer. "It has to be."

"Let's not jump to any conclusions," Jonathan warned, trying to look deliberately unexcited, afraid to be optimistic for fear he might jinx it. "It might just be a signal repeater."

"Way to kill the buzz, fearless leader," Osceola said, glaring at him from behind Kammy's chair. "How about giving everyone a minute to celebrate before trying to bring us all down?"

Things had been tense between the two of them since the "conversation" in the gym, but Jonathan had been trying his best to act as if it hadn't happened, which seemed to suit Osceola fine.

"Sorry," he said, grinning as he raised his hands palms-out in surrender. "For the sake of morale, I'll allow ten seconds of unrestrained cheering."

"Well, when you put it like that," Osceola griped, "I'd feel silly cheering."

Kammy didn't care; he whooped loudly, pounding a palm on the control panel hard enough to make the image on the screen waver, then jumped up and picked Petty Officer Nance by the waist and tossed her into the air. The woman shrieked but laughed through it, and the whole bridge crew was laughing with her, even Lyta.

Has it been that *long of a trip?* he wondered, trying not to stare at her for fear of the smile running away. *Or has being with Osceola changed her?*

"Okay," he said into the echoes of the laughter and applause, moving up to the Communications console, "I think that's ten seconds. Time to make the rest of the ship happy."

He hit public address, trying to imagine his mech company down in the cargo bay, working on maintenance with Chief McKee, Katy running simulations with her flight crews, all looking up at the sound of his voice.

"Wholesale Slaughter," he said into the audio pickup, "we have reached the system of origin of the signal, and we are going to be maneuvering into a deceleration burn in approximately two minutes. Secure for maneuvering, and once the braking burn starts, you're going to have two hours to prepare for orbital insertion."

He paused, eyeing Lyta and remembering what she'd said about delegating authority...and then recalling how it had felt walking into the Quonset hut and finding Marc Langella's body. He switched the intercom to another feed and continued.

"Drop-Ship One crew, prepare for launch. You'll be carrying a heavy platoon of mecha and a platoon of infantry, plus a research crew."

"Cover One will be flying overwatch." That was Katy's voice and it wasn't a question. His first instinct was to argue, but then realized it would only be delaying the inevitable.

"Yes, you are, Lt. Margolis. Prep your shuttle for takeoff."

He grinned, imagining her frown at the lack of an opportunity for an entertaining verbal tussle.

"Aye, sir," she replied curtly, signing off.

Another switch of channels.

"Terry," he said to his brother. "You're up. Get your team to Drop-Ship One and bring whatever gear you think you'll need."

"Got it. We'll be there."

Terry sounded eager, excited, which was an improvement over the glum introspection he'd been stuck in for weeks after the fight with the Jeuta and what had happened with Wihtgar. He hadn't tried to talk to his brother about it, hoping Terry would come to him.

"And who's going to be leading the landing party?" Lyta asked him, suspicion strong in her voice and in her expression.

"I am," Jonathan told her, then went on, not waiting for her inevitable objections. "This is the holy grail, Lyta, the end of the quest. The decisions to be made, the information I'll need to make them, it's all down there." He gestured at the view screen, at the image of the planet below. "It's where I need to be."

"Yes, it is," she agreed, and it was all he could do to keep his mouth from dropping open in shock. She spread her hands as if accepting the inevitable. "Mission first. It's one of the most important things they teach in Ranger school."

"Everybody hold on tight," Osceola warned, both to those on the bridge within earshot and over the intercom to the whole ship. He screwed a lid onto his spit bottle. "Things are about to turn upside down."

Aleksandr Kuryakin hadn't even bothered to leave his cabin for this jump. He had a moral conviction they wouldn't find the *Shakak* until the last possible moment, which was still one more drone-drop and four possible jump-points away and he preferred handling the post-jump nausea he'd always suffered strapped into his bunk with the lights off. Laurent could handle the disappointment of one more dry hole, could try to massage Captain Kessler's ego and listen to her whining and moaning about maintenance schedules and refueling and leave schedules.

Kessler was as bad as his wife. Holy Bull of Mithra, how Giovanna had ranted and raved about retirement and getting away from the backstabbing and politics of the capital, how she didn't *want* to be married to a minister, how she'd waited all these years for him to give all this up and move out to one of the more sedate colonies.

He'd told her he would be back when he would be back and that was it. If she didn't care for his career choices, she was free to move back in with her trash parents on their dirt farm and give up the cushy job as a civilian employee at the Supremacy Military

Command. It wasn't the best way to part, but their children were grown and gone, and maybe it was time to make a clean break.

"Damn," he murmured to himself. What was the use sitting here in the dark to avoid the drama on the bridge when he kept reliving his own drama inside his head? He was about to unstrap and sit up when the alarms went off and he gritted his teeth and braced for the jump.

He knew some people felt nothing during the transition from one universe to another, and he hated those people with the fire of a thousand suns. When it came, it was the metaphysical equivalent of his intestines trying to leave his body through his navel without the benefit of an incision. It involved pain, but not the sort felt in the nerves; this was the pain of losing a child, a parent, a beloved pet. It was the pain of heartbreak and loss and despair rolled into the point of a knife and rammed through the guts with the weight of a universe behind it and no researcher or doctor or physicist had ever been able to explain the "how" of it, much less the "why."

It lasted forever, yet it was over instantly, leaving a residue of psychic slime smeared over his soul. He moaned softly, opened his eyes and let the muscles of his neck unclench. And he'd had to go through this shit *fifteen times* in the last three weeks.

"Bugger me."

He yanked the zero-g restraints on his cot loose as he felt the fusion drives kick in, pushing him into the cushioned mattress with about half a standard gravity of acceleration, and sat up.

Maybe his wife had a point.

"Sir, are you there?" It was Laurent because of course it was. Another report on another disappointment, another system filled with the burned cinders of once-habitable worlds.

"Where the hell else would I be, Ruth?" he asked, tilting his head up toward the overhead speakers even though he knew the audio pickup was on the wall beside his bunk. "Get it over with, give me your report so we get to repeat all this again."

"Sir, we've found them!"

Kuryakin nearly fell back to the bunk with relief, but forced himself to pop up from the mattress instead. He slipped into his ship boots, grabbed his tunic from the locker built into the bulkhead of his private cabin, and headed out the hatch before he even had the shirt completely fastened. Crewmembers not currently on duty were making their way out into the passageways to take advantage of the thrust to get some food or exercise. He weaved his way through them, earning curious glances and more than one whispered conversation.

He didn't wait for the lift car, pounding down the spiral staircase of the hub instead, not slowing for upward traffic, forcing his way through by the power of his rank and his urgency. He ran his hands through the regulation cut of his hair before he hit the hatchway to the bridge, a moment's concession to the necessity of not looking like a wild-eyed madman in front of Captain Kessler and the bridge personnel.

"Situation!" he snapped, barging through the open hatchway into the kaleidoscope of multicolored displays and screens at the heart of the ship's control systems.

Captain Kessler made a face like a dog sniffing a rival and said nothing, but Ruth Laurent was already hustling forward, gesturing with a laser pointer at the tactical sensor displays.

She brought a damned laser pointer with her on this mission. I can't decide if that's dedication or just Obsessive-Compulsive Disorder.

"They're in this system, sir," she told him, her eyes lit up like a child at Yule, weight shifting from one foot to another as if she were about to break into a spontaneous dance. "They've moved into orbit around one of the interior planets, this one here." She highlighted the world on the sensor display with a touch of the laser. "We think they've been in-system at least a few hours, maybe as many as twenty or thirty; long enough to have made it from the jump-point to orbit at least."

Kuryakin squinted at the readout next to the computer-enhanced image of the world, comparing the spectral analysis to the brown, lifeless appearance of the planet. He chewed at his lip, leaning up against the Tactical console, ignoring the way the Navy officer crewing it leaned away and gave him a dirty look at the intrusion on his personal space.

"There can't be any life on that world," he declared. "What the hell do they want there?"

"We're picking up a repeating signal coming from somewhere on the planet," the Communications officer reported, stepping on Laurent before the woman could give him the news herself. "It's..." The man was young and fresh-faced and excitement glowed in his eyes, replacing the resentment and boredom the whole crew had sunken into over the last few weeks. "Here, let me play it for you, Colonel."

At the touch of a control, the image of the planet on the main screen was shunted to one of the smaller, side displays, replaced by the lined, worn-down face of a man. Even before he spoke, Kuryakin could tell he was a military officer. He'd been in the military, and in the business of Intelligence long enough to read the clues written across the hard edges of the rough-hewn features, the resolve behind the tired sag of the dark eyes.

"I am Colonel Walken Zeir," he said, tired and resigned yet still with an underlying strength and dignity the exhaustion couldn't quite erase, "of the 403rd Imperial Ordnance Battalion. My unit has been stationed here on Terminus for the last three years."

Terminus. Holy shit, Terminus!

There were murmurs across the bridge, not shocked or surprised as they'd seen the recording before he arrived, but excited or confused, with one crewmember explaining the old legends to another.

"When I came here," Colonel Zeir went on, "there seemed hope we could yet pull the fragments of the Empire back together. Now with the Jeuta invasion of the Homeworld, that hope is dead."

"That's over four hundred years ago," Laurent added *sotto vocce*, as if he couldn't remember his military history classes from the Academy.

"I'm going to send this message on a continuous loop as long as the generators hold out. I'm directing it towards the human worlds farthest away from the Jeuta incursions in the hopes rebuilding will begin there. It won't be in time to save us, I'm afraid." His face fell, his voice becoming even grimmer and more hopeless. "Food stores have been stretched to their limit and there is barely a two-month supply left. We have sent the few ships we have to search for outposts, for Imperial outposts or ship, but those who have returned report no living worlds remaining within a hundred light years. I will not starve to death, and neither will the rest of us. We have decided to end our lives with dignity before it comes to that." Zeir's shoulders shuddered with a steadying breath as he visibly collected himself.

"If anyone hears this... if there's anyone left who can, and who can reach us, this system has yet to be discovered by the enemy. There is safe haven here, and weapons to take the fight to them, if you have the personnel to use them and the ships to carry them. And if no one comes, if there is no one left, then this message is simply a grave marker. If there may yet be any other life in this universe besides humans, and if they ever hear this, let them know we died doing our duty to the Empire, and to all humanity."

The man straightened and saluted, fist to chest.

"Ave, Imperator, morituri te salutant."

The image froze on the salute and the Commo officer wiped it away with a swipe of his finger across the control screen.

"After that, it just keeps repeating," the man explained.

"It's been repeating endlessly for four hundred and twenty three years," Laurent jumped back into the conversation.

"Why haven't we detected it?" Kuryakin demanded, feeling light-headed and grabbing at the edge of the tactical console to steady himself. "It's been pointed right at us for centuries."

"The signal attenuates severely past a few dozen light years," the Commo officer explained. "By the time it reaches Dominion space, it's too weak and corrupted to separate from all the other ancient radio signals left over from the Empire."

"The Guardianship was able to figure it out somehow," Kuryakin mused, eyes clouding over, the planet on the screen losing focus in his vision as he let his thoughts travel back along the path of the message, watching its leavings sputter their way into Spartan space. "I'd bet it's one of their universities. The Guardian's younger son is an astrophysicist, and he's convinced old Brannigan to pour ridiculous amounts of funding into orbital observatories and the software and computer systems to analyze them."

"This is why they're here, sir!" Laurent was gushing. "If the weapons and military technology this Colonel Zeir was talking about are still on Terminus, it could permanently shift the balance of power in the Dominions! We have to get there and take control before they do!"

"Thank you, Captain Obvious," he said with strained patience. He turned to Kessler, who still seemed skeptical about the whole business. *Imagination has never been her strong suit, though.* "Get the drop-ships loaded, every mech, every pilot, every Marine we have. We're going to go down in history, Captain Kessler," he assured the ship's commander with a broad smile. "This will be the day we reunite the Empire, under the banner of the Starkad Supremacy."

Forget the damned Ministry, he thought, the possibilities racing through his brain like a drug. *Perhaps it's time Starkad came under new guidance. Even Lord Aaron wouldn't be able to stand against the technology of the Empire.*

Emperor Aleksandr the First. It had a nice ring to it.

13

The Sentinel swayed ponderously, a grizzly walking on its hind legs down the broad ramp of the drop-ship. It all seemed unnatural to Jonathan Slaughter, as if he had switched bodies with someone much taller and heavier. It was the first time he'd piloted the Sentinel outside a simulator and even with the neural halo on, he could still tell the difference between real life and virtual training.

He'd heard the old stories about how the Empire had virtual reality so advanced it was impossible to discern it from waking life, but the thought didn't appeal to him, no matter how useful it would have been for training. Some things needed to be lived through to experience.

The Terminus Cut was one of them. They'd seen it from orbit and known immediately it was where they had to land. Two thousand kilometers long and over a hundred wide, it was nearly ten kilometers deep at its lowest points. Terry had thought it might have been formed by tectonic or volcanic activity at some point in the distant past, but there were side channels formed by water, still filled by lakes fed by what had to be underground rivers.

The planet's atmosphere was too thin and cold for liquid water or human habitation everywhere except the deepest parts of the Cut, where they'd seen the greens and blues standing out like a searchlight among the lifeless browns and blacks of the world. It could have been natural, but he doubted it, not deep inside the Shadow Zone. The worlds in the heart of the old Empire were terraformed as a matter of course, even when it only gained a few thousand square kilometers of habitable ground.

The transmitter lay outside the Cut, but none of their scans indicated any means of accessing its power source from the surface there, so the drop-ship had touched down near the head-waters of the largest of the finger lakes, where the sensors had detected a spike in temperatures, a heat source deep underground. It might have been volcanic activity, but nothing else about the geology indicated an active core and he was willing to bet it was a big-ass fusion reactor still powering the signal, even after all these hundreds of years.

The walls of the canyon were dozens of kilometers away on either side of their landing zone, but he could see them even without his mech's optical magnification, like mountain ranges peeking through the wispy clouds hanging like a ceiling over the canyon. The light would have been dusk-dim even if the world hadn't been just past the edge of the habitability zone, with the cyclopean rampart of the front edge of the canyon looming ahead of them less than a kilometer away, like the edge of the world. Blue-green moss coated every rock, boring its way and breaking down the outer surface for nutrients, eroding the crenellated cliff face, wearing away grooves and recesses in a silent war that would someday bring the wall crumbling down.

To the left of the landing zone, the largest of the lakes lapped gently at the boulder-strewn shore, mats of the ubiquitous algae spread across it like a carpet. He'd seen it before: it was the work of the Empire, hardy and fast-growing and genetically engineered to turn bare rock into arable soil. On most of the older and more settled terraformed colonies, it had been supplanted by transplanted Earth life, but places like this, where no one bothered to live, it still did its work in patient silence.

The soil crunched under the thunderous steps of his Sentinel, flattened into the oval, four-clawed shape of the mech's footpads. He moved forward, instinctively drawn towards the cliff wall, needing to touch it to prove to himself it was real. The mass, the sheer size of the thing was hypnotizing, and he was startled when he noticed Kurtz's Golem striding up on his right, the radar dish atop the mech's flattened head only up to the Sentinel's shoulder.

"My platoon is in a defensive perimeter," Kurtz told him. "We got any ideas about where we want to deploy the Ranger platoon and the scientists?"

Kurtz didn't have to walk up to talk to him and Jonathan guessed the man was feeling as haunted by the place as he was. He shook his head at the question, about to confess his abject ignorance of where in the huge stretch of wall they might start looking, when a transmission from the cockpit of the drop-ship interrupted him.

"Jonathan," Terry said, "I tried using the drop-ship's radar and lidar to scan the face of the cliff and I think I've spotted something."

Nice to know one of us got some brains in the genetic lottery.

"Nice job," he said, resolving to try to treat his brother at least as well as he did his own officers. "You got a location?"

"It's...umm, about your eleven o'clock, where that overhang is. You see it?"

He zoomed in the view from the forward cameras and scanned to his left, where what looked like an old rockslide had left behind a huge pile of dirt and stone at the base of the cliff, with a slab nearly ten meters long hanging off the edge like a canopy. Except...there was something too regular, too rounded about the face of the piled rock and dirt, something that pulled his eye back to the shape over and over.

"Everyone stay here," he instructed Kurtz, doing something incredibly stupid by investigating the anomaly himself.

It was the only incredibly stupid thing I could think of.

The climb to the edge of the wall would have been arduous on foot. The aeons had built up hills of detritus, fallen slabs of rock, dirt piles and run-off ditches and even in the long-legged Sentinel, he found himself running a serpentine course to keep his footing as solid as possible. He was already missing his Vindicator's jump-jets and he hadn't even been in a fight yet.

He'd taken his attention off his goal to secure his footing, and when he was able to look away from the downward-facing screens, he was only a hundred meters from the rockfall, except it *wasn't* a rockfall, he could see that now. It was, or at least had been a tunnel. Whether the avalanche that had buried it had been natural or an attempt at camouflage, he wasn't sure; but close up, he could see patches of concrete through gaps in the dirt.

Maybe concrete, he amended. *Maybe whatever the hell the Empire used for construction back then.*

"There's something in here," he reported back to Terry, slowly and carefully making his way toward the concealed passage, thinking with each step how ridiculous it would look for him to come tumbling down the hill in the sixty-ton strike mech. "We're going to have to dig it out, but I think it's an entrance."

He reached down with the Sentinel's articulated left hand and grabbed one of the larger boulders, a jagged, uneven slab three meters long and about half that wide, nearly as thick as the arm of the mech. Absurdly, he wanted to grunt as he pulled at it, as if it were his own muscles straining against the mass and not the mech's servos. The Sentinel's left footpad sank into the loose dirt and its balance shifted precariously, but the boulder came loose as well, toppling backward, shattering into pieces on impact and sliding down the slope.

The missing keystone caused a collapse, and Jonathan pulled back instinctively, a river of dirt and rocks as big as groundcars slid past him, throwing up a billowing cloud of dust. He scowled at the precarious state of the remainder of the pile and made a command decision.

"Kurtz. I need two of your mecha up here. This is going to take a while."

It did.

A solid two hours of steady digging later, the door was visible. It was bigger than Jonathan had expected, taller than his strike mech and ten meters across, definitely a cargo entrance.

"I bet there's a ramp somewhere down under all this dirt," Terry said, echoing his thoughts.

It felt even creepier out of his mech, without the protection of fifty tons of metal separating him from the perpetual twilight of the dead world. Even this deep into the trench, the temperatures hovered just above freezing and as the day grew later, the wind grew stronger with its waning, lashing at Jonathan even through his heated jacket.

"Can you get us inside?" he asked Terry, feeling cold and exposed. He glanced back over his shoulder at the Sentinel, wishing he could have gotten away with staying in the cockpit where it was nice and warm.

Terry was shaking his head, gesturing helplessly at the blank, featureless expanse of the door. It seemed so much bigger to Jonathan here out of his mech, towering above them as if they'd discovered the home of some ancient species of giant.

"I don't see any controls on the damned thing," Terry admitted. "Maybe there was some sort of transponder signal they used to open it."

"What about the transmission they sent out?" The voice in the

RICK PARTLOW

ear bud of Jonathan's 'link was Katy's and he looked up automatically, as if he could see her shuttle flying cover for them. He knew he'd left his 'link open so Kurtz could let him know if there were any incoming threats, but he hadn't realized Katy would be listening in.

"They sent the message to try to get someone to find this place," she pointed out. "Maybe we should try the same frequency?"

Jonathan exchanged a glance with Terry and they both shrugged, a mirror image of each other.

"It's worth a shot," Terry offered. He touched a control on his 'link. "Lt. Cordray," he said to the pilot of the drop-ship, still nice and warm inside the aerospacecraft, "can you tune the ship's radio to the same frequency the old Imperial transmission was using?"

"Sure thing, Terry," the woman drawled casually, as if this was all just some routine training exercise. "Let me get that data from Nance, just take a second. What do you want me to transmit, anyway?"

Terry looked a question at his brother and Jonathan tried to remember what Zeir had said in his message. They'd been able to play the whole thing, video and all, once they were within range of the transmitter, and he was sure the Colonel would have left a clue of some sort in the message. He frowned in concentration. What had that phrase been he'd used? It had been Latin, a language ancient and dead even before the rise of the Empire, but he'd been able to look it up in the *Shakak's* database.

"Try this," Jonathan told the pilot. "Hail Caesar, we who are about to die salute you."

"Uh, roger that, sir." Cordray sounded bemused. "Give me just a second." She paused and he assumed she was getting the correct frequency from the ship.

A cold wind sent chills down his spine.

"Sending," she told him.

For a second, he was sure he'd made the wrong call, that he should have sent the phrase in Latin, or he'd been totally off-base and it wasn't even related to the transponder code; then he felt it. It was a scraping, grinding, less of a sound and more of a vibration deep in his chest. He wasn't even sure it was coming from the door until he noticed the movement. Just a shifting of shadows at first, so slow it was almost imperceptible, but increasing speed as it gained momentum. Ancient motors pulled the long-neglected door inward and, as it opened, lights began to snap on, one squared-off section of tunnel at a time. Jonathan watched in awe, wondering what sort of technology could create a reactor, a power distribution network, and a lighting system that could last this long.

"Mithra," Terry whispered, whether in shocked curse or awed prayer, he couldn't be sure. His brother had never been very religious but something like this could make a believer of an atheist.

"Kurtz," Jonathan said, walking deliberately back towards his Sentinel. "I'm going to lead the research crew and the Ranger platoon in. I want your platoon to follow and set up a relay chain for comms. Between your people and the Rangers, we should be able to stay in touch with the surface. I want you up here, with eyes on for regular sitreps."

"Got it, boss," the man said, his backcountry accent seeping through. "Umm...what do you think you're going to find down there?"

Jonathan paused, one foot on the lowest rung of the access ladder built into the side of the Sentinel's right leg. The broad tunnel curved downward ahead, leading under the cliff and below the surface, beckoning him with the timeless magic of a golden age long passed, with a flicker of hope for its return. But he was the commander, and he had to keep the troops focused.

"The end of this mission."

"They're inside," Lyta Randell said.

The words were redundant, of course; they could all see the video broadcast up by the drop-ship and relayed by Katy in the assault shuttle. But she felt the compulsion anyway, as if it were a religious ceremony and these were the words necessary for the ritual. Osceola's hand covered hers and she saw the grin flashing across his face. It was for the completion of their mission, but it was, she knew, more for her. The mission wasn't what motivated him, she was.

The thought was frightening. She'd let herself think he could change, once, and it had ended badly. She'd been younger then, perhaps more gullible and idealistic, and he'd been fresh off his disillusionment, dangerous and edgy and an outlaw... a good cover for a deniable operation into Starkad space. No one had traced it back to Sparta—the mission had gone off without a hitch. Their relationship, not so much.

And yet here she was, sharing his ship, his life, and his bed once more, against all her better instincts.

Who the hell says you get wiser with age?

"We're about to hit the terminator," Kammy reported. "Gonna be dark down there soon." He shrugged, his bulk bouncing against his seat restraints in the microgravity. "Darker," he amended. "Do you think..."

"Oh, *fuck* me!" Tara Gerard blurted, jabbing a finger at the tactical display where an icon blinked red in the computer simulation of the star system. "We got a bogey at the jump point!"

"What is it?" Lyta demanded, in antiphonal chorus with Osceola.

They'd hardly spoken the words when the sensor readout flickered and shifted along with their position in orbit, the planet now between them and whatever she'd seen.

"Hold on," she said, scrolling through the controls of her station and bringing up the sensor records, then running a highly-classified recognition subroutine Lyta recognized because she'd hand-delivered it to the woman for installation on their systems.

Lyta moved up behind her, watching and waiting, as the subroutine checked the thermal and lidar scans of the bogey against one recorded pattern after another until it came up with an answer none of them were going to like.

"That," she announced, perhaps just as unnecessarily as her earlier statement, "is a Starkad heavy cruiser." Her stomach dropped out from beneath her, and the feeling had nothing to do with the micro-gravity. "It's the fucking *Valkyrian*."

"That's the same one that boarded us back in Gefjon." Osceola's voice broke, the tightness around the corners of his mouth telling her he was experiencing the same gutpunch sensation she was. If they hadn't been in free-fall, he'd have been sagging in his chair with the realization. "That sorry fucker Kuryakin put a drone tracer on us the same way we did with those Jeuta."

"No time for recriminations, Don," she told him, trying to slug her brain into motion. "We have to recall Jonathan and get the drop-ship and shuttle back up here so we can make a run for the jump-point."

"No." Osceola ran his fingers over the stubble on his cheeks, something firming up behind his dark eyes. "What we need to do is get you and your Rangers and all the other mecha and all non-essential personnel into the drop-ship and get you out of here. The other assault shuttle, too. Fast, while we have time."

She stared at him, uncomprehending, mouth working but nothing coming out.

"Don," she finally said, grabbing his arm and pulling herself over to him, "this isn't like the Jeuta destroyer. This isn't some old design you can find a weakness in, this is a top-of-the-line Starkad heavy cruiser!" She grabbed the front of his flight jacket and shook him, as if she could bring sense back into his thick head. "There's no way you can beat them! They'll rip this ship apart and kill you!"

"They will," he admitted, something wistful in his voice but no give at all in his expression. "But not you. I want you and everyone you can take with you off this ship before we come back around the dayside."

"Why, Don?" she demanded, for once feeling helpless. The Don she knew would be jumping at the chance, grateful she was sensible enough to make the decision to run instead of trying to stand and fight. "We can get away…"

"Lyta, I have spent the better part of thirty years running away from who I am and what I did. Thirty years refusing to be the man I am." The corner of his mouth twitched upward. "Refusing to say my own name. And most of all, refusing to admit to myself that I did the right thing. Those men and women who died, they knew what they were sailing into, knew how little hope there was, and they did their duty anyway." He shook his head. "I've been trying to tell myself I was going along with all this because of you, because I wanted another chance with you. But the truth is, I'm here because this is important and it has to be done. If Starkad gets their hands on what's down there, that's it for everyone else."

She wanted to argue with him, wanted to scream at him and tell him she wasn't going to let him die.

But she was.

She grabbed the front of his jacket in both hands and kissed him fiercely, trying to burn every sensation into her memory, to carry it with her for the rest of her life.

"I love you," she told him, for the first time in twenty years.

"Love you, too, Lyta." The confession seemed easy for him, so much easier than it had been for her. He smacked her playfully on the butt and jerked a thumb at the hatchway. "Now get off my boat and go kick some ass."

14

B y the holy fire of God," Jonathan said, eyes wide, mouth dropping open.

He couldn't hear what the others were saying, couldn't even tear his eyes away from the forward camera views to look at them.

The tunnels had led them downward over a kilometer, through open cargo handling bays, through overhanging arches of automatic loader arms frozen for centuries like a saber arch at a military wedding. There'd been no cargo stored there, not a single box nor barrel nor crate, not as much as a speck of dust left over from centuries of disuse. It had been impressive, yet disappointing, a team of archaeologists breaking into an ancient tomb and finding it empty.

The next chamber in had been dark and impenetrable until they moved through it. The lights had snapped on automatically at their entrance in a chain reaction outward and upward…and just kept going. Fifty meters up, nearly a kilometer on a side, with cargo loading arms hanging from tracks crisscrossing the ceiling and aisles twenty meters across at the narrowest. And filling all the space between those aisles were mecha, hundreds of them, *thousands* of them, arranged by type and size and Mithra knew what else.

The largest dwarfed even his Sentinel or the Scorpion he'd left to Paskowski, towering at twenty meters, with four articulated arms, each carrying a different weapon, and trailing a damned *tail* to balance it. How the hell could one pilot control all that? Or was it a multi-pilot mech somehow, with a gunner like on an assault shuttle? Maybe it had some sophisticated targeting system to follow targets independently after the pilot marked them?

His mind raced, and not just fixed on the one design. Other mecha seemed to have foldable wings for long-range flight, or massive armor shells like a tortoise or a half-dozen other designs that should never have worked with any engineering he could imagine.

And above everything else, beyond the unimaginable arsenal of war machines in the chamber was the absolute certainty that there had to be more. This was one room, one cache in a massive installation of chambers just like this, if not bigger.

"Jonathan, I think I've found something."

It took him a minute to find Terry. The research group—which was a grandiose name for what was basically Terry, two members of the Spartan mech salvage unit who had physics degrees on top of their mechanical engineering certificates and one of the *Shakak*'s maintenance workers who claimed to have once been a weapons researcher for the Shang Directorate—had split up and begun searching through the room. The Rangers had separated to watch over the small team, and probably would have stopped them from wandering off if Lyta had been here.

He finally spotted his brother waving to him all the way over at the near wall, almost three hundred meters from the entrance. He wondered how Terry had gotten so far so quickly. Sure, the gravity here was a *little* below standard but...

He zoomed in with the mech's optical cameras and saw some

sort of control screen built into the surface of the wall, improbably active, glowing with what seemed like a holographic display. Holographic projectors were fiendishly expensive in the Dominions, usually found only in capital buildings and palaces as a curiosity, an ostentatious display of wealth and advancement. Argos had a public theater with a holographic projector for special occasions, but ViR goggles accomplished the same effect and were so much cheaper to produce, no one considered the projectors to be worth the expense. And certainly, no one used them for haptic control boards like this.

Terry was scrolling through page after page of text, diagrams, blueprints, still images and videos, pausing every few seconds to read something or play a video. He couldn't pick up the sound from this far away, but he assumed some sort of narration went along with them, because he saw Terry nodding to something, then yelling for the rest of the research team to join him.

"There are another five chambers just as big as this one," Terry said, transmitting again on the 'link after several minutes of apparently forgetting he'd called his brother in the first place. "They're stocked with experimental models of hovertanks, battlesuits…"

"What?" Jonathan demanded, the words all in a language he understood but not in those combinations.

"Wish you'd just come down here," Terry grumbled. "Hold on…"

Because it's fifteen meters up and down and I'm the only real security we have, he thought at his brother but didn't bother to say.

A video display box popped up in a corner of the Sentinel's communications screen, relayed from Terry's 'link. The picture flickered and flared, the holographic display meant to be viewed with the naked human eye rather than a video pickup, but

Jonathan could make out the images in the holographic display between the crackles of static.

He knew what a tank was from military history class. They were still seen sometimes, in colonial militias, but their biggest problem was power production in relation to size. You *could* make a tank big enough to fit a small fusion core into it, one the size of a mech's power plant, but once you squeezed in the power plant, the turbines, the weapons, and the drive train, you had something even bigger than a mech with less mobility. It was far too awkward to use jump-jets in a tank and all you accomplished in making a tracked vehicle that large was giving your enemy a huge, poorly-maneuverable target.

The power plants you *could* fit into a useful-sized tank weren't enough to mount a laser large enough to take down a mech or an assault shuttle, so what you wound up with was a mobile artillery piece you could only drive on fairly flat, fairly open surfaces. These tanks were *nothing* like the ones he'd seen. They were flat and disc-shaped with an armored plenum and they reminded him of the hovercraft he'd seen in the swampy areas of some colonies, except none of those hovercraft mounted what looked like tons of heavy armor and some sort of weapons turret with either a barrel or a beam emitter four meters long.

"There are specs here," Terry said, his hand straying into the image and scrolling away from the stills of the tanks to pages of text. "From what I can tell, these things can run over just about any surface and they have a top speed north of two hundred kilometers an hour."

"Mithra, what the hell could power that? Can you even fit a fusion reactor into something that small?"

"Well, no, you can't." Terry's face replaced the image of the tanks and the expression on it was grim. "You couldn't fit it into one of these, either."

Back to the shot of the holoprojector, only now the chamber it showed was full of what looked like nothing so much as a terra-cotta army in some ancient tomb, waiting to do the bidding of their emperor in the spiritual battles of the afterlife. It took Jonathan a moment to realize the scale of what he was seeing. When he did it was only because the computer system provided a handy, human-sized avatar beside the squat, bipedal shapes. If something three meters tall and two meters wide could be called, "squat."

He intuited what they were without Terry having to explain it. Powered armor had been attempted in the last two centuries, as Dominion military research and development agencies had tried desperately for an edge against their neighbors, but those researchers had run into the same problem as they had with the conceptual, fusion-powered tanks. If you made the things big enough to hold a reactor, you had a mech. If you made them smaller, you had something without the possibility of jump-jets, without enough power to take down a mech and without the maneuverability and versatility of regular, unpowered infantry.

These had obviously solved the problem, or the Imperials wouldn't have bothered to manufacture thousands of them.

"You've got one of those 'good-news, bad news' kind of looks, Terry. Give me the bad news."

"You ever hear of antimatter?"

"Sure, it's the shit they're always using for power in those stupid movies about aliens." Jonathan had rattled off the answer without thinking, but his eyes widened as he realized the implications of what Terry had said. "Wait a minute, these things are all powered by antimatter?"

"Yeah." His brother hissed frustration. "And from what I can see here, there's *none* of it stored in this installation." He turned the 'link's video pickup back toward the holographic display and scrolled through a menu to what could have been a spreadsheet. "It looks as if they were scheduled to receive a new shipment when everything went to shit. What they had left, they used to power the ships they sent out looking for help, and most of those didn't come back."

Jonathan's stomach began sinking through his body and down toward the center of the planet. All of the effort, all of the cost, the people who'd given their lives on this mission...

"You aren't saying all this is useless, are you?"

The words came out anguished, hopeless and he knew he should have been trying to sound more stoic and commanding, but the fraud was harder to pull off with his brother. Hell, he couldn't even keep repeating the lie about Terry being his cousin, not inside his head and not with the people who mattered.

"No, not useless," Terry insisted. "They all represent incredible advances, but..."

He'd been scrolling absently through one spreadsheet after another as he spoke, but he stopped scrolling at the same moment he stopped speaking.

"Logan...," he stumbled over his words, cursing softly, and turned the video pickup back towards his face, "...I mean, Jonathan, I think I have something here. It looks like one of the ships *did* come back, and it might still have fuel on board, maybe. I mean, assuming the containment didn't fail after four centuries. But I think if it had, it would have taken half this base with it."

"It wasn't in orbit. We'd have detected it visually even if they had some sort of stealth material technology we don't know about anymore."

Terry wasn't facing the video pickup anymore, but he hadn't bothered to turn it back toward the display, just holding it askew and giving Jonathan a view of a particularly uninteresting part of the ceiling while his brother did something with the controls out of his view.

"I think I see something about..."

"Captain Slaughter!" Kurtz's urgent call interrupted Terry,

coming in via a passive relay between the platoon leader at the base's entrance all the way down through the rest of his mecha stationed at visual range at intervals along the tunnel. "Captain Slaughter, do you read me?"

"I'm here, Valentine," he told the man, trying to sound calm, or at least calmer than he had with his brother. "Report."

"Sir, it's Starkad! They just jumped a heavy cruiser in-system and they're burning this way!"

Something almost physical hammered into Jonathan's gut and only the easy chair kept him from rocking back on his heels. A million questions raced through his mind, starting with an inane "do they know we're here?" to "how did they find us?" and finishing with something useful: "do they know the base is here?"

The answer to the last one was almost certainly a yes. The broadcast was loud and clear from inside the system; they'd have to be blind and deaf to miss it. They knew about Terminus and if they'd followed the *Shakak* here, they might know Wholesale Slaughter was a cover for a Spartan operation. It was the worst-case scenario, the one military units always trained for and never actually expected, and the reality of it crashed over him. There was no way the *Shakak* could take on a ship that size.

"We need to get back to the lander," he decided immediately.

"It's too late," Kurtz told him. "Major Randell is heading down with the rest of our troops in the other drop-ship and the assault shuttle. Osceola is taking the *Shakak* and going after the cruiser. Major Randell says we're going to have to make our stand here."

"What the hell?" he blurted. "Are they nuts?"

There was a shrug in Kurtz's voice when he responded.

"You got me, sir. I'm just the messenger. But they're on their way. All of them."

The words poured out of him without thought, a decision made from an intuition he hadn't been aware he'd amassed.

"We can't fight them in the air," he declared. "And the drop-ships would just be sitting ducks anyway. Get the crews inside and I want you and your mecha down here as well. We have probably a couple hours to set up a defense in depth." *And I've never done it before outside a training mission.*

"Jonathan," Terry interrupted, "what's going on?" His brother's 'link wasn't on the command frequency and he hadn't caught any of Jonathan's exchange with Kurtz.

"Do you know where that fucking ship is, Terry?" he asked, harsher than he'd intended. On the video pickup, he saw his brother blink in surprise at the demand but then collect himself and try to answer.

"I think I can find it. I saw what's supposed to be a hangar on a level up from here, but it's a long way inward...like five or six kilometers." He shook his head. "I don't know if I can get it to work, and I couldn't fly it if we did. We're going to need a pilot."

"Yeah," Jonathan agreed. "I can get us one. But she's not going to like it."

"What the hell do you *mean* you want me to land?" Katy demanded hotly, curving the assault shuttle around in a flat arc, her voice strained but her anger making it past the g-forces of the tight turn. "We have a freaking Starkad heavy cruiser inbound! Do you not understand the concept of aerospace cover?"

Francis Acosta wished he could see the expression on her face, but he'd learned months ago not to try any sudden movements while she was flying under combat conditions. He'd learned it the hard way, unfortunately, and paid for it with days of bedrest and muscle relaxants, so he just remained still and kept his eyes straight ahead, and his ears open.

"Katy," Jonathan replied, the strain in his voice nearly as

pronounced as hers, though not from the acceleration forces of a maneuvering shuttle, "it's a heavy cruiser. They're going to have four assault shuttles, minimum—*real* assault shuttles, not civilian landers rigged with a makeshift weapons package. You're a damned good pilot, so let's say you take down two of them before they get you. What does that gain us? Their drop-ships will still make it down and we'll still have to deal with their ground forces down here in these tunnels where their air superiority won't do them a bit of good."

"So, we don't *try* to take out their assault shuttles," Katy insisted. "Lee's already launched from the *Shakak*—together, we make a run straight at their drop-ships. We could take down one or two before they got us!"

And we'll fucking get killed! Acosta wanted to scream at her, but he'd learned that lesson too. Katy Margolis didn't make decisions based on fear, or on common sense, just on accomplishing the mission.

"Say you do that," Jonathan Slaughter replied, making what Acosta considered a tactical error by trying to reason with her, "and you kill two of their drop-ships, we're still fucked because there is no way the *Shakak* is going to take out the cruiser in a straight-up fight."

"Well, damn it, Jonathan," she raged, slamming a palm down on the control console of the pilot's station, "what are we going to do, then? Just huddle inside the Imperial base and starve to death like they did?"

And she had a point there, Acosta realized. Given the choice between dying in a rather painless explosion out here or going slowly and painfully from malnutrition over a period of weeks, he knew which he'd pick.

"Katy, there's a ship down here," Slaughter confided, his voice low as if he somehow thought he could keep the enemy from overhearing by speaking softly. "It's an Imperial ship with experimental weapons and a stardrive and it's powered by anti-matter. If we can find it and get it working, I'm going to need someone to fly it. It's pretty much our only hope of keeping Starkad from getting their hands on the Imperial tech inside this base, not to mention any of us getting out of here alive."

"Well, why the hell didn't you lead with that?" she asked him. There was a subtle change in her tone, something that wouldn't be noticed by someone who hadn't known her for a while, the shift from "we're going to argue this until you see I'm right" to "I understand you were right but I'm not happy about having to admit that."

"If you don't come down here and help us with this," Jonathan pleaded with her, "I'm going to have to let Lt. Cordray do it."

"Melissa?" Disbelief was strong in Katy's voice. "She's a damned taxi driver, Jonathan! You're going to let her try to fly a 400-year-old experimental spacecraft?"

"Unless you land that shuttle and do it instead."

Acosta wanted to keep quiet. He knew he *should* keep quiet. It was his *job* to keep quiet. But there's just so much a man can put up with and keep his mouth shut, and even the strictest orders had to give a little leeway.

"Lt. Margolis," he said, finally taking a risk and turning his upper body toward her, hoping against hope she wouldn't throw the bird into a violent maneuver out of sheer perversity, "would you do me a personal favor and land this fucking shuttle?"

Her eyebrow cocked upward, an odd mixture of annoyance and curiosity writ across her face.

"You didn't *have* to fly with me, Francis," she reminded him. "Lee said he'd trade copilots..."

"My name is not Francis Acosta," he declared. *And I'd like to get ahold of the bastard who saddled me the name Francis.* "I'm Major Patrick Bray, Military Intelligence."

Telling the truth felt like tossing off a backpack after a twenty-kilometer hike...or maybe more like finally hitting the bathroom after holding it in for three hours, if he was being honest with himself.

Kathren Margolis' mouth dropped open, her eyes narrowed in suspicion.

"Why the..." she began, but he cut her off.

"Did you really think General Constantine was going to send an intelligence operation into enemy space with the Guardian's son along, without sending one of his own people along to keep an eye on things?" He shook his head, slashing his hand sideways to forestall any attempt at an answer. "Forget it, the right answer is 'no, he wouldn't.' And since it's my job to both report back and to make sure this mission succeeds, I'd like you to make both of those possible by setting aside your remarkable and often admirable stubbornness and pride and setting this fucking shuttle down before the Supremacy shoots us out of the air."

She seemed nonplussed and he really wished he had the time to really appreciate the silence, but matters were pressing. He made a motion downward with his hand.

"Please? I technically outrank you, but I'd rather not make it an order." He grinned with perhaps more malice than he should have. "Orders require all sorts of reports and records and some things would just be better kept off the record."

"All right, all right," she conceded, pushing the control stick down fast enough for it to feel as if she were pulling the rug out from under his feet. "I should have known," she lamented, half to herself. She glanced over him and sniffed with disdain. "You suck as a copilot."

15

I do not remember this suit being so tight the last time I
wore it."

Aleksandr Kuryakin tugged at the wrist of the body sleeve, lip
curling in distaste. He looked ridiculous in the skin-tight outfit,
but it was necessary for the neural helmet to intercept the movement commands his brain was sending to his muscles before they
actually made it. Otherwise, he would have flailed around the
cockpit of the mech like he was having a seizure.

"I know I'm being insubordinate, sir," Ruth Laurent said,
staring at him in obvious disapproval, arms crossed over her
tactical vest, "but I think this is a very bad idea. How long has it
been since you were in the cockpit of a mech?"

"I'll have you know, young Captain," he informed her with a
self-righteous sniff, "I spend four hours every week in a simulator
and two weekends every month in mandatory training with the
Supremacy Guard. I am totally qualified to pilot a Scorpion strike
mech."

He didn't mention the Mbeki War or the half-dozen other
minor uprisings and engagements he'd fought in before transfer-

ring to Intelligence. If she was slack enough not to have researched her boss's record, she shouldn't be working for him.

"Yes, sir," she acknowledged, "but you're the commander of this operation. Wouldn't it be wiser for you to remain with one of the drop-ships while the mecha and the Marine troops clear the enemy out of the installation?"

He paused in pulling on his fatigues over the body sleeve, eyeing her balefully.

"Captain Laurent, consider this a professional development session." He snuck a glance around the nicely-appointed flag officers' locker room. It was supposed to be empty but for the two of them, but old and paranoid instincts died hard.

"This is not merely the most significant operation in my career, it may be the most significant operation in the history of the Supremacy. And as much as I appreciate the leadership abilities of Captains Jeffries and Singh, I am *not* going to trust the future of the Starkad Supremacy, not to mention the future of my career, to a couple of junior officers who've never once gone head-to-head with elite Spartan troops."

She didn't seem convinced, but she'd stopped arguing, which was good enough. Kuryakin pulled on his boots and strapped them tight, checking his wrist computer to see how much time he had left before the drive cut off and left them all in microgravity.

Ten minutes. Just enough to get down to the drop-ship.

He tapped a code into the security pad of a small locker set into the bulkhead and pulled out a pair of service automatics, the same 10mm caseless weapons the Starkad military had been issuing since before the last time he'd taken a mech into combat. He held them in the palms of his hands, feeling the balance, knowing they were identical but checking to make sure there wasn't some esoteric sense of advantage to one over the other.

He sighed. He hadn't even stepped into the cockpit and he was already indulging in soldiers' superstitions. He flipped the pistol in his left hand around and offered it to Laurent, butt-first. She took it carefully, hesitantly, but with a firm grip, her trigger finger kept straight along the grip just as they'd taught her at the tactical range. She popped out the magazine, then checked the chamber to make sure a round was loaded, not trusting the indicator on the side of the receiver. Satisfied, she slapped the magazine home, then shoved the pistol into the chest holster of her tactical vest.

Kuryakin nodded his approval. He didn't know if she would hit anything when the real bullets started flying, but he at least had confidence she wouldn't shoot herself in the leg by accident. He holstered his own weapon, the feel of the grip in his hand like the caress of an old lover.

"I've never been in combat before," Laurent admitted. It was an irrelevance; he knew her record and she knew he knew it. But he understood. It was her way of saying she was afraid without putting the admission into words.

"The way of the samurai," he quoted softly, the words coming on their own as if they were spoken through him by the beneficent spirits, "is found in death."

"Sir?" she asked, frowning with incomprehension.

"Something my military history teacher told me in my first year at the Academy. It means that to be a warrior is to accept the reality of death, not to treat it as a dreaded fate to run away from but an acceptable end to a well-lived life."

He smiled at the young officer, a gentler, kinder smile than he'd offered in the past.

"Death may be an undiscovered country, but it's surely more desirable than spending your retirement years fishing."

"They just launched drop-ships and assault shuttles," Tara reported.

She sounded normal, matter of fact; only someone who'd known her the last twenty years could have picked up the edge of fear.

"You could have gone down with the others," Donner Osceola reminded her. "I wouldn't have thought any less of you."

"Oh, right," she scoffed, a bit of her normal irreverence returning. "Like your overstuffed teddy bear here," she gestured towards Kammy, "could fight this ship for you."

"Hey now, sis," Kammy protested gently, more as if he was going through the motions than from any real offense taken, "I've helmed this ship before in a fight. Like the time you were sitting in your cabin crying over that Shang shuttle pilot who dumped you, and we got hit by pirates just out of Kochi. Or the time you were sleeping off the epic binge you put on for your fiftieth birthday and that Clan Modi customs agent decided he could blackmail us and sent three of his cutters after us. Or…"

"Oh, sweet Mithra," she blurted, "I know you're as big as an elephant, but do you have to have a memory like one?"

Kammy frowned. "What's an elephant?"

"Like a hairless mastodon," Osceola supplied. "We still on course for intercept?"

"Oh, yeah," Tara assured him. "The *Valkyrian*, she ain't changed her heading a degree. She wants a fight. Both of us accelerating at one gee for now, and I figure she'll try to reverse thrust and decelerate about halfway in to get more time on target for us with her beam weapons."

"You want I should flip us and hit the brakes, too, boss?" Kammy asked him.

"Naw," Osceola decided. "Matter of fact, when he goes into his braking turn, I want you to take us up to three gees. We need to draw this out as long as we can to buy time for those folks on the ground to figure something out. We need to take shots at him from max range with the railgun, rake him with the lasers as we pass. If we decelerate, we're just opening ourselves up for a missile attack."

"So, you think if we keep this a hit and run fight," Kammy asked, his rounded face lifting with a hopeful smile, "we might actually be able to take them out?"

Osceola looked carefully around the bridge, and the rest of the crew there met his eyes and they passed over them. Nance was still at the Commo board despite an offer to let her go with the drop-ship. Ortiz was at the Engineering station, having taken the place of Cheryl Mendelson now that Kenyatta was the nominal chief engineer. The woman was an enlisted reactor tech for the Spartan Navy, so she had the training to monitor the readouts from Engineering and relay commands back to Kenyatta and his people.

That *should* have been it. He'd tried to get everyone else to leave the ship, but some had refused. Norris was one of the stubborn ones. Osceola knew of him, knew he hadn't gotten along with Wihtgar and perversely resented him for it, even though the man had turned out to be right. Norris was another enlisted spacer from the Spartan Navy, a repair tech specializing in the sort of impromptu hot-patching necessary in combat. He'd plopped his stubborn ass down in the usually-uncrewed damage control monitoring station shortly after the drop-ship and shuttle had launched, and he hadn't moved since.

They seemed the sort who could handle the truth, and his people deserved it from him.

"No, Kammy" he admitted, facing back to his old friend. "We'll give them a good fight, the best we can, but the only way we'll beat them is a miracle straight from Mithra." Osceola laughed, not with the cynical bitterness he'd expected but honestly, openly. "Somehow, I don't think Mithra's going to waste a miracle on a beat-up piece of shit like the *Shakak*...or me."

"I dunno," Kammy said, only half kidding. "I mean, I've been a pretty good dude. You think he'd at least *consider* the fact I'm on board..."

"Just in case," Tara suggested, "maybe we all oughta' get into pressure suits while we got a little time." She shrugged. "God helps those who help themselves."

Osceola did the count in his head. There were maybe fifty personnel left on the ship and, with the extras the Spartans had brought with them, they should have just enough suits.

"Right." He speared Norris with a glance. "Make yourself useful, Navy boy, break out the suits."

While the big, pugnacious enlisted man followed Tara's gesture back to the lockers set into the bulkhead near the bridge hatchway, Osceola steeled himself with a breath and hit the all-ship intercom.

"*Shakak*, this is the captain. Get into your suits and lock down all pressure seals. We're sailing into the fight of our lives and whether we win or lose, we're not going to let these Starkad assholes forget us."

"Stirring," Norris commented with dry humor that belied his looks and his reputation. He shoved a suit and helmet at Osceola and the older man rose from his acceleration couch to accept them.

The suit went on with rote motions, practiced tens of thousands of times over a life lived in space, gaskets sealed to the gloves at the wrists and the boots at the ankles, and the helmet came down over his head, the darkness of its edges shutting out the bridge lights.

He felt his breath catch in his chest at long-suppressed memories of days on end spent inside a helmet just like this one, of the stale smell of air going bad as the recyclers slowly ran out of power and raw materials, of the bodies floating aimlessly, trapped inside a man-shaped coffin.

He snatched the helmet off his head, holding it at his chest, trying to slow down his respiration and heartbeat, fighting the panic.

"Something wrong, boss?" Kammy wondered, eyeing him with the shrewd insight of someone who'd lived on the same ship as him for almost two decades.

"Nothing," Osceola insisted, falling back into his acceleration couch, the helmet resting on his lap. "Just going to enjoy the fresh air while I have a chance."

Kammy nodded, accepting the lie even if he didn't believe it.

"Everybody set?" He saw helmets latching onto neck yokes and one thumbs-up after another across the bridge.

"All right then," Donner Osceola said, settling back into his chair and tightening the restraints. "Let's go show them who we are."

Katy didn't look happy. That was okay, though, Jonathan decided, because she was alive to look unhappy. She glanced backwards at her assault shuttle every few steps, as if she were afraid she'd never see it again; when she wasn't looking at the aerospacecraft, she was glaring at him. Acosta, for some reason, was wearing a grin like the cat who ate the canary. Maybe he was just glad they weren't going to get blown up by the Starkad ships.

"So, where's this ship you want me to fly?" Katy demanded, stopping in front of him, hands on her hips.

"Inside," he told her, motioning back at the tunnel entrance. "Terry is waiting there for you. It's a haul and he didn't want to go look for it without you."

"You better be right about this, *Captain* Slaughter," she said.

"Remember a little conversation we had about not trying to keep each other safe and putting the mission first?"

"I swear to Mithra, we need a pilot—Terry told me so himself. And are you or are you not the best pilot we have?" She frowned, seeming to consider the question. "Anyway," he went on before she could come up with another argument, "I have an ulterior motive for wanting all our aircraft on the ground."

"Is that why you're out of your mech and down here with us crunchies?"

The question came from behind him, but he wasn't surprised by it or by who asked it. Lyta had been inside, arranging her troops for a defense-in-depth, but he'd asked her to join him outside when she had a chance. He did a double-take at the sight of her, though—he rarely got a chance to see Lyta in full battle rattle, and it was an impressive sight. The Ranger armor added bulk to her, the helmet and the spiked soles of her combat boots bringing her height above his. Her carbine was tucked under her arm, hand always on the pistol grip, and he had the sense it wasn't from innate paranoia so much as a desire to be an example to her troops.

"Yeah," he admitted. "There are some things I don't want to say over open radio."

"Well, while we're sharing secrets," Katy interrupted, jerking a thumb at Acosta, "it turns out Francis here is a spook."

Jonathan couldn't see Lyta's eyes through her visor, but he had to assume they were as wide as his and staring at the copilot's bland expression.

"Yeah, yeah," he acknowledged, rolling his eyes at the theatrics. "General Constantine wanted an inside man to keep an eye on you. Are you shocked? Should I reserve a few minutes for righteous indignation?"

Jonathan had to admit righteous indignation *had* been his first instinct, but he bit down on it and used his forebrain instead of his hindbrain. It made sense and it made even more sense for him not to have told anyone. He'd been around Constantine since before he could walk and he knew how the man's mind worked.

"You're probably just the man I need to talk to, then," Jonathan told him. He let some of the anguish running through him show on his face. "I'd do it myself if I could, but I can't so..." He hissed out a breath. "How do I pick someone for what's probably going to be a suicide mission?"

16

The yawning mouth of the tunnel reminded Aleksandr Kuryakin far too much of a Venus flytrap, a reward too good to pass up but with a grim fate waiting those who tried to seize it lightly.

"You've checked the drop-ships carefully?" he asked Captain Jeffries, knowing he was repeating himself but also knowing young Marine officers could be headstrong and lose their attention to detail.

"And the assault shuttles," the man confirmed.

He was just another anonymously armored figure standing at the feet of Kuryakin's Scorpion, a toy poodle yapping at the heels of the fifteen-meter mech. He waved an arm back towards the four aerospacecraft lined up end-to-end across the shore of the lake, only a hundred meters or so from where their own landing craft had touched down.

"The systems are locked tight and powered down, and there's no one on board." An expressive shrug, exaggerated to be seen through the thick armor. "I suppose they could have sent some people up the canyon to find a hiding place, but if I were asked, my opinion would be all of them are in there." He pointed a finger at the tunnel.

"And you're probably right," Kuryakin acceded. "But humor an old man who's seen one too many sure things go bad. Captain Singh!"

Singh's Vindicator was ahead of his mech, standing just meters from the tunnel opening, poised like a sprinter waiting at the blocks.

"Yes, Colonel?" she replied. Her voice was as eager as the stance of her mech, ready to be sent into action.

"Detail one of your platoons to stay here with a platoon of Captain Jeffries' Marines and guard our rear while the rest of us head inside. Leave the Arbalests; their long-range missiles won't be very useful inside, anyway."

It wouldn't be a significant attrition of their forces—he'd called up two companies of mecha before they'd left on the Valkyrian and put them both under Singh's command. As for Jeffries' ground forces, his Marine company had been augmented by the reaction force platoon on board the *Valkyrian*, and if the man had any sense, he'd leave the platoon outside on guard duty so as not to mix up his command structure. He'd leave the decision to Jeffries, though, as he was not, nor had he ever been, a Marine.

Once he'd received confirmation the reallocation of forces had been achieved, he finally gave the word to advance. To Singh's disappointment, he sent the Marines in first.

That's what crunchies are for, he mused with the spiteful humor of a trained and experienced mech jock, *to spring the traps and detect the mines set for the armor troops.*

The tunnel walls blocked out the radios less than a hundred meters in, just as Kuryakin had suspected they would. It made the tunnel and whatever lay just beyond it a perfect place for an ambush. The possibility itched on the back of his neck, but he waited, forcing patience where none came naturally.

"What do we do if they don't come back out?" Captain Ruth Laurent asked him over his cockpit radio, too young to have learned that particular discipline. "What do we do then?"

It took him a moment to locate her: she was standing on the grounded belly ramp of the nearest drop-ship, one hand touching the hydraulic strut as if she felt letting go would make her too vulnerable and exposed.

"It would be troublesome," he admitted, "but not totally unexpected. We would send in a heavier force of Rangers, backed up by a platoon of assault mecha, and recon by fire, force them into open battle. It would be expensive, we'd lose more people, but we outnumber them too badly for them to win that sort of fight. But let's not give up hope just yet."

"The scouts are back, Colonel," Jeffries informed him just as he was about to give in to Captain Laurent's anxiety and start organizing the next entry force. "They reported no enemies detected but they discovered a huge storage area. I'm sending you the video they took inside."

He could see the returning Marines spreading out to take up the gaps in the defensive perimeter around the mecha, except for the squad leader who'd made the scouting run. She was tapping at her wrist computer and no sooner had she finished than he saw the video feed pop up on his cockpit commo display.

He didn't curse, though he surely wanted to. He allowed his jaw to drop open in shock and wonder because none of the others could see his face. The chamber was enormous, larger than any of the Starkad military depots on the homeworld, and filled from wall to wall with heavily armored machines. It was a toy shop for a mech jock, or for the ordnance officer who supplied them. He wasn't sure if he'd ever seen so many mecha gathered in one place, much less designs he'd only imagined in his dreams, impossible doodles by a child dreaming of fantasy machines.

"We're in the right place," he declared with affected casualness. "The question is, where are *they*?"

"What are your orders, sir?" Singh wondered. He half expected her Vindicator to be dancing from one foot to another as if it had to pee. "Should I lead the company inside?"

She was beginning to wear on his nerves, a puppy who needed her nose swatted, and he wondered if he shouldn't have given overall mech command to the junior of the two company commanders, Captain Byrne.

Gunfire erupted from off to his left, muted and distant through the filter of his cockpit, but experience and the mech's audio sensors told him it was close by, friendly, and outgoing. It jumped up in intensity gradually but inevitably as Marines shot at phantoms, hoping to get in on the action and "suppress the enemy" even if they had no real target. Kuryakin's eyes snapped to the camera view, searching not for the source of the rifle shots but for any sign of what they were trying to hit. He saw nothing, not on infrared nor thermal nor even active radar and lidar.

"Cease fire!" Jeffries bellowed. "Cease fucking fire!"

The order filtered through the company's First Sergeant, down through the gunnies, and on to the squad leaders. Then the raging thunderstorm died down to a spring shower before spluttering away entirely.

"Who the fuck opened fire?" Captain Jeffries demanded, his voice cracking with anger. Kuryakin had the sense he was angry at the thought of being embarrassed in front of a superior more than he was at the actual breach of discipline.

"It was me, sir," a woman's voice replied without a trace of fear. Kuryakin didn't recognize the voice but the Identification Friend or Foe transponder attached to her radio frequency told him it was a Sergeant Blasingame, one of the squad leaders. "I saw movement out by the lakeshore, at my two o'clock, about a hundred and fifty meters out."

"Are you sure you weren't just jumping at shadows, sergeant?" Jeffries asked her, still sounding doubtful but not as enraged.

"Negative, sir," Blasingame told him without a hint of uncertainty. "There's someone out there."

"All right," Jeffries sighed. "Though I don't know what the hell one person could..."

The only reason Kuryakin had a clear idea of what happened next was that he was looking straight at the enemy drop-ship. He wasn't sure what premonition, what sixth sense had drawn his eye to the bulbous lifting-body shape out of all the other aerospace-craft resting on the floor of the canyon a kilometer away. Perhaps it was his subconscious mind chewing the cud of the puzzle of the positioning of the thing. It had landed at an angle across the front of the lakeshore, forcing the Starkad drop-ships inward, closer to the entrance and he'd been wondering if there had been a strategy to its placement.

He thought he'd finally come up with a reason thanks to the added data point of an enemy trooper somewhere out there between the Spartan craft and their own. The equation summed up the combination of an observer, perhaps with a remote detonator, and an aerospacecraft filled with extremely explosive fuel...

"Get inside!" he screamed, his voice cracking with desperation, praying to Mithra he was in time.

He wasn't.

The drop-ship exploded.

"Patrick Bray. My name is Patrick Bray." He tasted the words, savored them, just wanting to hear his name spoken aloud again a few more times before he died.

It had been months since he'd heard it, months since he'd spoken it, and he was getting damn tired of being Francis Acosta. The guy was a wimp, bad at his job and no fun to be around. Bray had been undercover more than once in his career, and it was usually nondescript types no one would look at twice. It was difficult stepping into the role of an absolute cretin and not becoming one in the process.

"Patrick Bray," he said one last time.

The back of the volcanic rock felt nice and solid and comfortable, just like his name. He wasn't sure which he found more objectionable, leaving the cover of that rock or going back to being Francis Acosta. A few stray shots from the Starkad lines convinced him of the immediacy of the threat of leaving the rock, but he clutched the small transmitter in his hand and steeled himself.

You volunteered for this, dumbass.

The firing had stopped; they were probably trying to figure out if they'd really seen anything. He had to give them credit— he'd only been out from behind cover for a half a second, trying to get to a better position to transmit, but someone had spotted him.

Spot this, *assholes.*

He stood straight up, pointed the hand-held detonator at the drop-ship and pushed the trigger button. Then he tossed it down and ran like a son of a bitch.

This was the part where it was just about a suicide mission, he reminded himself, all the plastic explosives they'd had left wrapped around the fuel lines to the drive and the five-second delay that was all the time he was going to have. He threw himself into the water, the bitter cold driving the breath from him;

he ignored it and kicked away from shore, going deeper, hoping he could go deep enough before…

The concussion slammed into him and everything went black.

Aleksandr Kuryakin couldn't see a damned thing and he wondered for just a moment if he was dying. When he realized his chin-strap had come loose and his neural helmet had slipped down over his face, he nearly chuckled with relief…until he pushed it up and remembered where he was and how he'd gotten there.

His Scorpion was down on a knee, the pod-like torso tilted to the side, an indicator flashing yellow where something had slammed into the side of the mech's left leg. He saw most of Singh's reinforced mech company still arrayed around the entrance to the tunnel, some standing, some kneeling, a couple blown down onto their sides, but all of them moving and basically intact. Except for the Arbalests. She'd followed his instructions and left them separate, further away, ready to guard the external approach. The five missile-launcher mecha were down and wouldn't be getting up, twisted, smoking metal marking the place where their launch pods had been before the warheads had cooked off in the blast. Of their cockpits, nothing was left.

Nothing was left of the Wholesale Slaughter drop-ship, either. A mushroom cloud hung over the expanding cloud of burning gas where it had been, dust and debris hiding a crater at least a hundred meters across. The glow of the fireball lit up the night, rising into the sky like a funeral pyre. The words came to him before he realized the weight they carried. The Starkad drop-ship closest to the blast was a charred husk, its landing gear buckled, its hull fractured and burning. Ruth Laurent had been on that ramp.

The ramp was gone. She was gone. The Marines who'd been at the far edge of the security perimeter were gone, what was left of them buried under hundreds of kilograms of soil, debris, and volcanic rock.

Bastards. God-cursed bastards.

He should have been calling for an immediate, detailed battle damage report, a collection of the wounded, a sober and level-headed reassessment of their plan of attack. He should have been collecting data from his subordinates and calming them down. Instead, rage burned inside his chest with a fire hotter and brighter than the one consuming the wreckage of the drop-ship, rage he hadn't felt in decades, or thought himself capable of feeling anymore.

He pushed his strike mech to its feet, aimed both plasma guns at the opening of the tunnel and fired. Heat washed over him, searing yet still not matching the burning inside. The twin gouts of hyper-ionized gas exploded in impotent fury where the tunnel curved downward, charring the rock and gouging out twin grooves in the ceiling, but otherwise accomplishing nothing.

"Follow me!" he screamed, voice more frenzied and shrill than firm and commanding.

They followed him anyway, and like the mouth of the Venus flytrap he'd envisioned, the tunnel swallowed them whole.

17

The darkness inside his cockpit was oppressive and claustrophobic, turning his thoughts inward. He found it increasingly difficult to think of himself as Jonathan Slaughter. It had been easier when he'd been playing the mercenary, schmoozing with clients, playing things fast and loose, and making it up as he went along. It had been comforting, even, when Marc Langella had died, almost as if he could pretend the loss had happened to someone else. This was different. This was the mission, *the* mission, and those troops outside were Starkad Supremacy Royal Armor.

He squinted, trying to peer through the transparent aluminum of the Sentinel's cockpit, trying to see without the active display from the cameras and sensors. The mech was powered down, still as a statue, lined up perfectly between two of the Imperial-era strike mecha. They dwarfed his Sentinel, but they also made good cover. He hoped.

Had Acosta already set off the charges? It would be impossible to tell from down here; and, if he'd guessed wrong about how the Starkad forces would react to it, they might be wasting their time. If he hadn't guessed wrong but they were spotted by the enemy despite hiding powered down, the seconds it would take for them to boot up their systems would be a fatal delay.

So many things could go wrong, and if he screwed up, it wouldn't be Wholesale Slaughter LLC suffering, it would be all of Sparta. The wrong move could start a war, not just between Starkad and Sparta but throughout the Five Dominions. Letting them have what was in Terminus surely would.

This was a time when he needed to be Logan Conner, Captain of the Spartan Guard, when he needed to be the son of the Lord Guardian. And yet…he was beginning to wonder if that man still called this soul home. It was a disturbing thought and he shoved it away into the darkness behind him.

Out in the light ahead, he heard the thundering footfalls of the titans. The enemy was coming.

Mithra and all the warrior angels, give me strength and wisdom.

The Supremacy Marines *should* have come first—sending infantry ahead of armor was the tactically sound thing to do. When they didn't, Jonathan felt a surge of hope. Kuryakin was scared and pissed off, just the way he'd intended; and if Acosta had died pulling it off, at least he hadn't died for nothing. The very floor was shaking with the impact of a combined weight of hundreds of tons of heavy metal running hell-bent straight into the chamber, and at their head was the hunched-over, ostrich-legged mass of a Scorpion. Its camouflage was the grey-and-green tiger stripe of the Supremacy Royal Guard, but the grey was already charred to black at the muzzles of the twin plasma cannons, the emitters glowing white from firing at nothing.

The huge machine slowed its break-neck pace as it emerged into the chamber, the bone-shaking gallop turning into a plodding, cautious walk, the torso pivoting back and forth, scanning for threats. Behind it, a Vindicator with the same paint job emerged, grinding to a stop so abruptly it almost collided with the back of the bigger mech. It would have almost been comical if Jonathan hadn't been scared shitless.

You don't see us, he thought at the mech jocks. *We're just more empty armor. Keep looking for movement, keep looking for heat. We're not here.*

One step forward, then two, the careful recon turning into a resolute advance as the hunchbacked giant led one machine after another into the mech storage area. Four of them, then ten, still coming...*Holy fire of God, how many of them are there?*

The Scorpion passed by his position, so close he could see through the cockpit. He recognized the face beneath the neural helmet; this was Colonel Kuryakin himself. The man was no Customs officer, he was almost certainly military intelligence, and atop that, he was a mech jock. Jonathan thought of General Constantine and shuddered. One wrong glance, just a twitch of intuition and those twin plasma guns would swing around and he'd be dead. His father might never even discover what had happened to him unless Starkad tried to use his death for propaganda.

Kuryakin moved on, footpads scraping across the grooved surface of the floor and Jonathan let himself breathe just a little. He tried to see further to his right, through the archway entrance. He'd counted twenty mecha now, stretched out almost the whole length of the chamber and they were still coming in. The last mech in his line was Kurtz's Golem, and that was intentional; he had to trust the man not to power up until the whole force was inside, not to give away their positions unless it was necessary... but to be able to tell if things had gone to shit, if a change of plans was needed. It was a responsibility requiring more than just skill; it needed a steady hand, someone who wasn't likely to go get nervy.

He trusted Kurtz's judgement after these last few months. Which was why he didn't scream at the man when the fireball erupted from his Golem's position between two massive Imperial mecha, the ETC cannon round taking a Starkad Agamemnon through its cockpit at nearly point-blank range. He didn't panic, either, which almost surprised him. He surely *wanted* to panic and this seemed an opportune time for it. Instead, he simply hit the quick-start to boot up the Sentinel's reactor and power systems and tapped his hand against the control sticks, waiting for the seconds to pass and watching his nightmare unfold.

The enemy mecha seemed to be turning in slow motion, synchronous with the progress bar on his control display, crawling from red, through yellow and hesitating forever just before it reached green. Time jumped back into pace, flashing green and red and white and bracketed by a dozen chest-deep explosions. An enemy Golem had the poor luck to be standing directly in front of Jonathan's Sentinel when the strike mech powered up, and he fired his plasma gun through its cockpit. The Golem froze in place, suddenly lacking a pilot, Jonathan stepped his mech out from between the Imperial machines, and the easy part of the battle was quite suddenly over.

The Sentinel strike mech was the most advanced battle coordination platform in the Five Dominions, capable of handling the input from a full battalion of mecha and directing a battle on multiple fronts. If he could afford to pay attention to all that input, it would be invaluable; but wading into the middle of a knife fight, it was all just so much distraction and he shut it out and walked in swinging.

Lyta had been teaching him infantry tactics in the dead time on the *Shakak*, and they worked better here than the armor techniques he'd learned at the Academy. In a gunfight, she'd told him over and over, movement was life and cover was everything. The dead Golem was cover, and a long, sliding step put it between him and the mecha on the far side of the chamber, cutting his firing arc in half.

The bulk of his company was in front of him, surging far enough forward from their concealed positions to fire back toward the entrance, trying to avoid a circular firing squad. Lasers, plasma guns and ETC cannons streaked flashes of ionization and tracer rounds dotted their way between the two forces and Jonathan's indicators were flashing yellow in three places before he even had a chance to fire. He ignored the vibrating impact of a dozen tungsten cannon rounds smacking into his chest and leg armor and carefully picked out a target, a Goliath strike mech only fifty meters away. The broad-shouldered, humanoid-shaped machine was trying to fight three battles at once with three different weapons, and doing far too well at it. It needed to be taken care of.

Firing his missiles at this range would be close to lunacy, but the whole thing was lunacy and he doubted he'd have another chance to use them. And what was the old line?

They don't give you a bonus for bringing back unfired ordnance at the end of the battle.

Smoke billowed out in waves, enveloping half the chamber, and the four warheads barely had time to arm themselves before they struck the Goliath at the juncture of its right arm and shoulder. Flames from the bowels of Hell itself swallowed the gigantic machine whole and, when they cleared, the arm was gone, along with half the shoulder joint, and the entire upper body was listing badly to the left, stumbling off balance.

The frantic exchange of fire seemed to have paused for the barest of seconds in silent recognition of the inspired insanity of firing long-range missiles and the inertia of the heartbeat-long truce nearly froze him into inaction, but his hand acted on its own, squeezing off the go-to-hell shot with his mech's plasma gun. The right shoulder armor was nearly gone and the plasmoid burned through what was left, obliterating the cockpit, and once again, all was chaos.

He stepped forward, moved to the right, sliding past the burning hulk of a Golem, firing his twin 30mm Vulcans as he moved, subtly aware of a shift in the flux of the battle. Enemy mecha were flowing past him, moving to the other side of the chamber, fleeing the carnage and death of the ambush not back towards the exit but forward, further in. He realized he'd miscalculated, and Kuryakin wasn't *quite* as thoughtlessly enraged as he'd seemed or else the man had recovered quickly from the momentary madness.

The Colonel, Jonathan realized in a flash of insight, had realized his error and instead of doubling down on it and staying engaged with a neophyte's conviction of superior numbers, had broken contact. The Starkad mecha flowed away like water, moving through the Wholesale Slaughter kill zone to an angle where the Spartan mecha couldn't fire without fear of blue-on-blue casualties, leaving behind their own dead and disabled. It was cold-blooded and tactically brilliant.

The bastard knows I have to go after him, and he's right.

Jonathan hesitated for the space of two seconds, staring at IFF transponders flashing red, knowing he had at least five mecha of his own disabled, their pilots possibly wounded or dead...and knowing his brother and Katy, and Lyta's Rangers were deeper inside, searching for their only hope of winning this fight and there was no other choice.

"Get after them now!" he yelled, kicking his Sentinel into a gallop, the massive arms swinging with the long strides. "Before they have a chance to set up an ambush!"

He charged ahead through the chamber exit, deeper into the unknown.

"Just when I think I can't be surprised anymore," Katy murmured. "This place…"

Terry nodded wordlessly but didn't look away. He couldn't. The image was mesmerizing. He dimly recalled from his distant youth his great-grandfather sitting in his study, building models of old, ocean-going ships in glass bottles. It had been, he assumed, a hobby, though he couldn't figure out the entertainment value of it.

Gramps would love this.

It was a starship. Not a shuttle, not a drop-ship, a *starship*, nearly as big as the *Shakak*, and yet underground, nestled in a chamber even larger than the mecha armory, the largest indoor facility he'd ever seen in a life spent bouncing between military bases and university research labs. The ship was a monolith, a black and grey wedge of seamless armored hull nearly a kilometer long and somewhere over two hundred meters across, resting on—or more accurately, several meters *off* of—some sort of magnetic dry-dock skids, angled upward at somewhere just north of thirty degrees from level. The only way it had come to be in this chamber was if it had been assembled here, bit by bit. Not by some semi-retired military officer passing away his golden years, but by a team of Imperial researchers over months, bringing together the latest in cutting-edge technology.

"Why would something like this be way down here?"

Terry stared at Sgt. Montanez, wondering if he'd ever heard the man speak before. The Ranger NCO assigned to guard the research team usually did his job in silence and, if he hadn't seen the man with his helmet off on board the ship, he might have thought him some experimental and highly-illegal battle robot.

It was a good question, though. They'd followed the broad, ancient thoroughfares for two kilometers, passing through one chamber after another, past battlesuits and hovertanks and weapons large enough to have been designed for starships, and past machinery he couldn't even identify…until the tunnels had begun to slant upwards. Gently at first, enough it was barely noticeable, then steeper as another kilometer passed until he was sure they had to be only a few hundred meters from the surface, out of the Cut.

This had been the end, the climax, the culmination of their journey, as if the scientists working on this place knew it would be the most significant thing they'd designed.

"They wouldn't have put it down here without a way to get it out," he declared with more certainty than he felt. He tore his eyes away from the ship, looking for one of the control consoles like the one he'd seen back in the armory.

"It doesn't have a plasma drive emitter," Katy was saying from somewhere behind him, but he resisted the urge to inspect its aft end to prove her right, searching the walls instead. "How's it going anywhere without a fusion drive?"

"You see those things that look like atmospheric jet nozzles?" he said, his voice distracted, his attention on an unmarked section of wall that seemed suspiciously smooth and featureless.

"Yeah?" She was further away now and he could barely hear her.

"Those are antimatter drives. They suck air through intakes in the front and use that for atmospheric use, and they have a store of reaction mass to get them from high atmosphere to out of planetary orbit."

He touched the wall and barked a triumphant laugh when it lit up with a holographic projection, the seal of the Empire of Hellas, the rampant lion under a crown of stars.

"Those drive nozzles seem awful small to handle that kind of thrust...and heat." She sounded skeptical and he found her attitude mildly irritating.

"Well, we're here to get something new," he snipped off the words, losing patience with the question. He reaching into the Imperial seal and twisted the haptic hologram to the side, revealing a menu. "If you could figure out how it worked, we wouldn't need to be here."

Jackpot.

"Is that...?" Maurice Chaisson breathed, looking over his shoulder at the display, pointing at a three-dimensional diagram of the ship, at a spiral section of...something...running through the core of the vessel. It looked like nothing else so much as a strand of human DNA five hundred meters long, one end of it terminating in the antimatter reactor and the other splitting into axion-like tendrils reaching out to the perimeter of the hull.

Terry's finger scrolled text downward, the readouts appearing *ex nihilo* in mid-air beside the diagram and then disappearing just as abruptly. Some of the words might as well have been in another language, but he could make out enough of them to understand. He turned back to Chaisson and nearly laughed at the older man's bugged-out eyes. He was a Warrant Officer in the Sparta Guard, a mech repair and salvage specialist for the last fifteen years, and somewhere along the way, he'd picked up degrees in electrical engineering and theoretical physics. It would be hard to tell it by looking at him. He could have been the bouncer at one of Argos' rougher nightspots, with a nose crooked from one too many fights and one too few visits to the cosmetic surgeon.

"Yes," he told Chaisson, barely able to believe it himself. "That's a stardrive."

"Mithra's horns, lad, if you can make this thing work, we're saved, all of us!" The older man's pugnacious, uneven face was transformed into something awe-struck and almost reverent, a petitioner who had seen God answer his prayers.

Oh good, no pressure.

He finally found what he was looking for and stabbed a finger into a glowing icon fashioned in the universal symbol for stairs. Warning klaxons sounded as if from everywhere at once and Terry nearly jumped out of his skin, though he'd been expecting something to happen. Heads turned in every possible direction, a couple of the Spartan techs seeming like they thought a hideous monster was about to emerge from the walls.

"What the hell did you do now, Terry?" Katy demanded.

She wasn't panicking, but she was alert and her sidearm was in her hand. The Ranger guards had their carbines at the ready, but they always did, so he wasn't sure if they were being any more cautious than usual.

They scuttled quickly out of the way when the floor began flashing red. Not the whole floor, just a strip thirty meters wide and stretching from the chamber's entrance fifty meters across to the hull of the starship, glowing from inside as if the surface of the stone were infused with LEDs. He backed away a step himself, suddenly uncertain about what exactly he'd done.

He hadn't seen a gap in the surface of the floor, no delineation at all before the lights had begun flashing, but somehow, he wasn't surprised when the ramp began to raise out of it. It rose with a deep, earthquake rumble, giving more of an impression of crystals expanding in a growth medium than some mechanism extending a sectioned and compressed expansion unit hidden under the floor; and it didn't stop rising until the far end had reached a cargo hatch in the side of the starship. He hadn't seen the hatch, hadn't noticed it opening, but it was broad and circular and dark, and the inside seemed light-years away.

"Chaisson," he said to the warrant officer, "I need you to keep looking through the menus in this system." He motioned at the holographic display. "Somewhere in there is whatever control retracts the roof of this place, or opens the door or however they had in mind for this ship to get from under the ground into space."

"Gotcha, Terry," the older man said. "Shinawatra," he barked, waving for the *Shakak* crewman who had, supposedly, once been a weapons researcher for the Shang Directorate, "come help me with this."

The spindly little man looked spooked and doubtful, but he seemed to consider any movement away from the ghostly, ancient ship to be an improvement, and he stepped over to huddle with Chaisson.

"What about the rest of us?" Katy asked him, her gaze darting back and forth between him and the ramp and the suddenly-just-there opening in the side of the ship. "What are we gonna do?"

"You and I are going on board that," he told her, jabbing a finger up at the cargo door. "We're going to find out if there's still any antimatter fuel on her after over four hundred years...and if you can figure out how to fly her out of here."

"Shit," the pilot muttered. "I was afraid you were going to say that."

18

P asqual Jeffries was not a man given to fear. Fearful men did not make it through Supremacy Marine qualification, nor were they selected for officer training. When the drop-ship exploded, it had consumed a full platoon of his troops in an instant and left two and a half squads too badly injured to move and it would have been so easy to panic, so easy to stay on the surface and lick his wounds.

But when your commander yelled "follow me!" and ran into battle, there was only one choice for a Supremacy Marine: you grabbed your rifle and whoever around you could walk and followed your leader into battle.

Which was not to say he was a blind idiot, either. He'd left a full platoon behind to guard their rear and advanced carefully, keeping a safe gap between his Marines and the machines of the Supremacy Royal Guard.

"Hold up!" he yelled, raising a fist and taking a knee twenty-five meters short of the end of the entrance tunnel, squeezing to the side wall and motioning for those who'd followed him to do the same.

The mecha ahead of them had slowed from a forty-kilometer-an-hour trot to a ponderous walk, some of them stopping completely. His Marines had started out a good fifty meters behind the last of the machines and now they were nearly at the feet of the last of them. It was not a place he wanted to be. There was a reason mech jocks called infantry "crunchies."

"Top," he called over his helmet radio. "You in here, Top?"

"I'm near to the tail-end of this clusterfuck, sir," the old First Sergeant growled into his ear. "Whatcha need?"

He sneered in the privacy of his helmet. He'd known from day one the First Sergeant didn't like him much, but he couldn't bring himself to care.

"Get them reorganized and redistribute any survivors from Third Platoon. Lt. Marcus is dead, I saw that much, and small loss. Tell those worthless shits Nordegren and Ostermueller to get their asses up here for a recon."

"Roger that, sir."

Jeffries didn't wait for the two platoon leaders, partially because he wanted to get the lay of the land before they started asking him stupid questions, but also because they were both useless newbies who had to have their platoon sergeants hold their dicks every time they went to the damned bathroom. He sprinted across to the far wall of the tunnel, too close to the last of the mecha in the gaggle still pushing into the chamber but he needed to see for himself.

Maybe Nordegren and Ostermeuller will get stepped on and the next two platoon leaders Brigade sends me won't be fucking idiots.

He knew what to expect from the chamber after seeing Sgt. Leonard's video from her scouting run, but the seemingly endless line of Imperial mecha was even more impressive in person. They seemed like statues in a forgotten temple to some ancient and terrible god and it was hard to take his eyes off them. Maybe it was his lower perspective, maybe his training that had taught him to view every mech, friend or foe, as potentially fatal, or perhaps it was just luck, but he spotted the Golem before any of the Starkad mecha.

It was squatting in the shadows of the old Imperial mecha, a child hidden behind the legs of the adults at a military parade. The revelation slugged Pasquale Jeffries between the eyes like the air hammer in a slaughterhouse. This was an ambush, and the remaining ground forces of the Supremacy on this world were about to walk right into it.

"Look out!" he yelled reflexively, then cursed himself for not remembering to switch frequencies from his own Marines to the general net and wasted precious seconds clawing at the controls of his wrist computer. He didn't even try to scroll all the way down to the general net, just punched the first armored unit he came across, First Platoon of Alpha Company. "Look out!" he repeated, less shrilly this time but just as urgently. "It's a trap! There are enemy mecha between the rows!"

Mithra's blood, I sound like a primary school child acting out the Reconstruction Wars.

For a moment, he thought he'd had just as much effect as that playacting child. There was no reply, no cry of alarm on the channel, no eruption of gunfire. He raised his rifle to his shoulder, targeting the Golem, knowing the rounds would have no chance of harming the machine but unwilling to be merely a spectator. Before he could squeeze the trigger, one of the mecha near the end of the line slowed, stopped, its torso swiveling to the left toward the Golem he'd warned them about.

Jeffries felt a surge of relief along with a flash-image of himself receiving a medal from Colonel Kuryakin, a small piece in bringing the Supremacy to its rightful place at the head of the Five Dominions, but a key one.

The Golem fired first. The mecha directly in front of it, the Agamemnon he'd called the warning to, had been the Strike

Platoon leader's machine and it died along with him. Jeffries felt the blast from the ETC cannon deep in his chest, stumbled backwards from the concussion. Floaters clouded his vision and he'd barely shaken them clear when the very air was ripped apart by a fusillade of lasers, cannon rounds and plasma discharges. Heat washed out from the chamber in a wave, running point for clouds of billowing smoke, and Jeffries threw himself to the floor, covering his helmet with his hands, a helpless mortal in a battle of the titans.

A cool breeze splashed across his face, reviving him from heat-exhaustion stupor, and he realized with a start his suit's auxiliary air supply had kicked in, triggered by the heat and toxic gasses washing out of the embattled chamber.

Did I pass out? How long...

He pushed himself up to a crouch, fighting an almost overwhelming instinct to stay down, stay safe. Smoke drifted across the chamber, swirling in whirlpool spirals, drawn quickly and inexorably into vents still working perfectly after centuries with no maintenance, no resupply.

Whatever battle had raged in the armory chamber was over, or at least it had moved on. The wreckage of what could have been a dozen mecha burned and smoked and smoldered on a floor that refused to even be marked by the destruction. It was hard to be sure about the numbers; some of the machines were in pieces, melted and twisted and scattered. It was even harder to be certain who they'd belonged to, though he could see bits and pieces of Starkad camouflage patterns on several of the burning hulks.

It was a safe bet it hadn't gone well for Colonel Kuryakin because ambushes rarely went well for the ambushed.

Wait a second, I'm forgetting something. Oh, right.

Nordegren and Ostermeuller, always willing to follow orders blindly, had charged right through the hell coming out of the entrance to the chamber in their effort to report to him. What remained of the two men could have fit into a standard-size foot-locker with room left for all of a recruit's issue uniforms.

"Top," he croaked, his throat still dry and scratchy. "Get everyone up here. The actions moving and so are we."

"I've never been on the bridge for a space battle before," Ortiz said from somewhere behind him. "I didn't realize it would be this damned boring."

"Hours of boredom punctuated by seconds of sheer terror."

"What?" Kammy wondered, voice strained.

"That's how someone described space combat to me back in the Academy," Donner Osceola clarified, not turning his head to look at his navigator. He might have pulled a muscle trying to move around under high-g boost.

He still hadn't put on his suit's helmet. It was attached securely to the side of his acceleration couch with a magnetic anchor and even Kammy had stopped trying to nag him about it. He kept his eyes forward, glued to the computer-generated avatar of the *Valkyrian* still burning toward them as it had been, seem-ingly forever. Terminus hung off their starboard, a dark silhouette against the system's orange dwarf star, a disinterested spectator who'd grown bored waiting for the fight to begin.

"Well, you can tell that smartass he forgot about the minutes of misery," Tara reminded him, not sounding any happier about the four-gravity acceleration than he was. "By the way, those missiles are forty seconds out."

"Hit the ECM and open fire with the point-defense turrets," Osceola ordered. He tried to grin, but the boost plastered the expression backwards across his face, turned it into a manic leer. "At this rate of acceleration, they'll only have one pass at us before the boosters burn through their fuel. And that moron running the Starkad boat can't even fire lasers at us without hitting his own missiles."

"I'm sure we all appreciate the superiority of your tactics, fearless leader," Kammy said, nerves creeping into his tone. "But when do we plan on shooting back?"

"Range to target, Tara?"

"Just a second," she murmured, hands flying over controls at the edge of his vision. "Still trying to do the last thing you told me to do." Osceola tried not to tap his foot impatiently; more than once, he'd wound up with cramp in his calf doing that during a high-g boost. "ECM activated, anti-missile turrets targeting and opening fire now."

He sometimes wished the tactical display came with sound effects to go along with the visual simulations. He saw the dotted yellow flashes on the screen, converging on the arrow-shaped icons representing the missiles, but it didn't seem real. He couldn't feel the recoil of the 30mm rotary-barrel Vulcans, couldn't hear the roar they would have made in an atmosphere, just saw the effects via the sensor display. One after another of the incoming missiles began drifting off course or falling back, their boosters damaged or disabled by the hail of tungsten slugs, or their guidance systems fried by the microwave bursts from the ECM antennae.

"The *Valkyrian* is at 10,000 kilometers and closing," Tara finally reported. "Nine minutes till intercept at current acceleration." He appreciated the way she always managed to sound professional and precise when the occasion required it. "We've shaken the last of the missiles," she added. "They're still heading past us and none have tried to maneuver back."

"Power up the main gun," he ordered.

He hesitated for a moment. Should he wait until they wouldn't have the time to maneuver their deflector dish around, or should he try to *force* them to maneuver, to keep them from returning fire with their main laser batteries?

May as well find out where we stand now.

"Fire," he told her. "Keep firing as she powers up until we lose target lock."

"Firing."

This time he *did* feel it. The spinal-mounted railgun fired a big enough round at a high enough speed for it to actually decelerate the *Shakak* just slightly, sending a shudder through the ship's superstructure. The refresh rate for the railgun was slow, much slower than the laser batteries, but Tara still had time to fire off three shots before the first one struck home.

Minutes crawled by on their hands and knees, stranded men dying of thirst under the desert sun. Osceola wanted to curse, wanted to get a drink, wanted to cut boost back to one gravity so he could pace. All he could do was sit and suffer in the strait jacket of patience he'd strapped himself into decades ago.

Even at what was fairly close range for space combat, the *Valkyrian* was still just a reflective pinpoint of light and they had to rely on the radar, lidar, and passive thermal and spectrographic analysis, to build the computer simulation of the heavy cruiser. The rounds hit. He saw the glowing red dots merge with the wedge-shaped avatar of the Starkad ship, didn't see any sensor reflection indicating the enemy deflectors had managed to shunt the thousand-kilogram tungsten slugs aside, but...

"Anything?" he asked Tara, searching the display for any indication of damage, any thermal spikes or leaking atmosphere.

"We got some sensor scatter," she replied, her tone subdued. "That's probably from shedding armor. But I can't see any signs of real damage."

"Shit," Norris blurted, the first word he'd uttered since he'd handed out the space suits.

"Yeah," Osceola agreed. "Hey Ortiz, here's where you're

going to miss the part where it was boring." He sucked in as deep a breath as he could manage. "Boost us up to six gees, Kammy."

"Wonderful," Tara moaned, the sound squeezed off into a squeak as six times her normal weight pressed down on her chest.

"Keep firing," Osceola told her, forcing the words out and hoping they were still audible over the roaring in everyone's ears. "You might get lucky."

"That's what she said," Tara cracked, using precious oxygen on the comeback because some straight lines were just too good to pass up.

"Hey, Boss..." Kammy trailed off but Osceola could feel the eyes on him and knew what the big man had been about to say.

"I'll put it on when I need it."

"We've lost target lock on the railgun," Tara wheezed. "Firing angle's gone. Working on a solution for the laser batteries...but I think they're going to have one first."

Being hit by a laser weapon in a heavily armored starship was a strange thing. You felt nothing, you saw nothing unless you were unlucky enough to be in its path if it penetrated the hull. You just heard this incredibly annoying warning klaxon while the tactical display flashed red, just in case you weren't close enough to panic and needed some added sensual stimuli.

"We're getting penetration in the port cargo bay," Norris reported, surprising Osceola both with the fact he could even talk with six gees of boost and that he'd made the announcement at all. He hadn't realized the man knew how to read the damage control station display. "Losing some atmosphere, but it's sealed off already. No crew in the section so no casualties."

"Oh, they're not done yet," he assured the man.

He was trying to remain calm, matter of fact while his stomach roiled. The ship was his life, the child he'd never had, and every hurt she suffered felt as if it was a wound to his body.

"I've got target lock," Tara told him.

"Fire at will." The command was desultory. If their railgun couldn't penetrate the heavy cruiser's armor, their lasers wouldn't even scratch her paint.

Something rocked the ship, jerking Osceola to the left. He cursed, pain shooting through his neck, only the padding of the acceleration couch's headrest keeping him from snapping his spine.

"What the *fuck* was that?" Kammy demanded. Osceola already knew, but he let Norris answer the question. It didn't seem real if he didn't say it himself.

"They took out our port bow maneuvering thrusters," the Spartan spacer reported dutifully. "That was the reaction mass..." Osceola could almost hear his shrug. "...reacting."

The *Valkyrian* was close enough to be clearly visible on optical sensors as it passed, close enough to see the sparkling flares of sublimating metal tracking a black, charred line down the side of her hull as the *Shakak*'s lasers kept up their fire...and then she was past them and the warning klaxon ceased and the red flashing died away.

"Cut thrust."

Kammy had been waiting for the order and complied before the last syllable had left his tongue. The rib-creaking gee load died away to free-fall so quickly his stomach rebelled and he had to clamp his teeth shut to keep his lunch in his stomach. Ortiz wasn't quite able to manage it. He heard her retching inside her helmet, felt a pang of sympathy right along with a feeling of gratitude she was wearing a helmet at all. There wasn't much worse than someone vomiting in free-fall and having to watch the green and yellow globules orbit around the bridge, heading inexorably your way.

"Turn us around, Kammy," he gave the command he knew none of them wanted to hear. "Make sure you use the starboard thrusters," he added, though he was sure the big man had already thought of it.

A dull, distant roar vibrated through the hull, reaction mass heated by a fusion bottle the size of an assault shuttle beginning the end-for-end maneuver to bring their main gun back to bear on the enemy.

"But…" It was Ortiz, trying to speak while her helmet's regulator sucked the remains of her last meal out of her face and into the waste receptacles. "But we can't hurt them," she managed to squeak the words out. "Nothing we have can touch them. What are we going to do?"

He remembered what he'd told the crew of the *Paralus* during the Battle of Plataea and the words came of their own accord.

"We're going to fight," he replied. "We're going to fight until we can't fight anymore."

He reached down and freed his suit's helmet from its anchor on the side of his chair, staring at it for just a moment before he settled it onto his neck yoke and sealed it shut. The view seemed straighter, narrower through the faceplate of the helmet and his breath caught in the staleness of its enclosure before the hiss of air washed over his face.

"Deceleration burn at six gees, Kammy," he ordered, the words hollow and echoing in his ears. "Take us back into the shit."

There were, she reflected, some advantages to all-or-nothing last stands. You didn't have to hold anything back for next time, you didn't have to worry about what higher authority would think of your plan of action, and you didn't have to hang back in a command position and let some private take point.

Lyta Randell slithered out from beneath five centimeters of

black, volcanic soil and into a night still alight with the raging flames of the drop-ship. It had taken all her self-control to keep from hyperventilating on the auxiliary air supply built into her helmet, buried under the dirt, and it had taken every bit of patience not to jump up the second she'd heard the explosion.

But the plan had been to draw the mecha into the tunnel and leave the rest to her and the Rangers, and she had to give the plan time to work. When she raised her head far enough to see the entrance, she cursed. It had worked *too* well; it seemed as if all of the Marines had followed the mecha inside.

No, wait. Not all of them.

She spotted them on her second scan across the entrance, just the barest traces on infrared and thermal. They weren't dug in—there hadn't been time for that—but they'd taken up hasty fighting positions behind what cover they could find and she respected their professionalism.

Still have to kill them, of course.

"Abnathy," she radioed to her senior platoon leader, still a sub-lieutenant but one who'd worked his way up through the ranks as an NCO before attending officer's training. "Take Third Platoon around to the north and secure the surviving enemy drop-ships."

There were two of them, the third wrecked and burning just two hundred meters away, still close enough to feel the heat of the flames through her armor. They undoubtedly had an armed flight crew aboard each, and they'd likely left either Supremacy Marines or Navy Security guarding the landers. Either way, they couldn't leave the threat behind them.

"First and Second, follow me at a high crawl and deploy into assault positions."

It was a dangerous approach. She estimated a full platoon of Marines had remained behind, and they had the high ground. If they spotted her Rangers before they were in position, the Starkad forces could rain down hell on them and there wouldn't be a damned thing she could do about it. But they had one advantage: the fire would be playing hell with the enemy's infrared and thermal sights, and she was going to have to hope it was enough.

She tucked her rifle into the cleft of her arms and scrabbled forward on elbows and knees, the bulk of First and Second Platoons spreading out behind her into parallel wedge formations. She trusted their platoon leaders and NCOs, but she snuck a glance back every few meters just to make sure they were keeping their intervals. It would be easy to let it slip in this uneven terrain strewn with razor-edged volcanic rock, easy to detour around an obstacle and lose your way in the flickering shadows of the fire. Easy to get distracted by the discomfort. Ranger armor was well-padded and well-protected on the elbows and knees for situations just such as this, yet she could still feel the sharp edges gouging into her even through the segmented armor plating. Without it, they all would have been sliced to pieces; it would be easy to concentrate on the pain and lose focus on the enemy, but Rangers didn't lose focus and they didn't give in to pain. They just did their job and accomplished the mission.

They were less than a hundred meters from the enemy positions when she got the call from Abnathy, his voice low and muted out of habit despite the sound-proofing of his visored helmet.

"Third Platoon in position."

"Wait one."

Just a bit farther, seventy meters...

"Low crawl," she hissed, digging her helmet into the dirt, pressing her body to the uncomfortable, rocky ground and dragging it along, her rifle stretched out over her right arm, held by the end of the sling.

Fifty meters. It would have to be enough.

"Third," she ordered, "you are a go. Repeat, you are a go."

She waited. Ten seconds passed by and she began to wonder if something had gone wrong. She had opened her mouth to re-broadcast the directive when she heard the grenades. At this distance, they were sharp, snappy bangs and the stutter of the suppressed carbines was little more than someone clearing their throat beside you, but they attracted enough attention from the Supremacy Marines.

She supposed she could forgive them for the mistake. After all, they'd probably been left in haste, with no direction other than to guard against attack from the rear, and here they were detecting what looked just like an attack from the rear. So they stood and charged down the slope, intent on stopping the assault on their drop-ships, and ran directly into the guns of the Rangers.

"Now!"

She adjusted her aim just a centimeter or two and squeezed the trigger. The carbine pushed against her shoulder and tried to rise at the muzzle, but her left hand held firm on the vertical fore-grip. She let the target go slightly out of focus, not needing to remember the way the man's body jerked at the impact of the slugs, just letting herself see enough to know he was dead before she moved on to the next.

This one had realized what was happening, was trying to crawfish back up the berm, but it was way too late for that. He tumbled onto his back and slid a few meters down, arms flopping unnaturally, their strength gone along with his life. By the time she tried to transition to a third target, there was none. The Marines were dead, or close enough that they didn't move when a few extra shots splashed into them.

"Abnathy, report," she barked, coming up to one knee, eyes scanning back and forth carefully, checking for holdouts.

"Drop-ships secure," the man reported, voice calm and even, as if he'd just walked aboard with no problems. "No casualties. Ten enemy KIA."

"Stay with the landers," she instructed the man. "First and Second, we're heading inside."

"Hey Major."

She jumped at the voice, spinning around and nearly squeezing off a burst of fire before she saw the raised hands, the familiar face. The Military Intelligence officer who'd been calling himself Francis Acosta was soaked, still dripping water even after what had to have been nearly a kilometer hike back up to the entrance from the lake. She didn't know how the hell he'd made it all this way with no one spotting him, but there was a lot she didn't know about him, including his real name.

"Glad to see you made it," she told him, grinning behind her visor where no one could see the indulgence.

"Yeah, me too," he agreed. He motioned at the pistol holstered on her tactical vest. "You mind loaning me a gun? Mine's somewhere at the bottom of that damned lake."

She shook her head, but tossed him the pistol.

"You know, you *could* just stay out here and sit this one out," she told him.

"Oh, I could," he agreed, smirking in that way only pilots and spooks could get away with. "But I'm cold and wet and pissed off." He motioned to the entrance. "And all the fun's in there."

19

"C heck this out, sir."

Jeffries followed Sergeant Arsenault's voice around the curve of the hallway, shouldering past the trailing fire team, and found the squad leader crouched over what had once been a body. Centuries of dry, sterile air had turned it into a mummy curled on the floor, its stick-like fingers twisted in a death-grip around the butt of a pistol. It was dark in the back hallways; the lights in the offices and apartments where the base staff had lived hadn't come on automatically the way they had in the cargo bays and research labs. But he'd decided it was worth it to risk infrared illuminators and he could see the lines of the gun clearly through the night-vision filters in his helmet visor.

"Guess he decided he'd rather off himself than starve to death," Arsenault said, prying the gun out of the corpse's hand and sticking it in a pocket of his vest. Technically, battle souvenirs were against regs, but the squad leader knew Jeffries didn't care and Top was riding drag at the rear of the column.

"His problem," Captain Jeffries judged, "not ours. Keep moving, we need to get to that ship."

Pasquale Jeffries never ceased to be amazed at his own cleverness. Oh sure, it had been Top who'd noticed the diagram of the base displayed on the fancy three-dimensional projection by the wall, but Jeffries had been the one who'd found the perimeter passage. It was much smaller than the tunnels the mecha had followed, designed for personnel rather than cargo. It had made sense: there'd been a research and engineering crew here and they hadn't lived on cots in the middle of the storage bays. The great part was, the perimeter hallways took them to the same research labs and storage bays as the cargo tunnels without the danger of getting stepped on or blown up by mecha. He was sure even his prick of First Sergeant appreciated that.

Jeffries had spotted the inventory listing for the ship, too, though he hadn't quite believed what he was seeing at first. Why the hell would anyone have a starship underground? But the chamber where the ship was stored *had* to have access to the surface, and he knew it was where the Spartan forces would have retreated in the face of the Starkad advance. If he could get to it before their armored troops did, he could control the situation, use the Spartan research and salvage crew as hostages. *And* be the Marine officer who gave Starkad an Imperial starship as a present. Win-win.

Jeffries fell in behind Arsenault, between the squad's fire teams, letting the enlisted take the lead so he could afford to sight-see along the way. Doors hung open along the hallway and he saw this was some sort of housing block for military personnel. He could tell it was military rather than researchers by the uniformity of the rooms; some things didn't change, whether it was on old Earth, the Empire, or the Dominions. There was always some NCO or staff officer enforcing uniformity whether there was any good reason for it or not.

There were more bodies, too, though he didn't see any others who'd decided to eat a gun. Maybe the commander handed out poison or something less violent for those who wanted it. He shuddered at the idea, at the irony of starving to death sitting on a mountain of high-tech military hardware. None of it could create biological material out of thin air, though, and no one had been far-sighted enough to create a hydroponic farm down here before it was too late.

"We got stairs, sir," Arsenault told him.

He'd expected it; the facility maps he'd seen showed a steep incline on the way up to the chamber where they'd stored the ship. The stairwell was narrow and inexpressibly dark, even with the infrared flashlights doing their best to illuminate it. Arsenault was standing at the foot of the stairs with his lead fire team gathered around, weapons pointed outward. He couldn't see their faces through their helmets, but he was sure they were all looking at him for the call. None of them would want to go up those steps unless they had to.

"What?" he demanded, waving a hand forward. "You know which way we gotta go! Get up there!"

"You heard the Captain!" Arsenault barked. "Let's get moving! Follow me!"

The squad leader bounded up the stairs two at a time and both fire teams surged forward to keep up. Jeffries let them, let the whole squad run ahead of him before he took his first step up the stairwell. Arsenault, he reflected, was a hero. He loved heroes. They made great mine detectors.

"What in the hell am I looking at?"

Kathren Margolis had trained with every aerospacecraft in the Spartan inventory and a few flown by Starkad and Shang. She could probably fake her way through everything else in the Five Dominions. She'd also received enough cross-training at the Academy to work the helm of a starship at need. She didn't know the physics of star-travel the way she knew aeronautical engineering, but she knew the controls.

What was spread out before her on the bridge of the Imperial ship was like nothing she'd ever seen before, much less flown. She'd watched Terry play with the holographic displays, and thought she had an idea of how to manipulate them. The two of them had scrolled through menu after menu but there just didn't seem to be any flight controls. She tried to lean forward to peer more closely at the display, but the whole damned ship was at an angle back towards the stern and her butt kept slipping back in the acceleration couch.

"It keeps mentioning a neural linkage." Terry pointed to a line of text beside some sort of symbol she couldn't recognize. "Mech jocks use neural helmets, don't they?"

"Yeah, but that's just for reading nerve output to help keep the machines balanced. What would it have to do with flying a ship?"

Terry chewed on his lip for a second, then reached out to touch an icon shaped vaguely like a crown. A curve semicircle seemingly built into the helm console lit up with a red halo and he grinned, motioning towards it. She shot him a "who? Me?" look but reached out hesitantly and tried to pry the thing away from its mount. It came easily, lighter and flimsier than she'd thought it would be, as if it would crumple in her fingers.

"And what am I supposed to do with *this*?" she muttered.

The question was rhetorical. She knew exactly what he expected her to do with it, but the idea freaked her the hell out. She placed the halo across her forehead, letting the ends rest at her temples, then waited. And waited.

"Is something supposed to happen?"

Something *did*. A line of holographic screens lit up all across the curved bulkhead at the front of the bridge, the Imperial crest displayed over and over in sequence as they snapped to life before giving way to what seemed to be a series of optical camera views of the exterior of Terminus. The night sky shone brilliantly through the thin atmosphere above the Cut, a hundred thousand stars promising even greater mysteries than this place if, only they could be reached.

Maybe concealed cameras in the surface? she wondered. But the next screen showed the curve of the planet from high orbit. Had they missed a whole satellite up there? She'd seen the sensor readouts from their scan of the system and there'd been nothing, not a trace of any spacecraft. *Something so small we missed it?*

The next shot was even harder to explain: it was a live view from tens or hundreds of thousands of kilometers away, impossibly close to the wedge-shaped ugliness of the *Shakak* and the deadly, arrowhead lines of the Starkad heavy cruiser *Valkyrian*. The perspective was impossible; to see both ships in one shot would require multiple spacecraft matching velocities with them and broadcasting their signals to a computer powerful enough to...

Oh, for God's sake, woman, stop trying to figure it out. If we could understand their technology, we wouldn't need it so damned bad.

However they were seeing the *Shakak*, what they were seeing wasn't good. She had ragged, blackened rents burned through her armor in multiple spots, and even as they watched, a flare of vaporized metal erupted near her stern, the *Valkyrian*'s lasers striking home again.

We have to get up there!

It was an idle thought, barely formed, but something vibrated through the ship, just the barest of movements but strong enough to jar a craft weighing thousands of tons and she bared her teeth in panic, yanking the halo off of her head reflexively. The viewscreens went black, leaving the compartment dark and abandoned once again, a ghost ship haunted by the specters of the past.

"What the fuck did I just do?" she demanded, holding the device out at Terry in accusation.

"Were you trying to move?" he asked her, leaning over and examining the halo closely without touching it. "Were you picturing yourself moving?"

"I was just thinking we had to get up there and help the *Shakak*," she said, gesturing to where the image of the ship had been. "Then...whatever it was happened."

"I think it was the magnetic anchors outside starting to let go, just for a second. And I think that," he gestured at the halo, "was reading your thoughts."

She scowled at him. "That's not possible." She blinked, considering where they were. "I mean, it's not, is it?"

"If not reading your thoughts directly then somehow interpreting your intent through your brain waves, or your neural output, or something." He shrugged. "I'm a physicist, not a neurobiologist. But you were controlling it somehow and you've got to try it again."

"Does this thing even have any fuel left?" she demanded, trying to pull away on a tangent.

Terry sagged back into the acceleration couch beside hers, the expression on his face screwed up in obvious frustration.

"Not much," he admitted. "Not after they took her out looking for food sources. Thank the Beneficent Spirits the thing's been hooked up to external power all this time, or the containment fields would have failed and there'd be nothing left except a crater."

He scrolled through the display still floating over the engineering console, just to the right of the helm station where she sat and brought up what looked like a status bar. It was low, down under ten percent, what little was left glowing a warning red.

"But there might be just enough to get out there and save them," he went on. "If we can figure out how to fly her."

She let her head fall back against the padded rest and sighed in resignation.

"All right, I get it." She brought the halo back up to her head, wincing at the chill touch of the material. Was it plastic? Metal? It didn't feel like either one. "Let's get this over with…"

"Hey Terry! You there?" Chaisson's voice sounded tinny and distant over the external speaker on Terry's 'link. "Can you hear me in there?"

"What is it?" Terry asked. He sounded, Katy thought, much more serious than he had when she'd first met him, which was understandable but a bit sad, too. She wanted to think people like her did what they did so people like Terry could live their lives unaffected

"I've found…" There was a muted objection behind him that she recognized as coming from Shinawatra and Chaisson sighed. "All right, *we* found what we think is some sort of hatch or, I don't know, *something* to open up the roof. It ain't clear what it is, but we're pretty sure what it's for. You want I should go ahead and hit it?"

Terry's throat bobbed in a nervous swallow, and she saw something of the old Terrin Brannigan in the ashen expression on his face at the prospect of the decision. Whatever he was going to say, Chaisson interrupted it.

"Hold up, there's someone coming. Maybe it's Major Randell…" Katy's eyes went wide as an eruption of tinny static turned into the unmistakable explosion of gunfire. "Oh, shit!"

"Chaisson!" Terry yelled into the 'link, but there was no reply. The transmission had cut off.

"Son of a bitch," Katy snapped, pounding a fist against the armrest of her acceleration couch. She pushed herself up, yanking her handgun from its holster. "All right, I'm going to…"

"No." His hand on her arm surprised her, as did the calm determination on his face. "Give me the gun; I'll go."

"Terry," she sighed, "now is not the time to…"

"If I can get the roof open," he interrupted, fiercely insistent, "you can fly her out. *Someone* has to take out the Starkad ship and I can't fly this thing. Now give me your gun."

She bit down on her instinctive reply and handed him the pistol.

"You ever shot a gun?" she wondered.

"You know who my father is," he reminded her, checking the load and the safety with motions obviously practiced, if perhaps not recently. "I was shooting at the military ranges when I was four." He grabbed at the backs of acceleration couches to help him navigate along the sloped deck to the bridge hatch. "Get this ship ready to fly."

Colonel Aleksandr Kuryakin would have kicked himself in the ass except he was too busy running.

I am too damned old to be making these sorts of mistakes.

The mecha and the troops he'd lost, they were on his head. Laurent was on his head. He'd underestimated Logan Conner, thought of him only as a bargaining piece, something for him to gain and possess rather than as a military leader, which he quite obviously was.

He's one bold son of a bitch, he had to admit, much as he wanted to hate the boy. *To sacrifice his own drop-ship…*

Oh, it made sense. What good was a drop-ship if you didn't survive the battle? But it wasn't a strategy he would have expected from one so young and inexperienced, and now he was paying for it. He'd charged through the ambush, knowing the Spartans had to have a team deeper into the complex searching for Imperial tech to salvage, knowing Conner would have to chase after him, but he had to have a plan beyond running.

The first chamber was filled with some sort of armored exoskeletons, thousands of them; the Intelligence officer in him was fascinated with the idea and curious as to how the Imperials had made it work, but the mech commander he was pretending to be had to think of them tactically. He briefly considered trying to turn and fight, but the armored suits were barely three meters tall and offered little cover, so he pushed his mech harder, ignoring the heat building up in his cockpit, ignoring the blinking yellow indicators at his hip actuators, ignoring the blasts of plasma passing by only meters from his cockpit.

The next tunnel swallowed them up and the firing ceased as the narrower passage squeezed the pursuing mecha in tighter, where any shots could have hit their own people. He might have risked it were he in Conner's place, but the man was young and probably still fancied himself the good guy. Time and experience would teach him the realities of the world.

Kuryakin knew he needed somewhere to make a stand, somewhere to take advantage of his numbers, but the next chamber offered no help. The tanks were enormous and again, intriguing to the analyst in him, but still too damned low to offer real cover. On the IFF display at the right-hand corner of his HUD, he saw the rearmost of the mecha following him flash yellow, then red. Ehlinger was his name, a Lieutenant, a young man with promise and an easy, contagious laugh. Kuryakin remembered eating dinner with him in the mess, hearing him go on about his family and their little farm back on Loki. He'd gotten the young man killed.

Young men and women died in war, though, and he'd resigned himself to it. Back when he, too, had thought he was one of the good guys, he'd labored under the delusion he could save them all. He'd even changed career paths, thinking he could save more of them by making sure the intelligence the military acted on was more accurate. Years spent fruitlessly whispering in the ear of idiots like Aaron, Lord Starkad had taught him the truth of the situation: leaders acted on the intelligence they liked and refused to accept the facts contradicting the plans they'd already made.

Once again into the comparative safety of the next passage and he made a decision: the next chamber, they would turn and fight, no matter if it was empty.

It wasn't. Storage bins were stacked five high, twenty meters tall, row upon row, filled with Mithra knew what but at least they'd be concealment if not cover. The main aisle was the broadest, a shooting gallery, but if they could draw the Spartan mecha out toward the edges, the approaches would be narrow enough to funnel the enemy down to a single file. This was as good as it was going to get.

"Spread out!" He screamed the command, knowing it would take effort to shock the others out of the inertia of retreat. "Fight them here or they'll cut us down!"

He had to lead by example, despite a nagging worry he would peel away from the column only to have the rest keep on running, abandoning him to his fate. He was almost to the far side of the chamber, nearly even with the last of the branching side aisles through the storage bins, when he planted his right foot and pivoted, feeling the strain on the mech's superstructure without having to see the flashing yellow running up both legs in his damage display. Metal scraped on grooved flooring with a high-pitched screech, enough to set his teeth on edge, and for one terribly long second he was sure the Agamemnon was going to topple sideways, leaving him a turtle flipped on its shell, waiting for the next hawk to come along.

Gyrostabilizers, experience, and just plain luck kept him upright and he slammed his left foot to the floor with the echoing thump of a Lambeg drum, pushing off to the left and diving for cover behind a towering column of stacked storage containers, square and grey and ordinary but each likely worth a world back home. Something smacked against his mech's left shoulder hard enough to force it forward an unsteady step, and half a ton of armor sloughed off its back, lighting up a whole quarter of the torso in yellow on his damage display.

Kuryakin spat a curse and swung around, opening up with the Agamemnon's heavy laser before he even had a target, because fusion was free and so were photons. Micro-second pulses, fired in multi-second bursts ionized a scintillating lightning bolt of plasma through the air, creating the illusion of a solid line of fire splashing over the cargo pods for the space of a meter before it ripped into the left-hand chest plastron of a Sentinel strike mech.

Armor burned away from the Sentinel in a halo of sublimating metal and the temptation was to keep firing, but Kuryakin knew better than to give in to it. He stepped backward, putting more of the cargo container between them, only catching the edge of the sunburst of plasma offered in reflexive reply. He gasped, the interior of his cockpit as breathtakingly hot as a step out from an air-conditioned shuttle into the mid-afternoon sun at high summer in the desert. The 'Memnon's upper right arm showed an insistent yellow on the damage display, one of its actuators melted to slag.

He had a sense of the battle raging around him, sights and sounds and sensor readouts filtered through a haze of heat distortion and smoke and the need to be in the moment, to shut out the war and concentrate on his personal fight. The Sentinel was following him, stepping around the edge of the cargo pod, unleashing its own lasers on him while waiting for its plasma gun's capacitors to recharge. Kuryakin felt something unspeakably hot brush his right leg, knew on an instinctive level he'd been badly hurt, knew one of the lasers had penetrated the cockpit.

He shut out the pain and the panic, ignored the flashing red alarms on the damage display and forced himself to aim the

'Memnon's main gun before he squeezed the trigger. He'd been trying for a cockpit strike and he came damned close; the Sentinel pilot had known what was coming and had stepped just a meter to his right. Instead of spearing through the cockpit, the dazzling spear of light and ionized air destroyed the Sentinel's Vulcan cannon, melting it to a twisted, smoking piece of abstract art in the space of a half-second.

I almost killed him, Kuryakin realized. He'd come after Logan Conner to take him alive, as a bargaining chip, but wasn't this place, Terminus, worth more than the son of the Guardian?

Lord Aleksandr, he reminded himself. *I will be the Supremacy Himself, and no more young men and women need die because their leader was a headstrong idiot who refused advice.*

Then, *I am close to passing out.*

The cockpit was breached and heat was pouring through the gap from the laser burn, heat from both his own weapons and the Sentinel's. He was going to stroke out if he didn't end this. He was firing everything, squeezing three controls at once, pouring 30mm cannon fire from the twin Vulcans at close range into the other mech's legs and shooting burst after burst from the laser into the Sentinel's left arm and shoulder.

The Sentinel kept coming, its armor pouring off in smoking, molten sheets, heedless of the damage, a ravening beast out of myth, inexorable, immortal. And for the first time in decades, Aleksandr Kuryakin was afraid. He knew there was a man inside the machine, hardly more than a boy, but it seemed to him the metal had come alive independent of the pilot, like some ancient statue come to life with the spirit of a demon bent on striking him down.

Through the smoke and haze and the blinding flash of lasers and burning metal, he didn't see the plasma gun until it was slammed flush against his Agamemnon's mid-section, point-blank.

He wouldn't, Kuryakin thought. *The back-blast would kill him too...*

He did.

In the end, all was fire, and light, and heat, and Lord Aleksandr the First died a forgotten man on a forgotten world.

20

Despite what he'd told Katy, it had been four years since Terry—or Terrin, before that—had held a gun. You didn't easily forget the safety rules, or how to load and check the chamber, or how to hold it, or your firing stance, but you forgot how it felt. You forgot what the kick was like, how bright the flash could be, how *loud* it sounded in a closed room. How much your hand would sweat if you held the grip too tight for too long…

The gunfire still sounded distant from the top of the ramp. He heard the faint stutter, but he couldn't see the flash, couldn't see anyone, friend or foe below him. The main entrance, the broad, open cargo doors where the Imperials had hauled the components of this ship in piece by piece so many hundred years ago, was a straight shot down the broad ramp and he saw nothing all the way to it and through it. No shooting, no running, no bodies.

He wanted to be excited about the absence, but unfortunately, he knew exactly what it meant. There was a side entrance, a smaller doorway leading back to the housing blocks and office suites. Sgt. Corgan had found it and set a guard on it before Terry and Katy had headed into the ship; it was off to the right, out of sight of the top of the ramp, but it was where the sounds of the gunfire were coming from. The research team wasn't down there either, but two of them were Navy and the other had been an independent spacer long enough to know his way around a weapon. They were probably running to the sound of guns.

He felt a sudden, irrational urge to do the same thing, but throwing himself into the path of a bullet wasn't going to win this battle. He took a step down the ramp and felt another urge, just as irrational but twice as compelling, to run back inside the ship.

It's just fight-or-flight, he assured himself, breaking into a loping jog down the slope of the ramp. *It's natural. Too bad what I'm doing now isn't.*

The slope was steeper near the end and his jog transformed into a headlong sprint, nearly out of control and certainly irreversible. Which was why there was no option but to keep running, even when he saw the three Starkad Marines creeping around the stern magnetic couplings. The mechanisms were huge, each gleaming, metal strut twenty-five meters tall and ten meters wide, holding thousands of tons of starship off the floor in their magnetic field. The grey-armored Marines were insects crawling through the engine of a ground car, hard to pick out, impossible if he hadn't been seeing them first from above.

His breath was loud in his ears, so loud it drowned out the slap of his boots on the surface of the ramp, and was surprised the Marines couldn't hear it. He was sure they hadn't seen him yet, but they would when he reached the bottom, unless they were both deaf and blind. They were at least fifty meters from the right edge of the ramp, and the control board he had to reach was another fifty to the left, up against the far wall.

Say fifteen seconds to run the fifty meters for me, not wearing armor, not carrying a rifle and a full load of gear. Maybe forty, even forty-five seconds for them to run the hundred meters. That'll give me twenty seconds to figure out how to open whatever hole in the roof the ship launches through. Unless they just shoot me from fifty meters away...

He thought he'd be more afraid of death now, having come so close to it already on this trip, but the opposite seemed to be true. The idea of being shot seemed abstract, a mathematical problem to be worked out, as if it were happening to someone else and he was just observing it. He wasn't sure if it was denial or acceptance.

He nearly stumbled as the ramp transitioned into the floor, and his teeth clacked together with a heavy, pounding step to stay on his feet. Flailing his arms wildly to stay balanced, he cut to the left and threw all his momentum into a sprint for the far wall. They'd have seen him now, but he didn't look back to make sure because knowing wouldn't change what he had to do.

The control board glowed, a beacon in the dim light, and he prayed to a God he didn't believe in that Chaisson had left it scrolled to the screen where he'd found the switch for the roof. He thought he might be able to see it even from here, but he was running as fast as he had on three seasons with his college track team and fine distinctions were lost in the exertion. His breath chuffed in violent gasps that shook his whole body and his heart was pounding out of his chest. He wasn't sure he'd even hear if those Marines started shooting at him.

He was almost surprised when he actually reached the control display, nearly ran right through it before he stumbled to a stop just shy of running into the wall. He reached up with his right hand and realized he was still holding the gun. He tucked it into his belt and touched the haptic hologram, scrolling down just a line, then back up, trying to find whatever Chaisson had been talking about.

"Get on the ground!" The call was distant, still forty or fifty meters away, but definitely directed at him. "Put your hands behind your head and get on the ground right now!"

They wanted him alive. Probably figured he was one of the technical crew and wanted to squeeze him for whatever he might have found out. That could buy him a few seconds. He ignored the order and scanned the writing beside the icons hovering in space just in front of him.

There it was. A glyph shaped like a hemisphere splitting in half, marked "egress."

Damned military, always making things too complicated. Why couldn't they just label it "open the roof?"

"Get on the ground now!"

He touched the icon.

There was a rumble, not too different from what he'd heard when the ramp rose out of the floor, and he looked up. He didn't know if he'd expected the entire roof to raise up on hinges like a giant missile silo or maybe for the whole thing to collapse on top of them in a final, spiteful cave-in. Instead, part of the carved rock ceiling above them simply...melted away. It was there one moment, solid and substantial and as real as the floor beneath him, and then it was foaming, bubbling as if it had been a frothy liquid the whole time. It evaporated without even a puff of steam, and in its place was a gap, a darkness not nearly as deep as the utter lightlessness of an unlit cavern...the darkness of a clouded night sky.

"What in the living fuck is going on here?"

Terry didn't know for certain which of the three Marines had spoken, but he assumed it was the only one of the three still looking at him. The other two were staring up at the preternatural spectacle of the vanishing roof, seemingly having forgotten he even existed. The last one, though, she still had her rifle trained on him, the muzzle a relatively small 6mm and yet gaping like the mouth of hell itself as he looked down into it.

"You!" the woman, an NCO he thought if he recognized the rank insignia correctly, barked at him, motioning with the barrel of her rifle. "Get away from there and get on your knees or I am going to put a fucking bullet in your head, no matter what the Captain said!"

Terry raised his hands, buying time, and the cold metal of the handgun stuck in his belt was chill against the skin of his stomach. The untucked edge of his fatigue blouse partially covered it and he wondered if she had noticed it yet. An insane voice whispered in his ear, telling him to make a grab for the weapon, to go down in a hail of gunfire.

You're already dead, it hissed at him. *Just get it over with.*

It even made a sort of sense in an insane way. If he let them have the time, they might be able to reverse it. He couldn't imagine how the material he'd just seen disappearing could rematerialize, but then, he'd seen the ramp rise and couldn't explain that, either.

It didn't matter, because he wouldn't delay them a half a second if he pulled the gun now. The muzzle of her rifle was only two meters away, pointed right at him, and the other two were turning away from rubbernecking at the hole where meters of rock had just been. He sighed in resignation and slowly began to sink to his knees, his heart thumping hard in his chest, his breath just beginning to come back under control after the run down the ramp. In the sudden silence of his own head, he realized it was silent everywhere; the firing from the far side of the chamber had fallen off to nothing. Sgt. Corgan, Sgt. Montanez, and the Rangers with them were likely dead.

"Get some flex cuffs on him, Gregorian," the woman snapped, apparently not realizing she'd left her helmet's external speakers active. "Then get him on the ground and search him. I'm going to see if I can close that hole back up, somehow."

Shit.

Gregorian had just shifted the weight from one foot to the other and Terry was still debating whether he could accomplish anything by dying when the screaming, whining roar sliced through the air loud enough and close enough to make even the determined sergeant spin around to look for its source. Not Terry though. He knew the source, knew it was the sound of turbines larger than an assault shuttle spinning to life, sucking in air and running it through an antimatter reactor nearly five hundred years old.

Terry didn't even come off his knees, he just made a grab for the gun. The sergeant was the only one who noticed. She tried to spin back around, bringing up her rifle, when he pulled the trigger. Spartan military-issue sidearms had no manual safety, "just the one between your ears," as his father used to say, but the trigger pull felt long and mushy and when it went off, it surprised him. He was close, far too close to miss, and he'd aimed right into the woman's faceplate, knowing instinctively her chest armor would stop the bullet.

He didn't hear the gun go off, definitely didn't intend to fire again and was shocked when it kicked a second time into the web of his hand. The Starkad Marine NCO stumbled backwards, the inside of her faceplate suddenly smeared with something dark and liquid. He didn't watch her fall, though he could sense it; instead, he turned to Gregorian. It was harder. Gregorian had a name. Did he have a wife, a child? Parents who'd miss him?

He definitely had a rifle and the intent to use it. Terry shot him in the face. Gregorian spun away, gone from sight and perception into the tunnel-vision view where adrenaline had squeezed all his perceptions. He was making a mistake. He knew it in his gut but his brain seemed to have slowed down along with his perception and it took him all of a second to remember there was one more, to realize he was never going to be able to get the last of them in time. Inertia dragged at him, quicksand around his mind, slowing down decisions and actions and all he could think to do was fall.

An explosion of rifle fire blasted over his head, the tantalum slugs ripping through the space where his chest had been a half-second before. The flash of light, the thunderclap of sound and the solid impact of the floor between his shoulder blades shocked him into motion and he rolled off to one side, trying to gain distance and time so he could get to his feet.

Then getting to his feet was no longer a possibility.

He should have known it was coming, should have realized what would happen when a ship that size blasted out of the chamber, but the overpressure hit like a hammer in the back of the head, spinning him across the ground to slam against the wall. He couldn't see what had happened to the Marine, didn't even care enough to try to look. He had seconds to live unless he moved.

Later, he wouldn't remember actually clawing his way across the wall, wouldn't remember anything until he was in the tunnel and running and felt nothing but raging heat at his back and there was the control panel he remembered on the other side of the doorway. Nothing complicated, no haptic holograms, just a pair of large physical buttons, one red, the other green. He slapped the red one with a hand already beginning to blister and held it until the massive, metal door slid all the way down from its recess in the ceiling and cut off the source of his pain.

He staggered in sudden darkness, smelling something burning and realizing it was him.

I'm going to fall over.

He used the last of his consciousness to collapse to his backside, his shoulder hitting the wall and sliding down into blackness.

"Ahriman drag you bastards to hell!"

Pasquale Jeffries crouched behind the blast barrier, cursing inside his helmet as loud as he could and still barely able to hear it over the ear-splitting roar of victory slipping away. He'd had them, he'd had the Spartans right where he wanted them, he'd known it the second they'd reached the Imperial ship before their armored forces had arrived. All he'd needed to do was get the entrances secure and he could have held them off until the *Valkyrian* finished off that piece of shit cargo hauler and came back with some orbital fire support.

Then the fucking roof disappeared and it all went to shit.

It could have been a lot worse if the blast barriers hadn't been there, curving metal barriers centimeters thick and three meters high meant to shield what looked to be some sort of monitoring stations from the ship's exhaust. What was left of his people were sheltered behind them, along with the three technicians they'd captured. The Rangers...well, they were enjoying a Viking funeral on the other side of the barrier, along with the six of his Marines they'd manage to take with them.

"Captain," Top asked him with the annoying regularity of a bad case of venereal disease, "if I may be frank, what the fuck do you think we're gonna do now?"

He leaned forward and stared daggers at the First Sergeant, tucked in behind the shield about ten meters away, where it curved into the far wall. He had the Spartan captives over there with him and even though Jeffries couldn't see the man's face, he had this sense Top was holding onto them as leverage against him.

Still, it wasn't a bad question. He needed a plan, a way to get them out of this. Or at least a way to get *him* out of this. It also helped him to realize the roaring had gone...and with it, of course, the ship he'd come up here to seize. He wanted to go around the blast shield and have a look, but he knew the heat would still be enough to cook him even through his armor. You didn't lift something as massive as that ship off the ground without generating a shitload of heat and it would take a while for enough of it to radiate out through the hole in the roof to make the chamber passable again.

The cargo entrance was out of the question anyway, even if he could have seen it. The armored forces would be coming from there, which would be fine if it was theirs, not so good if it was the Spartans.

"We're heading back down the stairs," he decided. "We'll head back out with our prisoners to one of the drop-ships." *One of the drop-ships that* hadn't *been blown to hell.* "Once we're up there, we can communicate the situation to the *Valkyrian* and get instructions."

We can communicate it to them while we're blasting off this fucking planet, he amended privately. He didn't care what that fucking tight-ass Navy captain said, they were off this rock.

"Arsenault, get out on point."

"I'm down most of a fire team, Captain," the man reminded him, more sullen and less gung-ho than he'd been on the way into this battle. He hadn't moved to leave his protected position behind the blast shield.

"Reorganize into a single team, then," he snapped at the man, "and get out on point."

"What about the dead?" the NCO demanded with less deference than Jeffries would have liked. "Are we just leaving them here?"

He nearly put a round through the man's head but managed to control himself. Wouldn't want to give Top any reason to turn on him. Arsenault didn't have many friends in the company, but Top held the loyalty of the NCOs.

"We'll retrieve the bodies when we come back with reinforcements," he ground out, not happy about explaining himself. "Our priority right now is getting the enemy technicians back for interrogation. Now move the hell out."

"Yes, sir," Arsenault grunted, pushing himself to his feet with the butt of his rifle, waving at what was left of his people to follow.

One of the Spartan Rangers was sprawled halfway through the doorway to the stairwell, alongside two of Arsenault's squad he'd taken with him to the afterlife. Arsenault hesitated for just a beat as he passed by them, but Jeffries ignored them. He'd seen dead men and women before and one looked about the same as another. His only interest was in not becoming one himself and he debated for a long second whether he should let Top go ahead of him. He wouldn't put it past the fucker to frag him out here, where he thought he could get away with it.

No, I'm better off being up front, where I can react quicker and get out first. Plus, I look like I have balls, which will impress the troops and make it harder for Top to get away with defying me.

Military politics were complicated. Sometimes he thought he should have listened to his father and gone into the shipping business, married his old girlfriend from college, settled down and raised a family. But then he'd never get to kill anyone. Life was full of trade-offs. Like these damned stairs, dark and narrow and claustrophobic, but at least he didn't have to worry about anyone sneaking up behind him, not with most of two platoons tromping along back there.

He snuck a look back, saw Top dogging his heels, the Spartan prisoners close by, each with a Marine holding fast to their bound wrists. The enemy techs were beat up a bit, but they'd live to get their brains squeezed out with truth drugs and spend the rest of their days in a top-secret Starkad Military Intelligence black site. He might still get a medal for that, even if he'd let the Spartans get away with the ship. Not a promotion, but a medal, maybe a commendation...

They were nearly at the bottom of the stairwell and he was still debating whether the commendation would be enough to get him a post closer to the capital when something happened, something bright and loud and too close, and he found himself flat on his back on the stairs, not quite remembering how he'd got there. His vision was awash with stars and apparently someone had been beating on him with a baseball bat, because he hurt everywhere.

There had been an explosion...no, there had been *two* explosions. Out in front, where Arsenault had been walking point with what was left of his squad, and another behind them, at the back of the column. The memory of the double-thunderclap of sound seemed distant, something he'd experienced the last time he was on leave rather than a few seconds ago. Mines, he realized. Antipersonnel mines planted on the stairs, not aimed straight up the column or he'd be dead—the Spartans had oriented them crosswise, to take out the lead and trailing elements and knock the others down from the blast funneled up the stairwell.

Concussion. I've got a concussion.

What else? He patted at himself and found no rips or tears in his armor, but when he held his gloves up in front of his face to check for blood, he couldn't see his hands. His night-vision was out and so were his external speakers. His helmet was damaged. He knew he shouldn't have taken it off, but he felt a pressing need to see, to hear. He worked the neck yoke awkwardly with numb fingers, then twisted the helmet centimeters to the side to unlock it before yanking it off his head.

He still couldn't see shit in the utter darkness, but he could hear gunshots, suppressed but still loud inside the echoing confines of the stairwell. He heard muffled screams and footsteps, but still saw nothing. He was lying on top of his rifle and he tried to roll off of it, tried to work it free, but something hard stamped down on his hand and he yelped.

"Don't move."

The voice was familiar, even distorted through the external speakers of a helmet. He couldn't remember where he'd heard it, but he knew the deep, raspy yet unmistakably female voice from somewhere. She chuckled, an unpleasant sound, lacking any humor he'd appreciate.

"Well, if it isn't Captain Jeffries, Pasqual R. Guess I was right when I said I'd be seeing you, but you wouldn't be seeing me."

"Randell," he recalled. He settled back, knowing the muzzle of a rifle had to be pointed at him. "Hey, you know, we can work something out. I know stuff, I could be a valuable prisoner…"

"I'm sure you'd be a wonderful prisoner," she interrupted him. "Unfortunately, this is a covert-ops mission. You aren't here, we aren't here, and we *certainly* didn't engage in open combat with forces of the Starkad military. So, I'm afraid there wasn't anyone around to take you prisoner, Pasquale." She sighed with affected sadness. "If I had to guess, I'd say you died in a training incident."

Finally, there was light in the darkness, a flash of it right between his eyes that lasted the rest of his life.

21

K athren Margolis was riding a mountain into space.

It roared and strained, and spewed energy at a rate she couldn't even have imagined, but somehow, impossibly, something the size of a city block rose slowly into the night sky on columns of fire bright enough to light up the clouds for kilometers around it. She was guiding its flight, though she wasn't sure how and had decided it was best not to think about it too hard. She'd heard a story once about someone asking a centipede how it kept from tripping over its own feet; it had thought too hard about the question and wasn't able to walk again afterward.

She just kept her eyes on the display where she could still see the *Shakak* and the *Valkyrie* entangled in a fight to the death and concentrated on wanting to be there. And tried not to give voice to her doubts and fears, to the knowledge she was all alone on the ancient ship, to the worry the limited antimatter fuel remaining wouldn't last, or the very real fear she wouldn't be in time.

That one was harder to ignore. She could see the damage to the *Shakak*, could see the atmosphere venting in flares of burning oxygen through the huge rents in the hull. There was a ball of lead inside her gut, a sickening knot of terror not just at the question of how any of the crew could have lived through so much damage but also at the memory of Terry running out through the bridge hatchway with her gun to open the roof, at the realization Jonathan was back there, fighting for his life against a force twice his size. She knew she was doing the right thing, knew she'd left them so she could do her job, but that didn't make it any easier.

Clouds glowed with fire and burnt away to glowing stars, but the merciless mistress acceleration still punished her for the hubris of daring to fly into space. The gee forces didn't bother her, weren't even close to what she experienced piloting an assault shuttle.

Just get me there faster, you old-ass piece of crap!

She hadn't meant the statement as a command, hadn't meant anything by it but a fervent wish. The ship had other ideas. She'd expected the thrusters to switch from turbojet air intakes to on-board reaction mass once the ship cleared the atmosphere, just a brief interruption in thrust during the transition. Instead, the anti-matter drive cut off completely, leaving her in free-fall…but the tactical display showed the ship still accelerating, not at a just-barely-tolerable eight gees, but an impossible one hundred gravities.

The Imperial ship was already moving at sixty kilometers a *second* and still accelerating, somehow without a bit of gee force. She tried not to let the shock take over her thoughts, tried to keep doing whatever was making the ship speed up. She knew what it was, had known it was there before she boarded the ship, but to see it in action was like stepping back in time. It was the Alanson-McCleary stardrive, one of the lost arts of the Empire of Hellas they'd come to Terminus to retrieve. She'd just thought there'd be some special control, or alarms would go off, or she'd have to chant some weird magical incantation to make it work.

Instead, it just worked, the way you'd expect a military ship to work; and if she kept accelerating and the fuel held out, it would take her all the way past lightspeed and into another reality. For the moment, though, it was going to take her to a rendezvous with the Starkad heavy cruiser *Valkyrian* in less than five minutes, which meant she had exactly that long to figure out how the ship's weapons systems worked.

"We're losing hull integrity in section 39," Norris announced, sounding almost bored with the announcements. In fairness, he'd had to deliver the bad news every few minutes for the last hour. "Burn-throughs in decks three and four and I think I'm seeing a power fluctuation to the deflectors."

"Rotate the hull 180 degrees," Donner Osceola ordered. The words were automatic, rote habit, lacking any of the anger or outrage or deep sadness they might have contained at the beginning of the battle. "Take us back to four gees."

He'd been trapped inside his helmet so long that he almost felt as if he were talking to himself. The visor gave him tunnel vision and he didn't dare try to look aside to Kammy's station under emergency acceleration. For all he knew, his entire crew was Tara Gerard, his entire ship her tactical station directly in front of his. Certainly, the outside world might have not existed for all the forward screens told him. The last of the external cameras had been burned away twenty minutes ago and the clearest view the ship's tactical computer could give him was a two-dimensional animated simulation based on lidar. And it was depressing enough he didn't really *want* to see the optical view.

Here on the bridge, buried deep inside the ship, he could almost pretend this was a training simulation from back in his Navy days. The *Shakak* was falling apart around them, but here on the bridge, they might as well have been light years away in another system.

"We ain't gonna be able to keep up that burn for long, boss," Kammy told him. There was weariness in his voice, from the constant high-gee burns and from the stress of the losing battle. "We've lost the feed to fuel tank three, and one's burned dry. We're down to ten percent metallic hydrogen in tank two." The big man paused, breath hissing out with resignation. "We're just about done."

Osceola didn't respond, half because there was no real argument to make and half because he lacked the energy to make it. He felt a vibration through the hull, a stuttering bump he knew was the maneuvering thrusters turning the hull to expose a less-damaged section to the fury of the *Valkyrian's* laser batteries. It was a stop-gap measure, buying minutes by giving the Starkad heavy cruiser new bits of them to blow up. She was hanging just a couple thousand kilometers off their flank, matching velocities as pretty as you please, as if she were about to dock.

"Do we have anything left to shoot at them, Tara?" he wondered, his voice a dolorous rasp.

"Railgun's down," the woman ticked off, grunting in the middle of the sentence when Kammy activated the four-gee burn Osceola had ordered. "Primary laser battery is down. Hell, even the point-defense guns are down. I suppose I could stand in one of the hull burn-throughs and shoot a pistol at 'em."

"Kammy, try to put our drive towards them, get our plasma stream between us and their lasers."

"Roger that, boss. Brace for maneuvering..."

"Shit!" Tara snapped, fear infusing her voice with energy it had lacked a moment ago. "They've fired their railguns..."

Her terror was infectious and was almost welcome compared to the apathy Osceola had fallen into, but he'd barely had time to savor the sudden emotion when he heard it. He shouldn't have been able to hear anything. There was no air on the bridge to carry the sound, but he could feel the vibration through his acceleration couch, carried up through the deck from the hull for just the barest fraction of a second. Before his battered brain could process what was happening, there was heat and light and he was spinning through space.

Wait. Hadn't he been strapped in? Yes, he was *still* strapped in, but the acceleration couch had come unmoored and *it* was spinning across what was left of the bridge. Sparks and blackness and clouds of debris spun by him, a kaleidoscope of meaningless images until the seat assembly fetched up against the forward display screen and a painful, sharp impact robbed him of his rotational motion. And everything became clear, along with the reason for the screaming in his helmet headphones.

The bridge was deep inside the ship, but not deep enough. The rear quarter of the compartment wasn't there anymore. There was a gap in the heavy double-bulkhead, the radiation shields and insulation between the bridge and the compartments surrounding it torn and ragged, the edges glowing white from the kinetic energy of the two-meter-long tungsten dart. It had passed through, likely all the way into their reactor room since the ship had stopped boosting as well.

Norris wasn't going to be listing off the damage report from this hit. He and Ortiz were gone, obliterated along with their control stations. If there was anything left of them, it had been sucked away through the gaps in the hull. Tara was still at Tactical, and Tactical was still where it should be as well, though the controls were dead, the screens dark. The light panels were down, and only the pale glow of the emergency chemical light-strips shown in the dim, smoke-filled compartment.

Kammy…where was Kammy? The helm was still there, but his acceleration couch was empty. His eyes seemed to come into focus just ahead of him and he realized the big man was looming over him, his rounded, open face visible through the visor of his helmet. He seemed worried, and Osceola couldn't blame him for that. They had no weapons, no defense, no power, and now no control. They were dead. He tried to say something, tried to say goodbye to his old friend, but for some reason he couldn't talk. Breathing wasn't coming so easy either, and he gradually came to notice something at the very bottom edge of his view, something dark standing out from his chest, too close to focus his eyes on.

"Boss," Kammy was saying, his voice sounding distorted and tinny over his helmet radio. Or maybe it was his own senses that were the problem, not the helmet speakers. "You got a metal strut through your chest. You gotta' be still, I'm gonna get you to the med bay."

What difference does it make? He was thinking it and would have said it, if it hadn't been for the collapsed lung, the blood coming up in his throat. *We're all going to be dead in minutes anyway...*

"*Shakak!*" The voice in his headphones was urgent, insistent...and familiar. Was he hallucinating? "*Shakak*, this is Margolis! Hang on, I'm coming..."

At least I figured out how to use the damned radio.

Everything seemed to work instinctively, the way a mech's neural helmet did, except deeper and more intricately. It wasn't enough to just think about something, though, you had to *intend* to do it, which involved a combination of simultaneous concentration and confident relaxation she was having a hard time mastering. You couldn't merely think "I want to radio the *Shakak* on this frequency," you had to have a kind of certainty it would happen, the way you knew your fingers would wiggle if you told them to.

At least she was sure the *Valkyrian* had noticed her; the Starkad heavy cruiser had broken off from its attack run on the *Shakak* and began to align its weapons with her ship. Of course, she reflected bitterly, there wasn't much left the Supremacy ship could do to the *Shakak*. The ship was dead in space, drifting on her momentum, holed in a dozen places. If there was anyone left alive inside, they had hours to live at most.

She hadn't realized she'd ordered the ship to slow, yet it had...and it did not, as far as she could tell, require deceleration. It had matched velocities with the *Valkyrian* without reversing direction, without having to perform a braking burn. It made sense——she recalled reading speculation the stardrive worked on the fabric of spacetime the same way a boat propeller worked on water, contracting it and expanding it to move the ship, so there were no Newtonian laws to deal with.

Of course, matching velocities with the *Valkyrian* meant she was putting herself into firing range of the heavy cruiser's weapons...

She knew the laser pulses weren't in the optical spectrum and wouldn't have been visible outside the atmosphere either way, but the simulation in the ship's holographic display was so real, so lifelike she nearly ducked away from the scintillating red flashes, raising her arm involuntarily as a shield. The lasers...*bent*. There was no other way to describe it. The pulses of light twisted away like ribbons in the wind and she knew it was because the very spacetime they were ... traveling through had been bent out of shape by the stardrive.

They couldn't hurt her, but she couldn't let them get away to tell Starkad about this place. She lashed out at the Supremacy ship, striking out at it with the confidence of a punch to the face. And when it happened, she wasn't surprised. She couldn't be sure if the actinic bolt of lightning striking across the thousands of kilometers between her ship and the cruiser was actually visible or simply a simulation, but its effects were unmistakably real. Where it touched the *Valkyrian*'s skin, just aft of center, the armor split, burned, and vaporized, a halo of burning gas spreading out from the strike to surround the upper hull.

She wasn't certain if the beam was constant or pulsing so rapidly it just seemed that way, but it kept firing as if inspired by her desperation. It sliced backwards through the *Valkyrian's* hull as if the armor were wrapping paper, as if the deflectors weren't there, and when it touched the ship's metallic hydrogen fuel stores, the entire cruiser disappeared in a circular globe of fusion fire, a miniature sun shining in the darkness.

Katy's mouth opened in shock and the beam finally cut off. She drifted and so did the Imperial ship, rocked with disbelief and unsure what to do next. It was a transmission over the bridge speakers that woke her from her fugue.

"Katy, is that you?" It was Kammy, and she hissed out a prayer of gratitude the big teddy-bear had made it. And the prayer had gone, to her surprise, to her parents' God, the Father, Son, and Holy Spirit, rather than Mithra. "Katy, if you're there, we need help. The Captain's hurt...bad. And we have other wounded, too. You've got to get us back to Terminus."

"Oh, great," she breathed. "Now they expect me to land this damned thing..."

22

J onathan woke up.

He hadn't expected to. The last thing he'd had time to think was that this was as good a way to die as any, and probably overdue.

Is this the afterlife? He'd expected the bridge, and the final test of his worth, the balance of his deeds, though in honesty, he wasn't entirely sure which way the balance might have tilted. Instead, there were far-off voices and a certain stuffiness that wasn't quite comfortable enough for Heaven nor unpleasant enough for Hell.

There was a hiss of equalizing pressures and the voices were louder and the light behind his eyelids was brighter and it was *so* damned cold! His eyes blinked open and he shivered, hugging his arms to his chest and realizing with a start that he was naked as the day he was born.

His brother was standing over him, grinning like an idiot, his hair uncharacteristically short, as if he'd just had it buzzed.

"What the hell?" Jonathan blurted. *No, fuck it, this shit is over. I'm not Jonathan Slaughter anymore, I'm Logan Conner.* "Terry? Where am I? What happened?"

He was, he saw as his head and eyes began to clear, sitting upright in some sort of coffin-shaped pod, its surface clear but tinted dark, its curved lid hanging open beside him. The pod was just one in a room full of them, most of them open but a few shut tight. A few Rangers he recognized as trained medics were huddled with the medical team from the *Shakak*, both Osceola's crew and the Navy doctors they'd brought along, discussing something in hushed tones over one of the haptic holographic control panels Terminus seemed to be rife with.

"Take it easy, bro," Terry told him, clapping a hand on his arm. Terry was wearing some sort of dark utility fatigues instead of the civilian clothes he'd last seen him in, which also seemed strange combined with the haircut. "You've been out a while. Here." He had a bundle in his other hand, what looked to be the same dark grey clothing he was wearing. "We couldn't save your skinsuit, and all the clothes you brought with you got sucked into space."

Logan took the clothes, staring at them in utter confusion, squeezing his eyes shut for a moment just to try to organize his memories.

"The mech," he said, seizing on the last thing he remembered. "I was fighting that Agamemnon and..."

"I'm not a mechjock or anything, but I think a contact shot with a plasma gun is contraindicated by doctrine."

Logan turned inside the cabinet at the female voice coming from behind him, his legs coming halfway out before he remembered he was naked. It was Katy, and despite everything, he had to smile. She looked tired, overworked and a bit haggard with lack of sleep, but she was here and alive and the most beautiful woman he'd ever seen.

"Oh, Mithra's horns, I am so glad you're all right," he told her. There was a hint of pain in her eyes when she leaned in to kiss him, as if she'd been the one not expecting to see him. But she leaned her forehead against his and he could feel relief radiating off her, a weight lifted from her shoulders.

"What the hell *were* you thinking, brother?" Terry asked him, leaning against the side of the pod, shaking his head.

"I was thinking Colonel Kuryakin was the only thing keeping their forces from panicking," he said with more annoyance in his tone than he actually felt, shaking out the pants from the set of fatigues Terry had given him and trying to pull them on inside the pod. "But shouldn't I be dead? I seem to remember thinking when I pulled that trigger, I was going to die right next to that Colonel Kuryakin."

He fastened the waistband of the pants and hopped out of the pod, then had to lean against Katy when the room began to spin.

"Whoa there, sir!" one of the Ranger medics rushed in, taking his arm and holding him up. He was a big man, a head taller than Logan and a full twenty kilograms heavier, all of it muscle. "These things sort of drain your blood sugar. Try to get something to eat before you do anything too strenuous."

"These things," he repeated, finding his balance and straightening up, Katy still holding on to his other arm, having grabbed the fatigue shirt before he could drop it. "What things?"

"It's a long story," Terry said, pinching his fingers against the bridge of his nose, suddenly looking as tired as Katy. "These are what the Imperials called 'auto-docs,' some sort of medical repair pod. We think it uses nanotechnology, but otherwise we have no idea how it works."

Katy was helping him slip the shirt on, but he paused with it halfway onto one arm, eyes going wide, looking between the two of them.

"And you tested it on me?"

"Sir...," the Ranger medic began, in antiphonal chorus with Katy and Terry saying "Jonathan..."

"Fuck Jonathan," he cut them off with a slash of his hand.

"No more Jonathan. I'm Logan. Captain Conner," he added as an aside to the NCO. "And you're Terrin," he added to his brother.

"I've kind of gotten used to Terry," his brother admitted, shrugging.

"Logan," Katy interrupted, gently turning his face toward hers, and once again he could see the pain in her eyes. "You were dying."

The words seemed to wring themselves out of her, which shocked him. She was so forthright, so brutally honest, but this hurt her to talk about. He felt a sudden pang of guilt for putting her through it.

"You were really fucked up, sir," the medic agreed, his rugged face bleak with the memory. Sgt. Campion was his name, Logan recalled. "Third degree burns on sixty percent of your body. Out here, with just field surgery available, we'd have had to amputate your legs at the knees, and it's a fifty-fifty shot you'd have even been a candidate for cloned tissue transplants later as bad as your nerve endings were fried."

"Shit." The word went out of him with a breath, taking the strength in his legs with it and he nearly stumbled again. "Okay, I got it. Have you been able to use them on the rest of our wounded?"

"Yes, thank God," Katy said, finishing pulling his shirt on. "Otherwise, we'd have lost about half the crew of the *Shakak*. Even though it wasn't in time for..."

She winced, blinked as if something was in her eye.

"In time for who?" he wanted to know. He shook his head, pulling away from her and Sgt. Campion. "Can someone tell me what exactly happened?"

Kamehameha-Nui Johannsen gnawed half-heartedly at the protein bar for a few more seconds before tossing it down on the wrapping he'd spread out like a plate on the table. The mess hall was deserted but for him, the lights obscenely bright, like the waiting room of a hospital. He'd always hated hospitals, whether it was the little clinic back home or one of the giant medical centers in Argos or one of the other Dominion capitals. Hospitals reminded him of where his mother had died. He should have gone to visit Jonathan to see how he was doing, but the little med-lab reminded him too much of that hospital.

"You should eat that."

He didn't look up at Lyta's entrance. He'd heard her footsteps and recognized the pace. She walked like a cat, every step intentional and balanced.

"I'm not hungry," he said, staring at the unappealing lump of brown nutrients. "And even if I were, this sucks."

"Get used to it. It's all we're going to have until we get back to settled space."

She slipped into the chair beside him. The chairs, the tables, they were so much like what people still used, despite the centuries and the advanced technology. Maybe people just liked to hang onto home-like things.

He finally met her eyes. She looked older, he thought. She *was* older than the first time they'd met, of course, but somehow, he hadn't noticed it before. Just a few thin cracks around her eyes, where she'd squinted into so many alien suns, a few more around her mouth where she scowled far too much.

"How's the ship coming?" he asked her, changing the subject, hopefully steering it away from what he knew she'd come to talk about.

She cocked an eyebrow, knowing what he was doing but, thankfully, letting him get away with it.

"Slowly," she admitted. "We don't have much in the way of an engineering staff, though the fact everything is basically plug-

and-play with the Imperial ship has helped." She sniffed, not quite a chuckle because there was no humor in the words. "It's a good thing Lt. Cordray was able to get that drop-ship up to rendezvous with Katy in orbit, because if she'd landed the thing, we'd never have gotten it off the ground again. The antimatter fuel stores were totally spent."

"Who you got working on it?" he asked, curious in spite of himself.

"The drop-ship crews, what's left of Engineering…including Terry, about half the time, but right now he's down here on base since they called and told him Jonathan was awake. Also, the mech salvage and repair crews." She paused, eyeing him meaningfully. "They could use your help."

"I'm not a nuts-n-bolts kind of guy," Kammy demurred, shaking his head. "Especially when it comes to trying to bang together fusion reactors with shit from five hundred years ago. You really think it's going to work?"

"I think it's going to be a lot easier trying to replace the antimatter reactor on the Imperial ship with the fusion reactor from the *Shakak* than it would be to patch all the wholes in your hull and re-route the main power trunk."

"That stardrive isn't going to work without the power from the antimatter, is it?" He was dubious, though he didn't know if he had a right to be, given he'd just admitted he wasn't a technician.

"I'm not an engineer," Lyta qualified, "but from what Terry's been telling me, he thinks he can get it to run at a much lower efficiency. Not enough to boost at a hundred gravities and run us faster than light, but enough to get by as a sub-light engine to get us to the jump points."

"Can it even use jump points?" he asked, surprised.

"Apparently. Don't ask me how, Terry's the genius and even he has a hard time explaining the mechanics of it, but you can use the stardrive to access the jump-points just like a Kadish-Dean field generator." She paused and he could feel her staring at him even though he was studying the blank surface of he table. "The ship's going to need a captain, Kammy."

He glanced up sharply, shock and then anger running through him in quick succession before the overwhelming sadness beat them both out by its weight and persistence.

"Get someone else, Lyta," he told her. "I'm not a captain. I just drive the boat."

"You were his First Mate," she reminded Kammy, gently chiding. "He trusted you to have his back. He'd want you to take us home."

"I should tell you to go to hell." He smiled, or as much of a smile as he could muster. It felt like trying to move during a high-gee acceleration…but he'd done that, too. "But he loved you."

"And I loved him." Lyta Randell was as hard as a starship hull, but a tear was trailing down her cheek and she let it make its way down the unfamiliar territory, either not aware it was there or not ashamed of it if she was. "But he died doing something he believed in, and I think he'd want you to see it through to the end."

Kammy nodded, both in agreement and in resignation.

"All, right, *ho'onani.* I couldn't say no to you any more than the Captain could. I just hope they'll remember him."

"He'll have a star on the wall of heroes in Argos," she promised, finally wiping at her eyes. "I'll put it there myself."

23

S now crunched under Logan's boots and he pulled his jacket tighter against the morning chill, struggling to keep up with his father's long-legged strides down the old path. A gust of wind blew a shower of sparkling flakes out of the line of balsam firs lining the edge of the property and he brushed them off his neck before they could melt their way down his back. Fifteen meters tall, the firs hid the rustic lines of the family home, and hid them from anyone who might be passing by on the road. Beyond the gentle impact of their footsteps, the morning calls of winter birds were the only sounds.

"Why did you have me fly out here, Dad?" he asked, wincing at his own voice, loud and intrusive out here in the rural stillness of mid-winter. "I thought I'd just report to the palace."

"Too many prying eyes at the palace," his father tossed back over his shoulder, still walking.

The path, a dirt road when it wasn't covered in half a meter of snow, led from the old barn out through a forest of spruce and fir and bare, threatening oaks all the way out to the ponds. They'd been watering holes back when the place had been a ranch, but

Logan's great-grandfather had sold the stock off decades ago, and he'd never even seen a cow or bison or aurochs out here.

Jaimie Brannigan stopped at the edge of the biggest of the ponds, hands tucked into the pockets of his leather greatcoat, staring at the thin film of ice and snow on the surface as if he were considering whether it would hold his weight.

"I used to take you hunting out here in the fall," he said, the cold turning his breath into a fog blowing backwards across his beard in the breeze. "You remember?" A glance backward with the words, the big man's eyes soft with the recollection. "We'd take our fill of deer and elk. You even bagged that moose once."

Logan laughed softly, thinking of how much work it had been to gut and skin that damned moose…

"You remember," he asked his father, "that time we heard the rumors about a mastodon straying down here from the plains in the north and I made you come out here with me every day for two weeks to see if we could bag it?"

Jaimie Brannigan rumbled a low chuckle and he squeezed his son's shoulder in a one-armed embrace.

"I could never get Terrin interested in hunting." The big man sighed his lament. "Lord knows I tried. But he always thought it was more efficient to let others kill for his meat so he could stick to his strengths."

"Thank Mithra he did," Logan said fervently. "We'd all be dead without him…and Katy."

"And I wish your brother and your…" His father cocked an eyebrow questioningly. "Girlfriend? Fiancé?"

"Oh, Horns of God, father, that is a complicated question." The words had come out in a moan and a memory of a long and ultimately pointless argument. "Probably best discussed some other time."

"Well then," the Guardian went on, waving a hand in acquiescence, "I wish your brother and Commander Margolis were here to receive my thanks and congratulations in person."

"That's Lieutenant...," Logan corrected him automatically, then paused, seeing the glint in his father's eyes. "Wow."

"Indeed. We may not be able to hand out medals at a ceremony, but as the head of the Spartan military, I can and most certainly will issue promotions. Including yours, Colonel."

"Fuck!" Logan blurted, unable to hold the exclamation inside, his eyes bugging wide. "Colonel? What the hell, Dad? What happened to Major? You know what this is going to look like..."

"Like I am showing nepotism." Jaimie Brannigan held up a palm to halt his son's rant. "Calm yourself. There's a reason, and I promise to make it clear, soon. First though, I need some details and I had no wish to get them through channels." His mouth twisted in distaste. "And I didn't wish to have to ask General Constantine. Where is the ship now?"

"In the Aubergine system, at a drydock facility around the moon of the gas giant there. It's a secret Military Intelligence base, pretty remote." He chuckled maliciously. "We didn't even stop to ask for clearance when we blew through the Starkad systems on the way back. Without a fusion drive flare, they couldn't even see us. We didn't get off the drop-ships there at Aubergine, just left Terry and Katy and the engineering crew with the ship and transferred over with all our mecha and equipment to a Q-ship heading in to Clan Modi space, to Gujarat. We left the equipment with the Q-ship to take on in for refitting and the rest of us chartered berths on a corporate cargo hauler back into the Guardianship."

"Good tradecraft," his father said, nodding approval. "Lyta's work, I assume."

"Of course. I'm not a spy, as I've been reminded." *At least not a good one.*

"Now the bad news," Jaimie Brannigan prompted, motioning

for him to go on. "Come on, I've read the technical data your brother put in his report, but I want it in layman's terms from you."

"I wouldn't call it bad news," he protested, but then shrugged. "It's going to take a while, Dad. Reverse-engineering the weapons, the armor, Terry thinks we can do that in a few years, max. But those are just incremental improvements. Most of the really revolutionary stuff requires antimatter power, and we are not even close to producing it in quantity or being able to store it safely anywhere outside a laboratory."

"But the ship works." His father was staring out across the pond again, dipping beneath the frozen surface of his own thoughts.

"Yeah. It's not as fast as it would be with antimatter power, and the shields can't take quite as much of a pounding, and the weapons are only about half their normal effectiveness, but it works." Logan blew out a breath of frustration. "And in another ten years, we might be able to build another one just like it, if we can figure out how to manufacture the exotic elements in its drive core."

"It's a tool, son." His father's words were gently chiding. "In the military, we use the tools we have."

"Use it for what? Sir?" he added, sensing the conversation had taken a turn into something official.

"You asked how I could get away with promoting you to colonel without seeming as if I were engaging in nepotism. And I'll tell you how: because no one will know. I'm going to give you the greatest reward a military officer can receive for a job well done: another, even harder job."

"Father," Logan said slowly and carefully, "are you saying…"

"What I am saying, son," Jaimie Brannigan interrupted him, "is this isn't the end for Wholesale Slaughter." He grinned, as if he were getting used to the name. "It's only the beginning."

EPILOGUE

Heinrich Brunner slung the twenty-kilogram sack of rice over his shoulder, grunting involuntarily and bending his knees against the weight. It wasn't quite as much here as it would have been on his homeworld back in the Supremacy, but neither was it insubstantial, and for the hundredth time in as many days, he wished he could afford a powerloader. Or an elevator.

But Guajarat wasn't a world where powerloaders could be bought by every small-time restaurant owner, and Nashik wasn't a city where those restaurants were modern buildings with convenient freight elevators. And lunch was in two hours. He leaned into his load and the wooden steps up from the cellar storage room creaked under the combined weight of 120 kilograms of man and rice.

The dim light of the cellar gave way to the mid-morning glow through the rice-paper windows of the dining room and he kept his head down, trying not to let the sunlight dazzle his eyes before he stepped through to the kitchen. He stopped midway between the cellar and the kitchen. There was a shadow stretching out across the floor, a shadow he'd not seen in the five years he had run this place, in the five years he'd made the trip up from the cellar twice a day, every day.

He moved quickly for a man his size, ducking out from under the weight of the sack of rice and sweeping the curved blade of the karambit out of the sheath at the back of his belt, turning... and staring into the barrel of a gun. He couldn't see past the muzzle, couldn't see beyond a silhouette until the short, slender shape moved forward, just slightly, enough for the light to come in from the side instead of behind.

She was wearing a cloak of dark grey, the hood covering most of her face, and the only way he could tell it was a woman was the hand wrapped around the butt of the gun. It might have been delicate once, but he could see a keloid burn scar running up the sleeve of her robe, months old at most, and untreated.

"I don't keep any cash on hand before business hours," he warned her, letting the knife dangle by its loop from his little finger.

"I don't want your money. I want passage back to the Supremacy."

His lips skinned back from his teeth in a feral snarl, the knife swinging back into his palm.

"I don't know what the fuck you're talking about."

"Your commitment to your cover is commendable, Agent Brunner," she told him, her tone strained and desperate but with something beneath, an undertone of hesitance and officiousness. "But also unnecessary." She paused as if trying to make sure she recalled something exactly. "What is the most direct route to the city's central bank?"

"Main Street," he responded automatically, then scowled, beginning to relax. "You know, the point of a passphrase is that you can use it casually in a conversation without everyone knowing what you're saying. All this," he waved at her gun with his knife, "kind of defeats the purpose, don't you think?"

"Sorry," she mumbled, her voice muffled by the folds of the hood. She shoved the handgun back into her belt beneath the robes. "I'm afraid I'm new at this."

"All right," he said, slipping the karambit back into its sheath and waving her forward. "Let's get on with it. Who are you, and how did you get here?"

She pulled back the hood as she approached and he stifled a curse at the hideous network of burn scars running red and livid across the right side of her face, the empty socket where her right eye used to be. Her hair had been burned away along with the skin and she'd shaved the other side to match, but he could tell by the untouched half of her face she'd been pretty, once.

"I'm Captain Ruth Laurent," she told him. "And as for how I got here...it's a long story."

FROM THE PUBLISHER

Thank you for reading *Terminus Cut,* book two in Wholesale Slaughter.

W e hope you enjoyed it as much as we enjoyed bringing it to you. We just wanted to take a moment to encourage you to review the book on Amazon and Goodreads. Every review helps further the author's reach and, ultimately, helps them continue writing fantastic books for us all to enjoy.

If you liked *Terminus Cut*, check out the rest of our catalogue at www.aethonbooks.com. To sign up to receive a FREE collection from some of our best authors (including one from Rick Partlow) as well updates regarding all new releases, visit www.aethonbooks.com/sign-up